Ralph Compton:
Guns of the Greenhorn

A RALPH COMPTON WESTERN

RALPH COMPTON: GUNS OF THE GREENHORN

MATTHEW P. MAYO

THORNDIKE PRESS
A part of Gale, a Cengage Company

Copyright © 2021 by The Estate of Ralph Compton.
The Gunfighter Series.
Thorndike Press, a part of Gale, a Cengage Company.

LIBRARY OF CONGRESS CIP DATA ON FILE.
CATALOGUING IN PUBLICATION FOR THIS BOOK
IS AVAILABLE FROM THE LIBRARY OF CONGRESS.

ISBN-13: 978-1-4328-9515-0 (hardcover alk. paper)

Published in 2022 by arrangement with Berkley, an imprint of Penguin Publishing Group, a division of Penguin Random House, LLC

Printed in Mexico
Print Number: 01   Print Year: 2022

To my favorite outlaws:
Rose Mary and Dave.

— MPM

THE IMMORTAL COWBOY

This is respectfully dedicated to the "American Cowboy." His was the saga sparked by the turmoil that followed the Civil War, and the passing of more than a century has by no means diminished the flame.

True, the old days and the old ways are but treasured memories, and the old trails have grown dim with the ravages of time, but the spirit of the cowboy lives on.

In my travels — to Texas, Oklahoma, Kansas, Nebraska, Colorado, Wyoming, New Mexico, and Arizona — I always find something that reminds me of the Old West. While I am walking these plains and mountains for the first time, there is this feeling that a part of me is eternal, that I have known these old trails before. I believe it is the undying spirit of the frontier calling me, through the mind's eye, to step back into time. What is the appeal of the Old West of the American frontier?

It has been epitomized by some as the dark and bloody period in American history. Its heroes — Crockett, Bowie, Hickok, Earp — have been reviled and criticized. Yet the Old West lives on, larger than life.

It has become a symbol of freedom, when there was always another mountain to climb and another river to cross; when a dispute between two men was settled not with expensive lawyers, but with fists, knives, or guns. Barbaric? Maybe. But some things never change. When the cowboy rode into the pages of American history, he left behind a legacy that lives within the hearts of us all.

— *Ralph Compton*

CHAPTER ONE

"Far as I'm concerned, you'll never serve enough time." Tin Falls prison warden James MacNichol looked up from his desk and into the black eyes of the large, raw-boned, pock-faced man in wrist and ankle manacles standing before him. "You could serve two lifetimes and then some, and it still wouldn't be long enough for the likes of you, Skin Varney."

The big homely inmate did his best to look grateful, subservient, whipped, cowed, humbled, and honored to be in the boss man's presence. If he had to, he figured he could work up a trembling lip, maybe a tear or two.

Anything to get him out of Tin Falls Prison, the deepest hole in hell. He didn't need this simpering fool to tell him he'd served his time. But he nodded, kept his mouth pulled in a frown, and stared at his worn-to-a-nub boots. "Yes, sir, warden sir."

They loved that bowing-and-scraping stuff. And he'd dole out as much of it as he needed to, anything to get out of this rat nest.

The warden sighed, then stood. "Alas, the decision isn't mine. And I am, after all, a slave to the law." He leaned forward, fingers tented on the desktop. In a low voice he said, "And so should you be, Mr. Varney. Or you'll find yourself back here faster than you can say 'Skip to My Lou.' And then, by Jove, we'll see justice. Do you understand me, mister?"

Warden MacNichol strove for a menacing effect that was diminished by the fact that he had to look up at the prisoner before him.

"Sir, yes, sir," said the manacled man, returning the warden's hard stare until the warden broke away and thrust his hands in his trouser pockets.

"Escort him out, away from me. Now."

Minutes later, the warden heard the door in the front gate squawk wide on dry steel hinges and then boot steps on gravel, all punctuated with a chuckling that rose to full-throated laughter as the former prisoner walked slowly away from Tin Falls Prison.

The warden ground his molars tighter and his cheeks pulsed redder as he wondered, not for the first or last time, why he'd had to let a thieving, raping killer walk free.

Skin Varney's deep, rasping laugh echoed in the warden's head long after the man had slipped from sight.

CHAPTER TWO

The knocking was loud, loud enough to jerk
from sleep Fletcher J. Ralston — the young,
single dandy of Upper Creston Street, 442C
Chandler's Row, Providence, Rhode Island.
He groaned, then sat upright in bed, his
eyes wide and head fuzzy. Who in their right
mind would rouse anyone on a Sunday
morning, the workingman's day of rest?

He swung his feet to the floor and groped
with his toes for his house slippers. At least
he'd had good sense enough the night
before to remove his garments and pull on
his nightshirt.

He groaned once more as he passed the
wingback chair cradling the unsightly wrinkled mess that was his soft wool trousers
and coat. He'd indulged in rare extra rounds
of tipple with fellow junior clerks of Rhodes
and Son, the banking firm, at the club during their weekly Saturday night of celebra-
tion at conquering yet another week of still-

12

novel work.

The knocking persisted. "I'm coming, I'm coming. . . ." He fumbled with the dead bolt and opened the door as wide as the short safety chain allowed. "Yes?"

On his doorstep, Fletcher spied a short, thin youth whose unfortunate bristly red hair poked out from beneath a blue-and-red kepi, a symbol of the Coast City Telegram Co.

"Telegram, sir," said the youth. From his unhidden grin, it appeared the young man enjoyed rousting the innocent at such an hour on a Sunday morning. Well, the smug grin would cost him and be reflected in his tip.

"One moment." Fletcher closed the door and slid a nickel from the china dish he kept on a table beside the door for such moments. He opened the door once more, fully this time, and held out a hand. The youngster proffered the telegram and kept his own pink palm out, upturned, waiting.

Fletcher relinquished the nickel and turned his attention to the folded yellow note. The delivery boy's grunt of complaint at the meager tip was clipped short by the clunking shut of the heavy door.

Fletcher walked halfway to his demure

kitchen to heat water for coffee before looking at the telegram.

TO MASTER FLETCHER J RALSTON
OF PROVIDENCE RHODE ISLAND
STOP
YOUR AUNT MILLICENT JESSUP IS
DYING STOP
WISHES TO SEE YOU STOP
YOUR PRESENCE IS REQUESTED IN
THE TOWN OF PROMISE WYOMING
TERRITORY FORTHWITH TO DISCUSS
TERMS OF SIGNIFICANT INHERITANCE
STOP

Fletcher froze, read the telegram through a second time, then slowly walked to the kitchen and read it a third time, out loud. Despite his excitement, he gave voice to his skepticism. "Who is Millicent Jessup? Why is she referred to here as my 'aunt'? And above all else, what does this mean?" He wagged the telegram at the small cold room.

Fletcher had long believed himself alone in the world, bereft of blood relations — at least any who cared to acknowledge his existence. And now here was this shocking pronouncement.

He'd grown accepting of, if not comfortable with, the notion that he'd likely been

14

the result of an unfortunate extramarital dalliance, an illegitimate annoyance to someone of wealth and societal standing. Instead of spending his youth gnashing his teeth and weeping in self-pity over the notion, he had instead gotten on with the matter of living.

His formative years had been spent at Swinton's School for Boys, then later at Bilkerson College, both within the confines of his fair city. All the while Fletcher had counted himself fortunate — especially on witnessing poverty in the streets of Providence — that a conscience had accompanied the wealth and, presumably, guilt that had provided him with a fine education. On top of that, since college, he had received a modest sum from an unknown benefactor that had helped with his living expenses.

Not being the sort to indulge in numerous casual acquaintances with his fellows, save for his rather tame Saturday night revels, Fletcher found himself ill inclined to discuss the matter with anyone else. He knew few others well enough to trust them with information of such a personal nature.

Then Fletcher's thoughts turned to his supervisor, Mr. Heep, at his place of employ, Rhodes and Son, the banking firm where he'd been working these two months. This new position had come as a welcome improvement in his situation, both in pay and in challenge. But Fletcher had proven up to the task. Mr. Heep was a wise man — he'd hired Fletcher, after all. He might be inclined to advise his young mentee.

Due in large part to his increase in earnings, Fletcher had recently managed to leave Widow Silverton's boardinghouse behind to take up residence in his very own apartments in this modest yet respectable neighborhood. And now he was expected to leave it for the great raw frontier peopled with fiendish savages and beasts too vicious for words? It was unthinkable.

And yet the phrase "significant inheritance" was not tossed about with frequency. No, this demanded investigation. Fletcher drank a full pot of strong black coffee and paced his rooms. Then he shaved his face smooth, scented his dark hair with pomade, and dressed himself in his Sunday finery — a black derby, a storm gray waistcoat, a striped vest, a white shirt, a blue silk cravat, a stickpin, striped gray trousers, and black leather brogans with gray spats.

He then stalked the promenade of the waterfront park and pondered this most annoying, perplexing, and alluring telegram. Before the day was out, he had reread the thing dozens of times, searching for further clues that were not forthcoming.

And the more he thought on the matter, the more Fletcher realized that if anyone he knew would be able to advise him in his next steps, it would indeed be his supervisor, Mr. Heep. On the morrow, Fletcher would present the matter to him with all the grace and humility he possessed.

First thing the next morning, Fletcher arrived at the firm early and showed the mysterious telegram to his supervisor. Mr. Heep read it through twice, his pince-nez twitching at the tip of his long shining nose as if he were about to sneeze.

He looked up, tucked his spectacles into their pocket, and handed the telegram back to Fletcher. Then he smiled. "You have a promising career here, young Mr. Ralston. Therefore I will hold your position open for, shall we say, six weeks? Without pay, of course."

"Of course," repeated Fletcher, though he hardly heard what he was agreeing to. This was not the response he had expected.

"Late summer into autumn is rather a slow season for us, after all, and I speak for the company when I say we would hate to be the reason you passed up so promising and potentially exciting an opportunity."

Fletcher stood with the telegram in his hand and his mouth open. He had hoped the man might somehow talk him out of it, convince him that it was little more than a hollow ruse, yet here Mr. Heep was telling Fletcher to go west. *Oh, dear,* he thought. *Oh, dear, oh, dear . . .*

"But see to it that, should you still be inclined, you return in time. Or you will find yourself bereft of gainful employment at these premises and lacking in recommendation from Messrs. Rhodes and Heep. Is that understood?"

Fletcher cleared his throat and nodded. "It is as clear as polished glass, sir. I won't let you down."

"See to it. Oh, and, Mr. Ralston?"

"Yes, sir?"

"As you endeavor to solve this intriguing mystery, do try to enjoy yourself traipsing across the brute plains and dodging the gunfire of rapscallions and rogues." Heep smiled. "Every young man should have an adventure before he settles into a life of . . ." He looked about himself and a wistful look made his smile fade. "Before he settles in life, Mr. Ralston."

"Yes, sir. I'll return as soon as possible, sir."

18

Heep sighed and offered a thin smile. "Very well, Mr. Ralston. Safe travels to you."

Heep sighed and offered a curt smile. "Very well, Mr. Ralston, let me take to you.

CHAPTER THREE

Skin Varney refused to drag his feet on up the dust track. Sure, he was tired enough that nobody feeling the way he did would do much different, but he'd know that he was being lazy. That was enough to keep him lifting one foot, setting it down, lifting the other, and on and on. And he'd been walking hard for hours.

He had to get north — that much he knew. So: *Keep the rising sun to your right, the setter to your left, and you'll make out.* That's what the old buck who'd shared his cell at Tin Falls Prison, Chilton Sinclair, had said.

Skin didn't need the advice. He knew how to tell directions, thanks, but Chilton was due to die in a couple of months, and so Skin, feeling generous, had kept his mouth shut and let the old man dole out his worn tidbits of stringy counsel.

Chilton Sinclair was an interesting old

dog, to be sure. He had been chucked in that place for doing a whole lot worse than Skin ever got caught for. Sinclair never told him much about it, at least not in a direct way. Skin was told what had happened by another inmate by the name of Frijole before Sinclair even got to the prison.

Frijole wasn't even Mexican as far as Skin knew. In dim light, the man could take on the appearance of such, but it wasn't obvious. Whoever had named him was an idiot. Skin didn't tell that to Frijole, though, 'cause the man owned a hard temper.

Anyhow, he told Skin that Sinclair had gutted a drummer who'd bedded his wife, even though Sinclair himself was a drunkard accountant who'd left the woman and their young daughter to keep his own misfortune from landing on their heads. The story was as full of holes as an old mothy blanket, but Skin took a liking to Chilton just the same.

He was old, at least sixty, but looked about twenty years more than that, and he had a face like a stomped apple. Skin reckoned that was because Sinclair had spent most of those years squirming around in a bottle. Prison parched the old man out drier than a sun-puckered plank. Many nights, Skin would lie there in his bunk and listen to the man rave and howl and heave his dry guts even drier for hours.

After he'd passed through all that, turned out, Sinclair was a chatty old stick. When they weren't busting rocks for no reason out in the sun all day, they'd hole up in the cramped, dark stone cell and talk. Or rather, Sinclair would talk and Skin would grunt now and again to let him know he was still awake and listening.

He'd once told Skin about how to change certain numbers in a ledger sheet to look like other numbers. "Pennies add up, my friend," he'd said, then chuckled.

Skin had grunted, like always, but he was thinking that he'd be damned if he was going to take much to heart from a fellow who was concerned with pennies in life, not when there were whole banks and depot offices and payroll stages filled with dollars waiting to be cracked open like big eggs.

So, naturally, Skin found it funny that here on the trail, of all the yammering Sinclair had done when Skin would rather have been sleeping, he should call to mind that bit about keeping the sun to one side or the other.

That cursed sun, pinned high in the clear blue sky behind him and to his left, broiled the top of Skin's head and neck. It chased him as always, a hellhound nipping, nipping, nipping but never taking enough with each nip to bring you down. No, that wasn't the way with a coward like that big roasting egg yolk in the sky.

Skin came upon the man a few hours before the sun drew its curtains on the long, hot day. He smelled smoke from a campfire and let his sniffer lead him to the spot. It didn't take much effort, as it turned out, as the lone traveler was encamped for the night in a wide spot in the roadway.

By the unrolled blankets sat a small but lively fire bounded in a rough circle by fist-size rocks. Beyond that stood a bony black horse, muscled enough to keep him alive and lugging a sizable man. It was also old and thin and bone rack enough to keep from being made off with in the night by someone with an envious disposition.

"Hey, mister," said Skin. The man hadn't heard him approaching and Skin liked that. It told him he hadn't lost his old catlike moves. Skin was wearing a faded blue denim smock with a dark spot on the front where a patch had once told the world he'd been a recent resident of Tin Falls Prison, and that wasn't the sort of fellow most folks would want to see coming.

He'd been able to gnaw away the threads that held the numbers in place, then buried the patch the day before. No matter, because the back of the shirt still bore the prison name in big inked letters.

He'd been tempted to shuck it and bury it, too, but that would have left him without a shirt. And not having a shirt, even if it was only for a time, was not good thinking in autumn time in Utah Territory. As hot as it could get during the day, the nights grew downright shivery.

But good fortune, Skin decided, had finally shone on him once again. Here was a man crouched near a fire, forking over hunks of slab bacon. And the man looked as though he was about Skin's size, too.

"I said, hey there, mister." Skin walked up, forced a smile, and held out a hand palm up, as if trying to hold back something approaching. "I wonder if you could maybe help a fellow out of a hard scrape." He stopped some yards from the man and stood looking at him.

The man rose, still holding his three-tine wood fork in his left hand.

Yep, thought Skin. *Just about my height.* In fact, they both had similar hair — black but peppered now with the creeping in of whiteness that comes with age. It was curly enough that Skin's friends had picked on him when the war was on, claiming they were fighting to free him. Skin had never found that funny.

This man had a similar beard, too. Leaning toward thick, curly like his topknot, and about as untrimmed. Skin tried a smile again. It was not a facial feature he was accustomed to wearing and it pained him. He even thrust out a hand for a shake, knowing some men liked that sort of thing.

"I'm right pleased to make your acquaintance, mister. Again I ask, would you happen to be inclined to lend help to a starving fellow traveler?"

The man's overly bushy eyebrows came together in the center. "You" — he touched a fingertip to his mouth. *"Sprechen sie Deutsch?"*

It was Skin's turn to wince and flinch and squint. "What? Naw, naw." He shook his head. "I speak in English and that's all. Been enough so far, I reckon. You want to try English?" Skin tapped his own mouth. "English?"

The man almost smiled, but shook his head. *"Deutsch."* He shrugged and pointed the fork at his half-sliced brick of bacon meat. Skin took that as an offer of food, and he nodded with vigor.

He hadn't realized how very hungry all that walking had made him. Soon enough, following a strange stretch of silence while they watched the bacon and corn cakes fry, the pair of men, though strangers, enjoyed a meal together.

Skin figured he'd tend to business once he'd had his fill. Wouldn't make sense to commence before-hand, as he'd only have to cook the food himself. Avoid labors whenever you can. That was another of Chilton Sinclair's shavings of advice. Skin admitted it was a sound one.

"I guess you are my size, roughly, which I'll grant you is uncanny. Is it too much to hope that you also carry some decent amount of money and a working firearm about your person? Huh?"

The other man's vast eyebrows, the bushy look of them vexing Skin more by the moment, pulled together in the middle, creating one long, bushy rope of hair on the man's brow. "You . . . *Deutsch*?"

"Huh? No, no." Skin shook his head rapidly. "I ain't nothing but a man whose folks were maybe this or that. I don't rightly know, but don't try to pollute the subject now." Skin snatched a hank of jerky from an open saddlebag nearby and set to work on it. After a few moments of chewing, he looked up to see the man staring at him. "What's the problem?"

It was what Skin had been waiting for. He needed to see doubt drift into the man's eyes, wanted to see it. It would give him reason enough to set to work, as if someone had shouted, *Go!*

He had no knife, no gun, nothing but what that worm of a warden had turned him loose with. Wasn't supposed to be that way. He'd heard tell you were supposed to be given a few dollars, clothes that didn't mark you as a prisoner — someone had even said something about a train ticket to somewhere away from the prison, but he wasn't so certain of that part. Still, none of it mattered because none of it had happened.

The German fellow made no effort to hide the sheath knife hanging on his belt. It was laced at the top, knotted, but Skin reckoned he could surprise the man long enough to untie that thing. He hadn't wanted to have to drop the man with a split of firewood. That would take all the sport out of the task, but it seemed he was offered no other choice in the matter.

Skin sighed, smacked his hands on his knees, and rose to his feet. His host eyed him with raised eyebrows and looked as if he wanted to say something.

Skin didn't want to hear it, more of the same foreign gibberish. He was tired and wanted to get out of the prison clothes. Skin nodded, tried to smile back, and gestured toward a clump of trees. He thought maybe the man would take it to mean he needed to pee, but he didn't really care what the man thought. He just didn't want the other man looking at him.

When he walked back from his visit to the trees, he stopped halfway back to the fire, where the man's back faced him. He was scraping the bottom of the pan with a stick.

Skin palmed a round, smooth rock, gray with flecks of pink and veined with black. *This rock is as big as a baby's head,* he thought as he held it loosely in his long fingers.

The man still didn't look at him. *Good.* Skin stepped forward once, twice more. As soon as he was close enough to lunge, Skin's left foot ground into gravel, barely loud enough to wake a mouse yet loud enough to alert the man.

The German looked over his shoulder. Any doubt he had on his face was replaced with a messy mash of confusion, then fear as he took in Skin's crouching stance and the rock held loose in his fingertips. Then Skin saw anger draw down the man's face, his eyes narrowing as he tried to stand.

He was not fast enough because Skin was

already in motion. A smile — the first genuine smile he'd felt inclined to wear in a whole lot of years — pulled Skin's mouth wide. At the same time, his right arm rose up.

Instead of bringing the rock down on top of the man's head, he changed his intention midmotion because he realized the blow would spatter blood and bone and brain on the man's shirt. And what would the point be of going to all this trouble to get himself decent clothes to wear if he up and sullied them before tugging them on?

"No!" The man's voice was low and harsh, as if he knew he could not rise in time to ward off the coming blow. The best he could do was crouch and raise his left arm to receive the full force of the downward swing.

It didn't work.

The rock met the lone man's temple from the side. Skin felt the old comforting reassurance of bone collapsing beneath the swing's momentum, and that was about all there was to it. The German man's head jerked fast to one side — Skin thought maybe his neck had snapped — and he slopped to the ground.

The horse, still standing hipshot, flicked a long ear.

Skin let out a held breath, steady and

smooth. *Good.* He'd not lost his nerve while in prison. "Only one other thing to do," he said, tossing the rock toward the road. He bent, shoved the side-sprawled man over onto his back, and flinched when the man gasped.

"Huh," said Skin. "Tough bugger, huh?" He quickly untied the rawhide lace and freed the man's knife, a wood-handled, wide-bladed piece of steel that had decent heft in Skin's hand.

"Let's see how she works," he said, and with no hesitation raised it high and rammed the butt of the handle against the prone man's temple. A quick barking sound escaped the man's bearded mouth, then clipped off.

"Settle down, mister," said Skin, growing annoyed with the rascal. "Man ought to have sense enough to know when he's licked."

A close look at the man to see if he was breathing offered no sign, but Skin had been tricked in the past. Skin bent low, listening to the man's chest, knife held high and ready to strike downward. He heard no heartbeat. Still didn't mean all that it should, so he would strike the German a final blow once he relieved him of his clothing, boots, and such.

It took Skin a couple of minutes to strip the man down. He left the fellow the dignity of his long underwear. Besides, he didn't know what sort of man the German was, if he had slovenly personal habits. "Be thankful I am of a kindly disposition," he said, grunting as he dragged the man out of the campsite and behind a rocky, shrubby spot.

"There." Skin belched and looked down at his handiwork. He was tired once more and so not inclined to slice the man open. It was a messy task and made for a stink that clouded a man's nose for far too long afterward. He refused to believe that this meant he had softened in prison.

To prove it to himself and whatever demon whispered in his left ear, always the left ear, he found the same rock and once more slammed it into the fellow's head. That time something else inside crunched and there was no doubt any longer that the German was good and dead.

"By the time you draw flies, I'll be long gone from here. Won't be nothin' left to point to me but these trees." He looked up into the sparse web of aspen branches. "And trees don't talk."

Then he had a fine idea, perhaps one of the best he'd had in a long ol' time. He shucked off his raggy, baggy prison shirt and trousers and tugged them on the dead man. They looked enough alike that should anyone ever wonder, it might come about that Skin Varney had died on the road, done in by a vicious campsite marauder all because he'd been turned loose from Tin Falls Prison with scanty gear by that no-account warden.

"That Warden MacNichol is a menace," said Skin, dressing in the German man's garments and feeling a little sorry for his dead self.

Dark was still a couple of hours off, by his reckoning, and his belly was full and he had a horse and gear once more. *Why,* thought Skin Varney, *there don't seem to be much sense in sharing my campsite with a dead fellow. Not much conversation to be gotten that way.*

It took him longer to settle the lone traveler's scrap of a horse than it had taken to dispatch its previous master. It didn't help that Skin wasn't a patient sort, never had been. He knew this of himself, but couldn't help it, and he didn't care enough to want to.

Bulling his way through life had worked most of the time, but whomping on a horse that looked to be close to death wasn't going to get him far.

He sighed and saddled and loaded up the dead man's gear — now his gear. "Settle yourself, naggy! We'll get on fine until I have to plug you in the head. And I promise not to do that until we find a replacement for your sorry self. Okay?" He said this with as much kindness as he could muster.

He was tempted to rummage in the saddlebags. *No,* he told himself. *That treat will wait until later when I get to where I'm going. Then it will be special.*

For now he figured it would be wise to travel on, lest someone should stop and wish to pass the time of day with him and then get feeling so they had to visit the bushes themselves, where they might discover the German. It was more of a headache than he wished for that night. Best to move on.

He toed dirt over the fire, then urinated on it, steam rising up before him. "Okay, horse," he said, buttoning up. "Time we get acquainted. You will see I'm not as bad as all that." The horse offered a half-hearted hop, but it was too old for much more.

"I told you," said Skin as he swung up into the saddle, "we'll get along better if you know your place." They paced out into the roadway and pointed northward. "Gain us some hours, then we'll encamp once more. Might be you'll find I am a worthy companion of the road. Might not. Either way, I do not care."

And so they walked. Skin tested the horse's abilities to carry him, and he had to admit the bony beast was more impressive than he had thought on first glance that it might be. "Don't mean I won't be swapping you out when the opportunity shows itself. Keep that in mind, you cursed bone rack."

Skin smiled once more, this time for the good fortune with which he had presented himself. "Yes, sir, Skin Varney, you are still an enterprising fellow. There can be no doubt of that."

As he and the horse walked northward, far to his left the sun slowly dragged itself to sleep.

CHAPTER FOUR

Two weeks after he left Providence, Fletcher J. Ralston found himself sharing a rattling Concord stagecoach of the Bull and Bull Line, out of Schenectady, with an overstuffed woman in a garish green satin and black lace dress of a size she'd left behind some years before.

Beside her sat her equally bulging husband, a close-bearded fellow in a gray pin-striped suit and a gray bowler wedged atop his dimpled head. When he wasn't snoring and passing gas as if in competition with his perfumed spouse, he was tugging out a new and, as he took pains to explain several times, expensive pocket watch the diameter and thickness of a holiday meat pie.

"Where is it you said you were headed, Mr. . . . ? Ahh, I've forgotten your name, young man." The woman canted her feather-covered head and smiled at Fletcher.

"I didn't say, madam." Fletcher saw the

look of sudden shock on her face as if he'd slapped her. She looked at her husband. Perhaps he had been rude. He girded himself and said, "That is to say, I've not yet mentioned my destination, but I am happy to do so: Promise, Wyoming Territory. I daresay a city bearing such a bold name will offer all the goodwill and wonder of that most excellent word." He offered them a winning smile.

The portly pair exchanged glances once more, then turned forced smiles of sympathy on him. "Yes," she said. "Well, ah . . . yes."

"You are familiar, then, with Promise, I take it, Mrs. . . . ?"

"Cunningham. Our name is Cunningham," said her husband. "And yes, oh, yes, we have had . . . dealings in Promise, though it has been years since we have been forced to — that is to say, since we have had the opportunity to visit that fine town."

Their hesitation was revealing and failed to reinforce in Fletcher Ralston the hopefulness he'd been working his best to maintain. His journey thus far had been a headache enmeshed in a nightmare, and his Sunday togs were now sagged and near ruined — a metaphor, he thought, for his very soul.

"Not to worry," said Mr. Cunningham, seeing worry creep across the young man's features. "You have your youth!"

The bubbly pair slipped back into their not-so-quiet, gassy napping, and the stagecoach rumbled and swayed and bounced and slammed westward, drawing Fletcher J. Ralston ever closer to an encounter he felt less confident in with each passing dusty moment.

CHAPTER FIVE

Mr. and Mrs. Cunningham departed the stagecoach at Drover's Bend, Nebraska, after wishing Fletcher all the luck the world had to offer a young man. He swore he saw their smiles slip away, replaced with looks of horror as the stage rolled away from the stop.

He was now the sole passenger, save for a fresh sack of mail and a wobbly scatter of paper-and-string-wrapped parcels stacked on the floor and on the seat across from him.

Fletcher wedged his low black boots, topped with gray spats, now hopelessly dusted, against the bench across from him in an effort to stay seated as the coach slammed and rolled. His traveling finery was coated with a fine dust that seemed to work into and through the very fabric of each piece of his attire.

He had patted himself down regularly

early on in the trip, but soon realized the futility of doing so. For his black kid-leather gloves themselves picked up the sand-colored dust and left handprints up and down his sleeves and across his lapels. Fletcher vowed to visit a launderer as soon as he arrived in Promise.

Holding a once-white dust-clogged handkerchief to his nose and mouth, he gazed again at the vast depressing landscape. Never had he seen such . . . hopelessness. It was as if the very word had been rendered by a formidable artist who knew the futility of color.

And yet, when he allowed himself to see, truly see the land through which he was being driven, he admitted that the sky — and there was oh so much of it — bore a color not unlike hammered silver swirled with a blue as light as a fair maid's eye. And there was, surprisingly, green to be seen, too.

The porcine Mr. Cunningham had told him that this great sward of the most subtle and soft gray-green color was sage. Fletcher was aware, vaguely, of its scent as some herb used in cookery, but the aromas reaching him through the gaps in the slapping window shade told him of a perfume that refused to be bottled, so thin and rare was it.

At other times, he recognized the stink of his own sweat — too many days in the same clothes, without respite, wore on him deeper each day. It had long since become too much to bear. And yet . . . the allure of a "significant inheritance" still outweighed the inconvenience. But for how much longer? *A man, after all,* he thought, *can only take so much pushing before he turns and bares his fangs.*

Such were the increasingly violent thoughts of Fletcher J. Ralston as the two-brace team of horses pulled the begrimed Concord stagecoach down a slacking grade. It eased around a tight bend between narrow, rocky spires with rubble heaped at their bases. On each side of the stage, the tawny rock bore fresh scars of rockfalls and collisions.

They slowed to the pace of a man's brisk walk. Fletcher stuck his head out, a hand clapping his bowler in place, and squinted up at the shotgun rider. He was a coarse man named Clem or Cletus or Clell or some such. The well-fed fellow wore a brown wool coat two sizes too small, evidenced by the popped shoulder seams.

The burly man saw him looking up, and as they were rolling at such a slow pace, he shouted, "Rockslide couple weeks back!

Blocked the road in until they chipped and hauled it clear again!" He chuckled and spat tobacco juice.

It was that final parting guffaw that rattled Fletcher once again. He was about to shout for them to stop, to let him out — he needed to walk, for heaven's sake. After all, he repeated to himself, "A man can take only so much. . . ."

That was when the big shotgun rider bellowed once more: "Yonder is Promise!" Then he howled once more, and this time was joined by his seated companion, the heretofore silent Bob, driver of the spine-cracking, bone-rattling stage.

Fletcher was torn — excited to be so close to his destination yet concerned by the twin chucklers up front. He kept his bowler clapped to his head and squinted through the dust, craning his neck to see around the rock so close he reached out and grazed it with his fingertips.

They rounded the rocks and he caught his first glimpse of the town of Promise, Wyoming Territory.

Fletcher's jaw dropped open as he stared down the winding roadway through the half-treed pass. Dust swirled and clouded his open mouth, nose, and eyes, and finally he retreated back into the equally dusty interior of the stagecoach.

Surely, he thought, *a mistake has been made. If not, then never has there been a town that has failed to live up to its name any more so than Promise, Wyoming.*

His journey thus far had brought increasing difficulties, from rail travel to stagecoach, and one unfortunate two-mile stretch in between, when the train had developed some sort of coughing spasm in Iowa and refused to budge farther. The passengers, fifty of them, had been forced to trek the remaining distance on foot. Their luggage, they'd been assured, would follow along. It had, but nothing could have prepared Fletcher for the blisters he'd endured.

Now it was all coming to an end here. He flat-out refused to consider the fact that he had to repeat the entire journey, only in reverse, within days. He wished to be shed of the place, to be sure, but perhaps there would be a comfortable hotel at which he might enjoy a hot bath, a fine meal, and a clean bed.

The roadway angled downward to such an extent that he felt himself sliding forward. At least the jumble of packages and bundles no longer tumbled his way.

Fletcher poked his head out the door's window once more. The town, such as it was, lay several minutes' riding ahead. They were still elevated above it, though the roadway would take them downward out of the foothills and to flatland some distance before the town proper. Beyond the town, westward, the foothills rose up once more, leading to even grander mountains. In fact, it seemed the town was surrounded with an ambitious landscape.

For now he had a vantage point of Promise in full. It was typical, he'd come to learn, of many such Western towns, with a long central thoroughfare flanked by buildings. In this case, there were perhaps a dozen structures on each side, several in each row of significant size and bulk. Few of them wore fresh paint, and as the stagecoach approached, it seemed to Fletcher that even fewer than that had ever felt the touch of a brush.

Raw rough-sawn boards made up for many of the constructions; shade porches and worn plank sidewalks fastened the structures to the street as if they might otherwise spin away on a stiffening breeze.

Once more, the bulky man above half turned to him and, seeing he had the young stranger's attention, said, "Windy spot most times here, is Promise. Comes off them hills we just come out of. A real hat lifter!"

Fletcher supposed this was advice for which he should be grateful, should somehow show his acknowledgment and appreciation. "Yes." He nodded and patted his fingers, drumming them atop his hat, which he still held clamped to his head. "My thanks."

Once more, the big man shook his head and laughed, then without warning let loose a substantial stream of brown spittle that, due to the aforementioned wind, failed to reach the graveled earth alongside the turning wheel as intended. Instead, the ropy spew whipped along the thickly dusted side of the coach and across Fletcher's face, shoulder, hat, arm, and hand.

He saw the entire thing happen as if time itself had slowed, and he jerked too late back inside the coach. He held his breath, but soon realized this was not possible when one was at the same time gagging.

The spittle lashing proved to be the very thing that broke Fletcher's resolve. He sagged backward into the poorly padded bench seat and wiped with a trembling hand at his face with his handkerchief. It came away brown. His mind filled with thoughts of sickness borne through spittle.

The big man was obviously not well in his head. Why else would someone choose to wear such ill-fitting clothing and rove about unshaven and spitting in public? Fletcher continued wiping himself down as he stewed, quelling but not quite ceasing his gagging.

So woozy had he become, he did not notice they had descended down to the flat, and he barely noticed when the wagon slowed and then stopped.

He, Fletcher J. Ralston, had arrived in Promise.

CHAPTER SIX

"Well, well." Skin Varney had spotted the top of a small prairie schooner ahead, beyond an outcrop of reddish stone he'd seen more and more of in the past several hours. The rock and the ponderosa pines seemed to be competing. So far, the fight was even. Occasionally a third competitor, stands of aspen, entered the fray.

He slowed the bone rack of a horse and stopped in the trail to think. He sure was hungry, and he'd found precious little in the way of victuals in the German's traps some days ago on the trail. There had been jerky, but he'd eaten that within the first couple of miles.

Now he saw the possibility of food from what would likely be a migrating family. People in a wagon, in his experience, were travelers, and as such they would be carrying with them the makings of meals, maybe bread already baked, some choice meat, and biscuits.

"Oh," he groaned. "I can stand a whole lot of things, horse, but the thought of a fresh baked biscuit is not something I am able to resist. I drool like a dog chained out of reach of a gut pile."

The horse flicked an ear in response.

"You, too, huh? Say" — he shifted in the saddle — "what if they have tobacco? And dare I wonder . . . whiskey?" He sat in silence, musing on those toothsome prospects.

"On the other hand, what if they somehow saw the man who used to own you and these duds and whatnot. Just my luck he was their laggard kin, hoping to catch them up. Had to be a weak sort, near enough that he didn't value a good gun nor traveling with food." He shook his head and spat a gobbet of phlegm in disgust.

"I can do for them as I did to him, sure, but a whole family's more than I have strength to dally with just now. Give me a fine meal and a long night's sleep and I might well whistle up a different tune."

Then visions of fresh biscuits once more danced in his mind and Skin sighed. "All right, all right. I am a slave to my stomach, I tell you true, horse." He leaned forward on the saddle horn. "That brings to mind another thing: might be a new horse there who won't ignore me so much. Huh?"

From the moment Skin rode in sight of the wagon, he knew he should have given the camp a wider cut of the trail. It was a hardscrabble outfit; the top of the wagon he'd seen from afar was about the only thing in sight that didn't show signs of hard wear.

A man had seen him and stood beside the rear of the wagon and a too-smoky fire, eyeing him. Skin sighed and rode forward.

The man held his bony fists resting on his bony hips. The remnants of his long underwear cuffs, pinked with age, wagged in a breeze. His hat looked as haggard as the rest of him, and one side of the brim looked to have been gnawed away by a rat.

"Hello there, you at the camp!" said Skin, once more working to conjure a smile. It pained him. Then a thought came to him. He could ride on by. It was a trail, after all — well, not far off the trail. Anybody might travel it.

He could claim he was a lawman or some such tracking a fugitive and he had seen their wagon and figured he'd give it a look-see. And with no further thought, that became his plan — until the wagon's rear canvas flap rustled, as if someone inside was unknotting the ties that held it closed.

A dark-haired head poked through and raised its chin. And a pretty, whisker-free chin it was. That dark hair turned into two long braids draped down either side of that squint-eyed face.

She caught Skin looking her way and stared right back, bold as you please.

The ragged man visored his eyes and looked from Skin to the wagon, back to Skin, then to the wagon once more. "Here now!" His shout was thin voiced, high-pitched, but filled with instant anger.

The girl tugged her head back inside the flaps like a spooked turtle pulling into its shell.

Skin knew why the man was enraged. *Good,* he thought. *Let the devil think what he will. He's likely right. And I think perhaps I will stop and pay these fellow travelers a visit, after all.* A true grin worked its way onto his face. Been a long time since he had dallied with a woman. More years than he cared to recall, in fact. He expected the particulars would come to him.

"I say again, hello." Skin offered a wide, hearty, and, he hoped, friendly wave. Were he at the receiving end, he'd take it as such.

"What you want?"

Varney let his mouth droop as if he'd been told he was the homeliest man alive. "Why, mister, I don't want for anything, not unless you count the brief companionship of fellow folks of the roadways. Maybe somebody to share my evening sampling of whiskey with. That's all." Skin smoothed the reins between two fingers. "But I'll shove along now and I am sorry to have troubled you."

The raggedy man rubbed fingers over his lips. "Now hold on there. Never said you wasn't welcome. Just wanted to get the cut of the man I share camp with before I come to a decision."

Skin nodded with solemnity. "Oh, I understand that, mister. It's some of the people you meet along the way who cause the fuss." He wagged his head to indicate commiseration. "Yeah, I had a nickel every time some fool come along and wasn't what he said he was . . ."

"You what?"

"What's that you say?" said Skin, trying not to look at the wagon. He thought maybe the flaps were parted a sliver. He wondered if there was somebody else about the camp.

The man sighed and walked toward Skin, hands back on his hips. "You said if you had a nickel, you'd do something."

"Oh, well, I reckon I'd be wealthier than I am at present." He shrugged. "That's all."

"Uh-huh. Well, you can light down for a

spell, share the fire, such as it is. My daughter, she's of no use to me, gimped as she is, so I have to make do myself. It's a sore trial, I tell you."

"Oh," said Skin, glancing toward the wagon. "I guess that head poking out before was your daughter, then?"

"Yeah. What of it?"

Skin slid down out of the saddle. "Nothing to get worked up over." He held up a shushing hand. "Only being friendly." Skin noticed the man had once more become surly. "Had me a gimpy dog long ago. He was a bunch of work for my folks. Ended up dying, can't say the family wasn't relieved."

"You saying my daughter's like a dog?"

Skin sighed. This conversation was testing his patience. "I ain't saying nothing of the sort. Now, look, I'm going to move along. You don't seem the sort who wants company anyway. That's fine. I'm of such a mind myself. Good day to you and yours, mister."

Skin mounted up. This time when he tugged the horse to leave, the sullen man didn't make a move to stop him. Could be he'd read Skin's intentions. *Must be the prison taint still clinging to me,* thought Skin. He angled away from the man, not taking his eyes from him. He'd keep the rascal in

51

sight until he reached the bend in the trail by the big rocks. Besides, he didn't intend to dally with no gimp — that much was certain.

Then, he'd be jiggered, didn't the flaps on that wagon cover part once more? This time, the girl showed herself in full. Clothed, to be sure, in a floppy ol' dress that had started life as sacking, but it didn't hide the comely shape beneath. Skin slowed his sidelong progress.

He didn't pay as much attention to the scraggly man, who still watched him, but now with the perkings of a grin. Instead, Skin's eyes were fastened on the creature who was climbing out of the back of the wagon.

She returned his stare, save for a few seconds when she cut her gaze down to her feet. One of them appeared to be oddly shaped and swung as if it were a rock swinging at the end of a rope. The leg beneath the raggy skirts peeked out now and again as she grunted and fumbled with getting herself free of the back of the wagon.

It was a thin leg, not much meat on it, that ended in a man-size boot that bent in no way a foot should. None of that put Skin off, though, because the rest of her looked as tempting as a fat trout crackling and spitted slow and smoky over glowing coals.

She made it out of the wagon and stood by the tailgate, one arm resting in the wagon, the other propped on her hip and grinning at him as if she deserved mighty praise for doing what most folks could have done in half the time. But Skin was about to praise her anyway. She was something.

That's when he cut his eyes back to her father. The rascal was openly smiling at him. Skin didn't think that was such a good thing. The man had sidestepped away, not even toward the fire, which needed attention. "Here now," said the man over his shoulder to his daughter.

Before Skin knew what all was happening, the girl's arm that had been resting in the wagon lifted into view a short single-barrel shotgun. She wore a similar vicious grin as her pa on her own unwashed face. She lifted the butt of the stock, squashing it into her chest, not bothering to aim the thing, and not losing a smidgen of that grin. Then she cut loose.

Skin knew that whatever she had in that thing was capable of traveling the twenty, thirty feet between them. It was also likely a whole lot faster than he was able to draw the poor example of a six-gun he'd taken off that fool back yonder up the trail.

The only thing he had time for was swinging his near leg up and not quite over the saddle as he dove to his left, shoving away from the saddle and the old bone-rack horse and praying to a god he had long before lost faith in that his boot didn't snag in the stirrup.

It didn't.

As the shot rang out, he heard a guttural belching sound — not a scream, not a howl, something deeper, more animallike. The horse.

Even as his left shoulder hit the dusty earth and he rolled to cushion his fall, Skin was already boiling with rage. He felt hot, raw anger worse than that old raggedy bastard and his no-good gimp of a daughter could ever feel.

He was angrier with himself than them, for he had allowed himself to be overtaken by this pair of killing thieves. What did they think he had on him anyway? He'd all but told them he had whiskey, sure, which he didn't have, but the pickings he'd taken from that fool up the road didn't amount to all that much. They wouldn't know that, of course. They were vultures swooping in to pick him clean.

He came to rest on one knee, his right hand snatching for the paltry revolver. He lifted it free and saw the horse had been knocked to its left side. It jerked its old legs to stand, its head thrashing and whipping, smacking the ground as it screamed and flailed. The sounds made Skin shiver. He'd as soon put a bullet in the damn thing's head to shut it up because it gave him the creeping willies to listen to it. But he didn't want to waste the bullet just yet. He had a feeling he'd need it soon.

The horse thrashed between him and his prey, the beast who had shot at him — the girl. He looked over the horse's flopping barrel of a rib cage and saw weak squirts of dark red bubble up, subside, bubble again, then leak down along its back and belly, soaking into the saddle blanket. She'd laid into it with what looked to be a round of buckshot — intended for him.

Before Skin could squeeze off a shot, she'd reloaded. A second shotgun blast boomed, and the horse, behind which he crouched, jerked and screamed. Its long legs trembled, then stiffened and it jerked once more, then lay still.

It took him two shots from his less-than-impressive gun for Skin to drop the gimpy girl and then her father, who stood with his hands resting on his bony hips, smiling as if Skin's death was a sure thing. The look of surprise on his face warmed Skin's belly as much as a drink of whiskey. Then it was all over and done.

He ran a finger in his right ear and jiggled it. All that blasting, booming gun noise had left a ringing in his head like a blacksmith's hammer pounding steady on steel. He made certain the revolver was loaded and ready to go, then he stood and advanced, gun drawn, toward the pair he'd dropped and the wagon. You never could tell when there was somebody lurking about a camp.

He found nobody other than the father and daughter, and they were both good and dead. The wagon yielded more surprises than he thought possible, considering the state of the camp and its occupants. Not only were there fresh baked bread and a shank of some sort of salty meat, but there was coffee and two unopened bottles of whiskey.

He checked the pockets of the dead man and found nearly forty dollars as well as a decent pocket watch. The woman's pockets yielded nothing more than a much-folded crude drawing of a child that looked not unlike a monkey he'd seen at a circus many years before. He wasn't certain what that might mean to the woman, and he didn't much care.

Despite all this, the best discovery of Skin's day came when he scouted farther from the camp and found a single bay mare grazing on sparse grasses twenty yards away. Leading it back to the wagon, he tied it and searched for a saddle and anything else that might prove useful.

He dragged the two dead people off behind a jumble of boulders and decided to spend the night in their camp. He'd only have to build his own in another hour or so anyway.

As he revived the fire and set two roughly sawn slabs of meat to sizzle, he sipped from a bottle of whiskey.

" 'Never trust a woman, Skin Varney,' " he told the new horse. "I forgot that important lesson. Heck, it may be the biggest one of all. The most important of them lessons Chilton Sinclair told me in the cell. 'Never trust a woman.' And darned if that ain't about right, too."

He swigged the liquor. "Just look at what happened here. Why, you can't hardly forget it was a woman who got betwixt you and your pard back in the old days, could you? Night of the big takings and he up and scampers off with the money, leaves you to swing for it. And why? For his woman, plain as day. All he talked about half the time.

57

Should have known better. Well not this time, Skin Varney."

He prodded the sizzling meat with a stick. "This time, this time will be different. That town that locked you away behind the strap-steel walls of Tin Falls Prison? That town's going to pay. Pay until I get every flat penny owed me — and then some." He cackled and glugged back a few gurgles on the bottle. "I got me a promise to keep. A promise . . . with Promise!"

There was raw humor in there somewhere — he was certain of it. But right then he didn't care to probe it. He was feeling too fine. He had money, a horse, food, and whiskey, and he was close, so close to reaching the end of his long, long trail. A trail he'd been traveling in his mind for twenty-four years.

Soon, he thought. He let loose with a giggle and swallowed back more of that hot liquor. It burned him all the way down, and he liked it just fine.

CHAPTER SEVEN

"He been drinking?" said a townsman in a sweat-stained brown felt hat to the burly shotgun rider as he cast a sidelong glance at Fletcher.

The brown-coated, chaw-dripping man shrugged. "We don't recommend it. But you can never tell about folks. Never can, no, sir."

With that, he walked into the station, leaving Fletcher J. Ralston standing before the stagecoach. His leather satchel dropped from on high to land smack beside his feet. He winced, thinking of the bottle of bay rum cologne he'd packed, wrapped in spare underthings, to be sure, but a drop like that — and then he smelled its pungent reek drifting upward and groaned once more.

"Why?" he said, forgetting for the moment he was still being scrutinized by three women, a small boy, and an even smaller black-and-white miniature bulldog with a single protruding tooth and a breathing ailment. The aforementioned man, whose suspicions about drinking Fletcher had done little to quell, eyed him.

"Pardon me," said Fletcher, straightening his vest and doffing his bowler while trying to force a smile.

Before he could continue, the man said, "Maybe, maybe not."

"I . . . uh . . . I'm looking for" — he pulled the worn telegram from his inner coat pocket and read the address there — "Millicent Jessup. Might you know where I can find her?"

The eyes of the women rose high as if he'd just uttered foul words before them and the child. One said, "Well, I never!" and yanked the child's arm and stomped down the sidewalk.

Inches behind him, Fletcher heard a creaking and squawking, and the stagecoach jerked forward, close enough that the hub of the rear wheel grazed the back of his leg. He leapt away, catching the toe of his right boot on his satchel's loop handle and pitched forward, face-first, to the dusty, dung-riddled street.

Fletcher saved himself, barely, with outstretched gloved hands. The gravel pocked, tore, and scraped the kidskin gloves, ruining them yet saving his hands from the same fate. As the stagecoach rumbled down the street, Fletcher looked up to see the townsman, whose face hadn't changed, say, "Uh-huh, figured as much."

"I'm afraid I don't understand. . . ."

"I'll just bet," said the man, then made a sniffing sound, his head canted upward as if he'd sniffed a vile odor, and refused to look back.

Other people, Fletcher saw now, had gathered along the sidewalk and paused in crossing the street to catch sight of what he realized was a double oddity in their midst. Despite his recent misadventures, he was still a well-dressed stranger in their midst, and he was at present sprawled in the street. He remedied that situation forthwith.

As he stood, forcing a smile and a nod toward the nearest of the onlookers, Fletcher brushed at his clothes once more. Dust poofed upward.

A new, more pungent odor filled his nostrils. His eyes watered and he noted it wafted from his very own self. He looked down, held out his hands as if they had somehow betrayed him. They were green with . . . horse dung. Fresh horse dung.

Thankfully, it was cakey rather than sloppy, as the coachman's spittle had been.

Nonetheless, Fletcher now found himself the possessor of more stains and smells befouling his once-fine clothing than he'd ever before encountered intimately in all his twenty-four cautious years.

His eyes watered and his head thudded as if cannons were competing for rank as loudest. He'd never felt so thoroughly filthy.

"Pardon me," he said, catching the eye of the beefy townsman in his stained brown felt hat. The man turned to face him once more and rested his hands on his waist. Beneath each hand sat a gun of some sort, sheathed in leather and hanging by his side.

But it was the round metal badge riding high on the man's suede-leather vest that caught Fletcher's eye. He'd not seen it earlier.

The man seemed to be staring at him, as if he were trying to figure out something about him, trying to place him somehow.

"See here," said Fletcher. "That . . . that brute. That uncouth brute" — he fluttered a hand toward the end of the street where the stagecoach had ventured — "nearly killed me. He . . . he nearly ran me down!"

"Hardly," said the man, squinting at him.

"But surely you saw him. . . ."

The man crossed his arms. "You in the street?"

"Well, yes, but . . ."

"You come in on the stage?"

"Well, yes, but . . ."

"You think maybe the stage should have taken to the sidewalk?"

"What?"

"Maybe you ought to get out of the street." The man cut his eyes to Fletcher's right, nodded, and looked at him once more.

How Fletcher did not hear the mule team clomping at a decent clip toward him was a testament, he would later think, to the fact that he was still addled by the vicious ride and by the foul treatment he'd received at the hands of the stagecoach operator.

At that moment, however, Fletcher J. Ralston dove for his life. He ended up in a heap once more in the street, this time closer than he had been to the sidewalk. He piled up at the feet of the lawman as the mule team stomped and rolled right over the spot where Fletcher had been standing. And where, he now saw, his leather satchel still stood. The team eased to a halt directly over it.

A bearded man in a straw hat and a blue shirt, black braces, and denim trousers set the brake and looped the reins.

"Hello, Marshal," he called from the wagon's seat. He looked down at Fletcher.

"It looks as if you have your hands full with a public drunkard. And here it is not even a Saturday night!" This struck the man as a comment worth hearty laughter. He was joined in a mutual chuckle by the lawman.

Once more Fletcher stood, hastily slapped the dust from his clothes, and glared as brutally as he was able at the assemblage of townsfolk all staring at him. A good many of them had also joined the newly arrived farmer in laughing.

"When you've had your fill of braying at my expense, sir, could you kindly move that . . . that apparatus? You have parked it atop my belongings."

"Hey?" said the man, looking down through the traces toward whatever it was the young arrival was pointing at. "Hey?" he said again.

Fletcher sighed. "Oh, never mind." He started forward, edging between the near mule's rump and the wagon, reaching and bending.

"Hey now!" roared the man in the wagon. "You want to get a good kicking? Get out of there, mister!"

Fletcher backed up, eyes wide, and spun to the lawman. "Did you hear that, sir? He" — he pointed at the man in the wagon — "he just threatened me with bodily harm!

Make yourself useful and arrest that savage! I demand satisfaction."

The lawman hadn't moved a whit, but stood with his arms folded and stared at Fletcher. Finally he said, "Gustafson here" — he nodded toward the wagon — "or, as you refer to him, 'that savage' was trying to tell you that nobody — that is, nobody in their right mind — would get between a mule and a wagon and not expect to come away with a kick or worse for their trouble."

While the marshal spoke, the man in the wagon had climbed down and peered under the wagon. He used a hayfork from the back of the wagon to drag the dusty and by then stomped and rolled leather satchel out from beneath the wagon. He nudged it with a toe, then scooped up the two loop handles with one long callused finger and carried it over and held it before Fletcher.

The marshal said, "I've known Gustafson since we were both young, strapping lads, and I don't recall him ever threatening anybody with . . . bodily harm. Seems you owe him an apology."

Fletcher assessed the situation, took in the now more than one dozen people lining the street and staring at him, at the marshal, at Gustafson. Then he looked at the mules. He swallowed and nodded. "Yes, it would appear I do owe him an apology." He reached for the bag.

The marshal's hand shot out and held Fletcher's wrist in a tight grip. "You still do. That was anything but, stranger."

Fletcher J. Ralston gulped.

CHAPTER EIGHT

Fletcher had gone over how this meeting was to unfold many times in his mind. He would arrive in town, gather his bag, and without hesitation, he would find the location of this Millicent Jessup.

He'd march there with the most serious expression he could muster. There he would demand to know what sort of person would keep him in the dark about being a relative, would then demand to know what, of all things, could be so valuable that after all this time he was commanded to journey halfway across the nation to claim it.

He had nurtured these intentions for much of the journey. But as the days ground on beneath the wheels of trains, then stagecoaches, his resolve had dribbled away, leaving him spent, wrung out. And this very day, the prized day, the pinnacle of his journey, had arrived, and it could not have unspooled in a more depressing, more exhausting fashion.

Now as he stood on the sidewalk feeling the eyes of the ill-bred, uncouth rabble staring at him, all he wanted was to find a hotel room and a hot bath, a hot meal, and a laundry service. Then, perhaps, after all that, if he felt up to it, then he might deign to pay a visit to this mythical aunt.

But looking about him, Fletcher was suddenly uncertain as to whether or not Promise, Wyoming Territory, could offer a weary traveler any of those vital things he required. Surely there was a hotel, perhaps a boardinghouse, something of the sort nearby.

His gaze roved up and down the street; then he heard a sound at his elbow. He turned and there was the lawman. Fletcher could have sworn the man had walked away as soon as Fletcher had offered the necessary bows and scrapes and noises of apology the farmer had needed for the affront Fletcher had apparently caused him. *Great,* he thought, *not only are they all dim-witted and slovenly, but they are thin-skinned as well.*

"Well, fella, what do you think of Promise?" The marshal waved an arm wide, smiling as he indicated the long main street. A bone-rack, tail-tucked dog scurried across the road and disappeared in a cloud of dust kicked up by a small buggy with a definite lean to the right. Fletcher saw it bore mismatched wheels. The very sight of it annoyed him, and something he felt deep in his innermost self snapped.

"If you must know — and keep in mind you asked, sir — I am disgusted by the very stink of this back-water burg."

The words, a flurry of which Fletcher was quietly proud, had the effect on the man's face he expected.

The marshal looked as though he'd been slapped across the mouth with a dead rat. "You know, boy, it might not be up to back East city standards —"

"I'll say."

"But the folks hereabouts like it just fine. Besides, you get more flies with honey than you do with vinegar, son."

"Did you just offer me a bit of sage wisdom?" Fletcher smirked. "This day keeps getting richer." He walked away from the lawman.

The marshal slipped a matchstick between his teeth and watched the kid, squint-eyed, before shaking his head and walking back to his office.

Fletcher strode up and down the street twice. He'd be damned if he was going to ask for directions now, especially from a resident of Promise.

He passed by something called Hanson's Emporium, the front window of which showcased all manner of tinned foods, dishware, and bolts of plain spun and flowered cloth, none of which he would have dared consume, eat from, or wear clothing made of. Style, it appeared, was another of life's many vital elements among the missing in Promise.

"All I want," he muttered to himself, "is this mysterious inheritance, preferably in the form of cash, though a bank draft will do. Yes, that would do nicely. Then a quick trip whisking me back to the glories of the civilized East forthwith."

He paused before a sagging sign that had seen more years than its initial paint job was able to bear up under. It wagged once in a slight, dusty breeze. He read it aloud: " 'Millie's Place.' "

It was the closest he'd gotten to anything resembling the name Millicent. But this seedy hovel? With red velvet curtains in the windows? And drawn closed at this hour?

With his nose held close to the clouded glass panes, that velvet appeared to have been sun-bleached such that it glowed with a faint green tinge, as if mold had grown over the original deep red. And dangling from the bottoms were faded gold tassels.

Fletcher sighed. *It obviously can't be the abode of anyone I might be related to. But perhaps Millie's Place might be a place of accommodation,* he thought. *It can't be worse than standing in this dust-clouded street on legs weak from thirst and hunger. Perhaps someone inside will know where I might find this aunt of mine.*

With another sigh and a slight hesitation, Fletcher J. Ralston thumbed the brass latch and pushed inward. The door resisted, and for a finger snap of a moment, he felt relief that he might not have to talk with anyone inside the hovel, after all.

But no, its slight resistance gave way and the heavy door slowly swung inward, squawking on hinges in need of lubrication. Then a brass bell tinkled above his head. It was attached to a coil of hammered brass that held the bell just above the door's lintel.

Dimness gripped the inside and he waited for his eyes to adjust. He closed the door, and as he looked about, he saw dark woodwork and darker furnishings. A wide staircase bore wine red carpet that even in the dim light looked to be threadbare, as if it had been trod much upon by heavy boots by many people. Surely, as indicated by the sign out front, Millie's Place was a hotel of some sort. And yet nothing indicated this was so.

"Hello?" he said, his voice thin and small-sounding. He cleared his throat and repeated himself.

From high above, seemingly many floors up, though the place looked from outside to have only two stories, a woman's voice said, "Keep your boots cool. I'm coming."

Now that Fletcher's eyes had adjusted to the low light, further details emerged from the dim gloom. A tall grandfather's clock stood in an alcove to his left. Beyond that hung a thick line of glass beads, but with so little light coming through, he could only guess at their color — perhaps ruby red. They hung straight and unmoving.

The reddish carpet beneath his feet was worn in places such that threads showed through the ornate design, as was the carpet on the stairwell to his right. The carpet runner led straight ahead down a hallway that continued beyond an open doorway past the stilled clock. He guessed it led to a kitchen.

The place, for all its seedy trappings — velvet curtains, glass beads — appeared to have strong bones and carved-wood craftsmanship he had not expected to find in this town. How long had this settlement been here? He had mused very little on the place itself, as his curiosity had begun and ended with the inheritance he was to receive.

He was about to part the glass beads to his left and peek into the room beyond when he heard heavy footsteps descending the stairs.

A woman in a long silken robe of black-and-blue design and belted about the waist stopped on the bottom step, one hand on the newel post. She was striking in appearance, thick in a buxom, wholesome way, and was, he guessed, a mulatto. She gazed at him through narrowed eyes down a long nose. Her head was canted to one side, and her dark hair was partially covered with a scarf that matched the robe.

"Huh," she said. "A stranger in Promise." She nodded and stepped down to the floor.

She was still taller than him.

"Okay, then," she said.

Fletcher cleared his throat. "I wonder, ma'am," he said, hoping to rein in the edge of annoyance these thin-skinned folk of Promise apparently felt whenever someone from the East spoke. "I wonder if you might help me. I am looking for a . . ." He suddenly doubted himself. Was that the name on the telegram? He should know it by now, having read it hundreds of times in the weeks since receiving it.

"Excuse me," he said, fishing it out of his inner pocket. He unfolded the worn paper, its memorized creases so hinged and worn, it had begun to come apart here and there. He held it to his face and squinted at it once more. "Yes, that's it. A Miss Millicent Jessup."

The woman snorted. " 'Miss.' " She held a hand to her nose and shook her head. "Pardon, but Millie'll like that."

"Like what?"

"Being called a miss. Been a long time since anybody's done that."

"Oh, you know her? Do you know where I might find her? I've been up and down this godforsaken street for what feels like days."

"Well, why didn't you come in here to begin with?" She shook her head and turned, holding the time-worn railing. "Come on, she's been waiting on you. We all have."

"What?"

She turned and looked at him. "Are you hard of hearing?" Her brows knitted and she spoke in a loud voice. "I said, follow me. I'll take you to see Millie."

"You don't mean . . . Millicent Jessup is the Millie of Millie's Place?"

She looked at him as if he'd just asked her if the sun had risen that morning. "Are you simple in the head?" She tapped her temple. "Millie didn't say so but . . ." She shrugged. "Come on now. I'm busy. Got one waiting and it's been a lean week."

Again, he had no idea what she was talking about.

She stopped again and looked at him. "You are him, aren't you? The one from back East, I mean."

Fletcher cleared his throat. "I am Fletcher J. Ralston, yes."

"I know." She eyed him up and down again. "I'm Hester."

"Pleased to make your acquaintance," he said, not feeling pleased in the least. "I do indeed hail from back East, as you say. Specifically from the fine city of Providence, in the fair state of Rhode Island."

"Yeah, I figured it was you. Just checking. And I know where Providence is. We've been hearing all about it — and you — for years."

"I . . . I don't understand."

"Course you don't." She began trudging upward once more. "You being a dandy and all, how could you know?"

Fletcher thought he saw her smile. He was too tired to respond, but he'd be damned if he was going to follow this obviously some-what deranged woman.

She stopped again and sighed. "Leave your bag there. Nobody in Promise is going to steal from you. Especially you. Now come on. She won't hold out much longer."

He did as she said, in part because his arms were tired from lugging the battered satchel. As Hester and he trudged up the stairs, the woman said, "There's four of us, plus Millie. I imagine you'll want to know that."

Fletcher could not imagine why anyone should presume such, but grunted as if it were information of value to him. "Why?"

But she kept climbing. Perhaps she hadn't heard him.

As they ascended, there appeared to be more light. Hester paused a moment on the first landing, but said nothing, then resumed her climb before he reached the landing himself. The second half of the staircase continued at an angle to the first.

They reached the top of the stairs. "Here's where most everything takes place." She waved an arm behind her down the long hallway.

He saw three doors on each side of the hallway and a window at the far end. The carpet runner continued down the hall.

To his right, a dented pail stood wedged in the corner. Hester must have been glancing at him because as he looked at it, she said, "That's to catch a leak. Of course, it hasn't rained here in I don't recall how long, so it's not much of a concern."

He felt as though he should offer something to the conversation, so he said, "That's a shame."

"About the leak or about the rain?"

"Oh, well, both, I imagine. Yes, both."

She chuckled. "I wondered if you'd be the serious sort. Should have placed bets on it."

Again, Fletcher was confused and on the verge of asking her what she meant when she gestured to the door facing them at the top of the stairs. "That's Millie's. She'll be waiting."

Then Hester stood and folded her arms. "Well?"

"Well, what?" he said.

"Aren't you going in? She's been waiting on you for . . . well, for a mighty long ol' time, Mr. Fletcher J. Ralston."

She shook her head and walked away, her heavy steps making the floorboards creak down the hall. "Everybody here knows who you are, Fletch. Everybody." Her chuckle petered out as she opened a door on the right at the far end of the hall. "Okay, you ready?" she said to someone inside her room. Then her door closed.

More confused than he'd ever been in all his twenty-four years, Fletcher J. Ralston, whom the woman had had the audacity to call "Fletch," nonetheless straightened his back, ran his hands down the front of his dusty, rumpled, and soiled suit, and slid his tongue over his teeth. They felt as though they needed a good cleaning, too. Everything about him did. Too late for all that.

"In for a penny," he muttered, and stepped forward, then knocked lightly on the big wooden door.

There was no response. He stretched his neck, ran a finger under his sagged collar, and knocked once more, louder this time.

"Come in," said a thin, frail voice.

CHAPTER NINE

Fletcher pushed open the door, a heavy thing with carved angles and filigree that caught dust and held it.

The door swung slowly, emitting a low, long squawk. He peered in. Across from him, afternoon sun offered dim light through gauzy once-white lace curtains.

"Come in, come in," said the voice of an old woman.

He nudged the door wider and looked to his right. There sat a huge four-poster bed, again built of dark wood, decorated ornately with pineapple carvings topping the posts and what looked to be green velvet drapes tied back at the corners. In the midst of the bed, against mounded worn pillows, lay a thin old woman with a long face framed in silver hair.

Fletcher supposed in her youth she had been considered a beauty. It was difficult to tell what the years had done to her. But she

79

was old — that much was certain. Seventy or perhaps eighty. He had no idea.

She raised a bony hand and beckoned him with bent, knobby fingers to step closer. "Come on in. I can't see so well that far away."

Fletcher nodded and, leaving the door open behind him, stepped into the room. The scent reminded him of old flowers dusted in talcum powder and something else, a liniment that tickled his nostrils and cloyed at the back of his throat, threatening to make his eyes water.

To the right of a bedside table on which were stacked books and a tall drinking glass half filled with something tea colored, another window let in light. He also noted it was partially raised at the bottom, letting in a light breeze, as the softly swaying curtain told him.

"Closer, for Pete's sake. I'm not going to bite." She chuckled. "Those days are behind me."

He walked closer until he stood beside the right side of the bed. If he leaned forward, he could have grasped her hand, which he had no intention of doing. She didn't move, except for her watery old eyes. They studied him with an intensity that made him uncomfortable. He wanted to say something, but somehow could not speak yet. Instead he returned her stare and saw an alertness in her eyes that belied the rest of her haggard, worn appearance.

He became aware of a steady, soft, regular sound and recognized it as a clock tick-tick-ticking somewhere in the room. It was faint, combined with the near-silent whistling of the old woman's breathing.

"Who . . ." He paused and found he didn't know where to begin. He had gone over and over so many questions in his mind throughout the long journey, but now that he was here, none of them felt clear enough to ask.

She interrupted his thoughts with a quiet, wheezy, chuckling sound. "I expect you have more questions than I have answers for."

That annoyed him. "You . . . Pardon me, but you had better have answers for me. I have journeyed quite far. . . ."

She stared again for a long minute. Then she sniffed and waved a long, bony finger at him, let it drop to the quilt once more. "You look like your father, but you remind me of your mother."

"You knew my father?"

The old woman nodded. "Of course. And your mother."

"Well, tell me," he said, crossing his arms and looking about himself, wanting a chair, wanting suddenly to know every single thing this old crone could think to tell him. He felt certain he could commit to memory every letter of every word she uttered.

She smiled and waved to the bed. "Sit down. I still don't bite."

"Thank you. I'll stand."

She nodded again. "Just like your father. So prideful. And I bet the big reason you're here isn't so much that the telegram mentioned you had an aunt, but that there's an inheritance. Am I correct?"

Fletcher felt his face heat. "Tell me about my parents. Please."

She surprised him by shaking her head. "Not just yet."

"What?"

She sighed. "After I've rested. I don't have the strength just now. Go to the lawyer's office. His name is Chisley DeMaurier. He's been instructed. He knows what to give you. You'll have more questions. Come back after you've read through it all, and then I'll tell you everything. I'd thought to be dead before you came to Promise. I didn't think you'd actually show up. I didn't think I'd ever see you."

"Why?"

She shrugged. "Not so sure I'd have come if I got such a telegram."

"Then I guess you didn't grow up alone, not knowing your family."

He thought he saw her face tighten, as if he'd insulted her. And for a moment, he felt good about it.

"Don't be so sure of yourself, young man. You assume too much in life, and someone's going to call you on it. And they won't always be a feeble old woman knocking on death's door."

Her face pinched and her eyes closed. A dry cough caught hold of her and seemed to rattle inside before echoing up and out. It stopped and she looked as if she were remembering something painful. She pulled in a long, fluttery breath and let it out, then opened her paper-thin blue eyelids and looked at him once more. "Go see the lawyer. I'll be better later. Then I'll answer any questions you have. I promise."

From behind him, a familiar voice said, "Leave her be just now. Come back in a few hours."

It was the woman who'd let him in. She'd said her name was Hester. He wanted answers, but she beckoned him to the door. Fletcher looked down at the old woman, but her eyes were closed. Hester waited while he passed back into the hallway; then she swung the door closed and made for the stairs. Fletcher didn't move.

"I want answers. I've come across the nation to get here."

She sighed. "Look. Half of what I know about you I expect isn't right, and the other half you can't trust, so save your questions for the lawyer and Millie. Later. Give her time to rest."

"But she called me here."

"Yeah." The woman nodded. "But she didn't expect she'd still be kicking when you got here."

"This doesn't make any sense!"

"Keep your voice down, mister. Or I will show you the fast way down these stairs. Do you understand? Now get gone and come back in a couple of hours."

"Will she last that long?" he said, his voice harder than it had been.

"That's an awful thing to say."

"That's rich, considering you just threatened me. Is there a soul in this forsaken town with a modicum of couth?"

He snatched up his satchel and stomped out the big front door. As it closed behind him, he turned. "Hey, wait a minute! Just where is this lawyer's office anyway?"

The door slammed.

"At least remind me of his name."

The door remained closed.

CHAPTER TEN

The lawyer, as it turned out, was easier for Fletcher to locate in the bustling burg of Promise than had been Millicent Jessup. His office lay across the street and down but one building.

From the start, Chisley DeMaurier, Esq., as his name on the shingle out front read, was a conundrum of a man to Fletcher. Beyond his burning desire to know the why behind his summoning to Promise by Millicent Jessup, he found he wanted to ask DeMaurier, Esq., just what brought such a learned man to Promise. And so he did.

The thin, well-dressed, obviously cultured man smoothed his shining black hair and twisted one, then the other of the ends of his waxed mustaches. "Why, whatever do you mean?"

Fletcher had assumed the man would speak with a French accent, but in that he was further stumped. The man's accent was of the Deep South and bore a touch of Cajun, perhaps. Judging from his perpetual half grin, he was obviously pleased by it.

"Now," said the lawyer, "if I may ask a question of you . . ."

Fletcher noticed that the man had not answered his own question, but he lost his urge to know as quickly as it had come upon him. "I am —"

"Wait!" the lawyer held up a long finger, a smile spreading on his thin face. "I do believe I know who you are." He looked Fletcher up and down, nodded, circled the room, one hand in his watch pocket as if he were about to pluck out the timepiece, but not quite doing so.

"A stranger, yes, yes, one who has had of late a rather difficult time of things." The man stood behind him. Then as quick as Fletcher turned to see what he was doing, the lawyer circled around to face Fletcher, that sly smile still on his mouth.

"You have acceptable taste in clothing. Indeed, in fashion. Though your clothes could use laundering in the worst way."

"Sir," said Fletcher, "I ask you to please excuse the sorry state of my appearance, which has resulted from more hardship than I care to go into at this point."

"No need, good fellow. I already know of

your rather surprising arrival in town."

"News travels quickly."

"That's why it is called 'news' and not 'olds.' "

"Hmm. As to my second point, I wish to know the details Millicent Jessup assured me you would provide."

"Indeed," said the man. With a sigh, he settled himself in a chair behind the large desk. "Very well, then. Your arrival is a bright spot in the pervading dull brown shade my days normally wear."

The lawyer ran a fingernail through a stack of papers, stopped midway down the stack, and tweezered out a sheaf. Settling pince-nez at the end of his nose, he cleared his throat. "Yes, yes, I recall drawing this up some time since."

"Some time?" said Fletcher. "How long has she been cooking up this scheme to get me out here?"

"Millie isn't devious enough to cook up anything, Mr. Ralston. She was planning for her future and she kindly included you in it. Do you want me to continue, or would you like to insult someone else for a while?"

Fletcher felt his face heat up and shook his head.

The lawyer cleared his throat once more. "Very well, then. Since you seem like a man bent on progress . . ."

The lawyer rose from his desk once more, tugged out his watch, from the chain of which dangled two small brass skeleton keys. One of them unlocked a tall chifforobe, which apparently doubled as office furnishing. He opened one door, careful to not swing it wide enough for Fletcher to see inside.

He pulled out a wooden box and tucked it under one arm, then reached back into the dark interior and pulled out a flour sack bulging with something heavy, judging by the whitening of the man's knuckles as he shifted it in the crook of his arm. He re-locked the door and seated himself at the desk once more.

He set the sack down beside the box, tapped the box, and looked at it, nibbling his top lip as if considering something of importance. Fletcher scrutinized the box, too, admiring it. Polished unadorned dark wood, perhaps mahogany. It was half as long as a cigar box and twice as tall.

The lawyer spun it around and pushed it toward Fletcher. Fletcher leaned forward and was about to set his hands on it when the lawyer said, "You know, Mr. Ralston, haste in youth is forgivable, to a point. Then it becomes mere greed."

Fletcher sighed. "Mr. DeMaurier, I understand how my seeming briskness may appear as such to you, but you, sir, have not been through what I have been through. If the contents of this box are life altering, then, perhaps my efforts — Herculean they have been, I don't mind saying — may have been worth it. If not, I must return to my home forthwith. Or I risk my position."

The lawyer regarded him. "Home . . . position. Hmm." He shoved the box another couple of inches forward and nodded. Then he leaned back and steepled his fingers beneath his chin, watching Fletcher.

Fletcher lifted the latch-free top. It was hinged at the rear and the soft scent of oiled wood and something metallic rose to his nostrils.

Atop the contents sat a small white envelope with faded indigo ink writing on the front. It read plainly: *To: The Treasure.*

"The treasure?" whispered Fletcher. He glanced at the lawyer, but the man's face was unmoving as it studied him.

Fletcher lifted the envelope, felt its thickness, several sheets inside at least. Then his eyes rested on what sat beneath the letter in his hand.

A gold locket on a thin gold chain sat in the middle of a soft green cloth. The locket was worn but polished and offered a warm glow. Scrollwork on its face was so ornate that Fletcher could not make out the letters represented. He picked the locket up and for the first time noticed how grubby his fingertips had become. He was usually fastidious about his appearance.

With a grimy thumbnail, he popped open the coin-size locket and it butterflied wide, revealing two tin-types. They were tiny, facing each other, a man on the left and a woman on the right.

The man was young and black haired and he wore trim but thick mustaches and bold dark eyebrows. His hair was slicked and parted in the middle, and he wore a stiff white collar with a high-knotted black tie and the slope of his shoulders was black.

The man appeared to be smirking, and instead of gazing across the hinge toward the young woman, he looked ready to shift his gaze toward Fletcher. The man looked oddly familiar.

A worm of suspicion wriggled in Fletcher's gut. Then he looked at the woman. She, too, was young, perhaps the same age as the man. *Twenty, if that,* ventured Fletcher. She was handsome, her hair gathered behind her head, lighter in color than the man's.

Fletcher imagined it to be auburn. Ringlets framed her pleasant smiling face. She, too, bore a strong chin and a long, pretty nose above a near-fully smiling mouth. This struck him as odd because most people did not smile when photographed.

She wore a brooch pinned at the throat, high up beneath the chin, securing a tall lace collar.

"They look like a happy couple," said the lawyer, who, unbeknownst to Fletcher, had walked over to peer over his right shoulder.

"Yes, it would appear so."

"The man, if I may say so, could well be your brother. The resemblance is strong."

"Yes, well . . ." Fletcher wished the man would leave him be.

As if his unspoken desire had been heard, the lawyer returned to his chair. "There is a reason for that, but of course by now you must be able to tell for yourself."

Even though Fletcher knew it, hearing the lawyer practically say so confirmed his suspicions. The people in the locket must have been his parents. They had to have been. So how had he come to be an orphan, then? And what was Millicent Jessup to him? She had said "aunt" in the telegram. Was she a sibling of one of these people in the locket?

"I suggest you open the letter here," said

the lawyer. Then he held up his hands. "You don't have to read it aloud, but I have other items to share with you, and it would be in your best interests to know the contents of the letter before we proceed."

Fletcher regarded him, then nodded. "Okay, then."

He turned over the letter and noted it was sealed with a wax stamp bearing the initials *MJ.*

"Millicent Jessup," he whispered.

"That's the one," said DeMaurier.

Fletcher found this scrutiny annoying. He wanted to take the letter to a cool, quiet place, a polished reading room in a library back in Providence. But he was here, in this dusty office. He worked a thumbnail beneath the wax seal and popped it open. His lips felt dry and he ran his tongue over them. The lawyer once again appeared to read his mind. He poured two glasses of water and set one before Fletcher.

"Thank you." He drank the glass dry and set it down and the lawyer filled it once more. Fletcher opened the envelope and pulled out four folded sheets of stationery. He unfolded them. The faintest scent of rosewater tickled his nostrils. The first sheet faced him, bearing the same indigo ink, slightly darker than that on the envelope.

The hand was fine, graceful, the lines straight and did not meander, and looked to him to be the writing of a woman — a lady, cultured perhaps, of breeding. Someone to whom penmanship was a mark of distinction.

The top right corner bore a date. With a start, he realized it was his birth date. The same date that had been in his personal files that he'd snuck in to the headmaster's office at Swinton's School for Boys to read when he was eight years old.

He'd learned nothing that he'd wanted to know, no hint of parentage or place or date of birth differing from which he'd been told. He sipped from the water once more, then read the letter:

Dear Fletcher Joseph Ralston.
If all has gone according to some sort of plan (I never have been all that great at making such things work in life, but who knows? Maybe this time.), you will be reading this in the office of Chisley DeMaurier, attorney at law (tell him I said hello), a man I trust eminently. I, however, will be among the dead. I have been failing for some time now and I find that there are certain of my affairs that require tending to.

You'll no doubt have found the items left for you, as now that you are of age (whatever that means), they are no longer mine to keep watch over. Your mother's name was Rose McGuire. She was the woman pictured in the locket. The man is Samuel Thorne, and yes, he was your father. About him, I'll say no more, except that the guns in this box were his, though in truth I deliberated much over whether to give them to you or not. In the end, I decided they were not mine, but yours, and you should do with them as you see fit. I hope you will dispose of them in the manner befitting a gentleman such as I know you have become.

Your mother died shortly after birthing you. I was there and helped bring you into the world. Your mother was in my employ. In addition, she was a good, dear, and trusted friend. Of your mother's family, sadly, I know nothing I might pass on to you. I am sorry for that. It is good to know of one's family.

On your birth, your mother knew her time was short and so asked me to see to it that you be given the opportunity to receive a fine "back East" education. And so I did, the wherewithal to do so having come up unexpectedly yet fortuitously at that time.

At the last, she held you, swaddled, and gazed on you with the love only a mother can offer her very own and called you her "treasure."

That brings us to me. I have referred to myself as your aunt, and in truth, I feel as though I am and have been throughout your years, firmly occupied in that venerable role of not-quite-mother. That I chose to maintain a distant, aloof demeanor or relationship with you has been a decision that troubled me the entire time.

I told myself, however, that you were better off not tied to the peripatetic vicissitudes (how about those words, eh, college boy?) of once-promising Promise, Wyoming Territory. Time has proved me somewhat correct in this. And yet, as always, I feel there is promise in Promise, enough so that I have maintained a life and, what's more, a business here. And that brings me to the aim of this letter.

The money I have relied on to fund your schooling and your lifestyle of somewhat conservative finery has, alas, dried up. I had hoped that by the time this finite resource should have reached its end, you would have found a pastime, an occupation that suited you, as the locals say, "down to the ground."

That you have somewhat done by clerking at Rhodes and Son. This has the whiff of possibility lingering about its edges. I take it to mean you have a keen interest in figures and in business. I will climb farther out on the wagging limb and say that you secretly wish to be the owner of a business. A proprietor, a merchant, a businessman. As I have been such for many years, a longer time than I care to recount here, and as I have come to regard you, albeit from a distance, as my only heir, I suggest you may as well take your life by the collar and drag it along — speed the plow, as they say — and go into the family line of work. Lawyer DeMaurier will kindly provide the details to you.

I wish you the very best this life has to offer you, young man. May the past be dead and the future be alive.

Finest regards, and all my love,

your ever-doting

"Aunt" Millicent Jessup

Fletcher's mouth hung open, slack and as wide as his eyes. His mind writhed in question like a tangle of snakes.

That's where the letter ends? he thought. He flipped over the pages, then spied one last, separate sheet of paper, smaller than the others, and with a faded pen-and-ink illustration of a rose in the top left corner. It bore two simple lines, once more in Millicent Jessup's hand:

This is from a poem I found to be most fitting to your circumstance:
   "From a rose, a thorn / and so, a thorn a rose."

Did that mean at his birth he had been considered a thorn begot by a Rose (clever) or a Thorne meant to beget roses? It sounded silly any way he considered it. He blew out a breath and folded the sheaves back together into their memorized creases.

Fletcher was angry and more confused than ever. "She is obviously dotty in the head," he said, leaning back for the first time in the stiff wooden chair across the desk from Lawyer DeMaurier. He looked at the man for the first time in long minutes. The man was studying him with intent.

"This is . . ." Fletcher held up the letter and envelope in his hands, let them drop to his lap. "Is there nothing else? The telegram said, and I quote: a 'significant inheritance.' "

The lawyer held up a long finger and slid both the mysterious heavy flour sack and the open wooden box farther forward on the desk. Fletcher looked at the box and reached for it, saw that the locket and the letter had not rested at the bottom of the box. He probed the depth, found a finger-hold, and lifted. There sat, on soft emerald felt, a pearl-handled two-shot derringer with a dozen shiny silver bullets nested beside it.

"Ghastly," he said. He'd never owned a weapon any larger than his penknife, which he used primarily to clean and trim his fingernails once safely at home in his rooms. "What am I to do with that?"

"Paperweight?" said the lawyer, no hint of a smile on his face when Fletcher looked up.

"And that?" said the young man, nodding toward the flour sack.

The lawyer spread his hands. "Open it."

Fletcher did so and his eyes widened. Two nickel-plated six-shot revolvers, also with pearl handles, sat polished and in their respective holsters, coiled about with a black leather gun belt with tasteful carving and stamping on the leather's smooth, shining face. The belt was studded with a full complement of silver bullets as well.

"I . . . I've never owned weaponry before."

"You now have quite the arsenal. Hand-some, too, as well as deadly."

"But what am I supposed to do with them?"

"They are your father's, after all. Perhaps you could keep them as is until you've had time to decide."

"Yes. Yes, I'll do that." Fletcher swallowed, and his gaze fell on the letter. His plight consumed him once more.

"What of this family line of work she mentioned? And who does she think she is, intimating that my hard-won appointment as a junior clerk at Rhodes and Son isn't a sound career move?" He leaned forward, eyes blazing. He felt his face heating. "Dotty in the head!" He circled a finger beside his temple and shook his head. He wagged a finger at the locket. "She's confused me with a charlatan whom someone has mistaken as my father!"

The lawyer sat behind his desk, fingers steepled before him, now a slight smile on his face. He waited for Fletcher to silence his sputtering. "If you're quite through . . ."

Fletcher's ears reddened once more and he nodded.

"Okay, then." DeMaurier leaned forward, his wooden chair creaking. "The family line of work Millie mentioned is her business, the one she has run for . . . oh, since the town came to be many years ago. She was one of the first wave of gold seekers to settle here. Then there was silver, and then there was . . . well, not much else. But by then the town had been established, people were raising families, and the stage line came through. Rumor has it, too, that two railroads are showing interest in running through these parts. If that's the case, Promise is well sited to be an important hub for commerce. The future is bright."

"That's all well and good, Mr. DeMaurier, but the business?"

"Ah, yes, sorry about that. I tend to wax rhapsodic where Promise is concerned. You live here long enough and you'll feel it, too."

"Ha. I don't intend to stay here any longer than is required for me to claim my significant legacy."

"Well, yes, as to that . . . You have inherited Millicent Jessup's business, lock, stock, and barrel."

"Her business?"

"Yes."

"What . . . what exactly is her business?" Fletcher felt he knew the answer and he wasn't certain he wanted to hear it.

For a moment, DeMaurier looked confused, then smiled. "I see. You have a subtle sense of humor about you." He lost his smile. "Oh, you're not joking."

"No, Mr. DeMaurier, I am not joking."

"Millie's Place is . . . Well, it's a bagnio, Mr. Ralston. A bordello." Fletcher showed no sign of recognition. "A home for wayward doves. A brothel, Mr. Ralston?"

Still, the young man wore the knitted brows of confusion.

The lawyer sighed. "A whorehouse, Mr. Ralston. You have inherited a whorehouse."

Fletcher's mouth dropped open.

"Oh, it's true, Mr. Ralston. And what's more, it's a business of much promise, no pun intended."

"But . . ."

"And there's more, Mr. Ralston." He picked up a paper, perched spectacles atop his long nose, and read. Finally he saw what he wanted. "Ah, here it is." He cleared his throat. " 'Mr. Fletcher J. Ralston, aka Samuel Thorne II, is to inherit the business, which includes all physical property including the home on Main Street, as well as the double lot on which it sits. Provisions are made for the women who currently reside there. They must be retained and kept on as employees and residents of Millie's Place for a period of no less than five years, and the business is to be run as a going concern for at least that period of time."

He finished, set down the paper, removed

his glasses, and regarded the younger man. For a moment, neither spoke.

Then Fletcher leaned forward, slid the paper toward himself, spun it around, and read it. "Samuel Thorne II?" he whispered, his brows pulled tight. Then he stood and wagged the paper, all his previous bluster and bravado crowding back in. "How legal is this?"

"It is as legal as it gets."

"But . . . but what am I going to do with a . . . a brothel of all things!"

"Seems to me it's an enviable position for a young man to be in." DeMaurier smiled, but was not met with one in return. The lawyer sighed and stood, his face tight. "Perhaps you should talk with Millie. She's a fine woman, and she has nothing but your best interests in mind."

"My best interests?" Fletcher thumbed his chest. "How does she or anyone but me know what's best for me? Hmm? They weren't the one left orphaned by whoever these damn people were!" He shook the letter's pages, still clutched tightly in his left hand.

"But you are correct, sir. On one count, at least. I will most assuredly go talk with Millicent Jessup or, as she prefers to be called, 'Auntie.' " He opened his broad-mouthed satchel and stuffed his newly acquired possessions inside in a jumble, thrusting the letter atop and strapping the bag closed once more.

The lawyer stood by the door. "If it's any consolation, I'm sure your arrival here surprised Millie. I believe she had thought she'd be deceased before you were able to venture out this way."

"Yes, well, if you lived a modest, quiet, unassuming life in a city back East, with a circle of few acquaintances, and you received a telegram promising a significant inheritance, I just bet you would pursue it with all haste. Am I correct?"

"You are, yes. I cannot deny it."

"As it turns out, however, Aunt Millie's definition of 'significant' and mine differ. Vastly." Fletcher stepped through the door. "Good day to you, sir, and thank you for your time."

"Drake's Hostelry," said the lawyer.

"Pardon?"

"The best and, at present, the only hotel in town. Two blocks up thataway." He pointed northward. "Can't miss it. Duck on the sign. Good food, clean beds, real walls, not those canvas affairs they used to put the miners in. Only place I'd recommend to a fellow gentleman." He nodded. Fletcher didn't detect any hint of condescension in the man's tone.

"That's good to know. And again, I thank you." Fletcher offered a quick bow with his head and departed, still seething inside.

Out on the street once more, he said, "Okay, Aunt Millie, here I come. And I demand answers. Even if it kills you."

CHAPTER ELEVEN

Fletcher J. Ralston passed a half dozen people on his way back up the street to Millie's Place, not that he noticed. He stalked by the toddler Dickerson twins and their stun-faced mama just emerging from Doc Hoadley's office with the confirmation of Miss Dickerson's seventh pregnancy echoing in her head. Then there were Mr. and Mrs. Baskers and young Bo Dover, part-time deputy.

They all paused along Promise's main street and watched the young dandy in soiled, wrecked clothes and reeking of dung and who knew what else as he stomped his long legs back up the street to Millie's.

Most folks in town knew, or thought they knew, who he was. Millie's nephew. But none knew the full story. And so they were more than happy to tease apart what scant, choice tidbits they felt they did have, then suture them back together to suit their own purposes and desires.

Not knowing the full truth didn't keep them from trying to find out. Barring that, they made up their own facts, out of convenience, nosiness, and a general lack of entertainment. Even poor, pregnant Miss Dickerson stared after Fletcher a moment, though hers was a longing look at someone roughly her age who seemed to have much to look forward to, free of a life on whom so many mouths depended.

Of all this, Fletcher was oblivious. He was also still livid, tired of feeling ill-used by everybody and everything; even the place in which he found himself felt as though it jeered at him. He was sick of these games, and he would get to the bottom of it all, by gum, as old Teaberry, the night cleaner at the bank, would have said when he found Fletcher still hard at it. Fletcher was often burning the lamp low in hopes of impressing the big men in their big offices.

And yet here I am, thought Fletcher, stomping along the sun-puckered puncheons of the boardwalk toward Millie's. He was armed with a bag of dust-smothered clothes, newly presented guns — three of the awful things no less — as well as a nonsensical letter. Not least of all, however, he had been given the knowledge that two people pictured in a gold locket were indeed his long-lost parents.

They were the two people in all the world, if he dared admit it to himself, that to this day he still pined to know. But why had he been denied a childhood with them in a loving or hating household?

He had also gained not only an aunt who was not really an aunt, but, worst of all, the knowledge that the very thing he had ventured out on this grand quest for, the "significant inheritance," was nothing more than the wreckage of a broken-down old woman's broken-down sordid old business and its attendant sordid dealings.

The very notion of owning a brothel made him shudder. Yet perhaps it also intrigued him. Was he not, indeed, a man, young and in his prime years? But this deluge of newfound information, of revelations, was overwhelming.

Then a thought stopped him two strides before Millie's front door. The letter had said the money had dried up. What money? *The money,* it had said. The money that had paid for his life, the money he'd received without cease all these years from what he'd been told by the man at the bank was a trust account set up by someone who wished to remain anonymous and who had taken considerable pains to remain so.

He'd pursued the matter very little after being told that some dozen years before, mostly because he didn't want to lose the money he'd come to expect and depend on to live. It had been a comfortable crutch his entire life, and now, the letter told him, it was gone.

Of course, he'd assumed once he received the letter from this mysterious "aunt" that she had been the one behind the money all those years. But he had harbored the deepest hopes since receiving the telegram and on the journey west that she was a fabulously wealthy woman who wished to meet him one last time, perhaps, but certainly one who intended to leave her entire vast fortune to him and him alone. A final act of magnanimity.

And he supposed from Millie's point of view, that was the case.

Fletcher transferred the now-weighty satchel from his left to his right hand and pulled back his free hand to rap once more on the big old door of Millie's. He paused, held his knuckles poised. Why knock? Was he not, after all, the heir, the new owner of the business and, so, of the building in which it was . . . transacted?

With a snarl, he snatched the brass handle

and thumbed his way in. The door once more swung inward and squawked for want of oil. This time he hesitated not a whit, but slammed the door behind him, wiped his shoes once each on the frayed ornate runner, and stomped up the stairs.

He could not say later what came over him at that moment, but he began shouting as he mounted the steps. His shouts raised footsteps and he was greeted at the top of the stairs by the same woman who'd greeted him on his first visit but a few hours before. Behind her was another woman, shorter, thicker, though younger, and with a great swoop of red hair piled poorly atop her head.

"Just what are you doing, mister?" said Hester.

At the top of the stirs, he shoved past her. "I demand to speak to Millicent Jessup right now!"

"No. She sleeps in the afternoon. She's not well," said the second woman.

"And at this very moment, neither am I. And as her time is limited, my time for gleaning answers from her is also limited. Do you understand?"

Before she could answer, Fletcher said, "I really don't care if you understand." He shoved past her, too. He twisted the knob on Millie's door, pushed inward, and closed it promptly behind him.

He expected the flustered women behind him knew at least as much as he did about his relationship to Millie and that he would want and deserved answers. They did not barge in behind him.

Dusk was falling fast on the dusty little town of Promise, Wyoming Territory, and darkness had claimed much of Millie's close-smelling room. The window beside her bed, near her nightstand, was open, and a soft breeze made the wispy curtains dance.

Seeing her supine form in the bed, sleeping away the time he felt he deserved, angered Fletcher. "How dare you . . . ?"

His voice came out low, a growl that surprised himself. Then the anger bubbled up once again when she did not move. "How dare you?" he said louder. Louder still, he began to shout, "I want answers, Millicent Jessup — and I want them now! Wake up!"

She did not stir. He mumbled loudly as he set the bag by his feet and fumbled with matches in a short glass holder beside the lamp. One strike, two, and then the match flared. He levered up the globe and lit the wick. The light bloomed bright and filled the space. He lowered the globe and adjusted the wick's height.

"Now," he said, turning his gaze once more on the bed, "you had better wake, Millicent Jessup, because I have traveled far too long for far too many days — no, make that far too many years of my life, for that's how long this journey has been — only to have you tell me scant news in a letter. A letter? How dare you!"

Still, she did not move. He leaned over her, laid a hand atop her shoulder, and shook her, albeit gently. She was an old thing, after all. The lightness of her body when he shook her surprised him. Still, she did not wake.

He pulled her toward him, and her head flopped to the side, eyes wide and sheened with . . . tears? She seemed to be staring up at him.

A puff as light as a girl's quiet breath bloomed in his face, the same cloying, close smell he'd detected when he'd burst in earlier. For the briefest of moments, he felt pity for her and thought she was crying and unable to answer him. And then he saw her neck.

In the dim light, a ragged stain had bloomed across her neck and gown, covering part of her shoulders and the nightgown's breast as well as the top of the folded sheet and blankets. One old veined claw of a hand rested half curled atop the blanket as if she'd been about to grasp something or else cuff something away. But Fletcher barely noticed this, for the welling darkness about her neck glistened wet. Between that and the old woman's eyes, he didn't know what to think.

But by then somehow he knew that he was in real trouble. This wasn't just some nearly dead, half-crazy old woman. He felt some sort of allegiance to this woman. She was someone he realized he needed.

"Millie?" He bent low with caution and reached for the blankets to pull them up. Some instinct told him she would be cold. Where he'd grabbed the blankets, his hand felt wet, sticky. He pulled his fingers away, held them up before his eyes. His hand was smeared with the same darkness he'd seen at her throat.

She was not moving, and he knew she would never move again, in fact.

Fletcher's breath held in his throat. He reached for the lamp, lifted it, and ran it low over her form. The front of her blankets, which he'd grasped and pulled up, he now saw was a smear, a pool, a saturated, sticky, sopping mess. It was blood. Had she somehow hemorrhaged? What was her affliction?

As he stood half bent over her, the light illuminating her torso and the bloody, savaged mess that had been her neck, he saw the cause for what it was now, a brutally sliced throat. The papery, powdery soft wrinkles and folds of the old woman's neck had been sullied, soiled forever by a savagely dragged knife blade.

His breath was stoppered in his throat once more, and in that pause of quiet, a gasp, then others sounded from behind him at the door. He straightened, surprised, holding the lamp higher, half swinging toward the sound.

There stood Hester and the woman with the mass of piled red hair. Behind them stood others he could not quite see.

"What have you done?" whispered Hester at the fore of the clot of faces. She shuffled forward, her hands before her mouth, her eyes wide and white in the low light of the softly guttering lamp.

"I . . ." His voice was hoarse, catching in his throat. "I . . ." The woman's words soaked into him as had the blood into Millie's blankets. "No . . ." He shook his head. "No, it's not . . . not that. I would never . . ."

Behind her, the other faces drew closer, two or three women in dresses and corsets and thin shawls crowded into the room. They shoved closer to him, and he looked back over his shoulder and saw the sight for what it was: the gore-riddled body of their mother hen, their protector, their madam.

She's now dead, as dead as dead can be, thought Fletcher. Not only would he never get to know her, but he would never get to hear the answers to so many questions he had for her. For the one person in all the world who could have answered them.

And then the screaming commenced. It seemed to set others off, and they, too, screamed, at least three of them. It stopped when he held up his hand. He saw in the lamplight that the hand he held aloft glowed like an eerie, sticky crimson glove of gore.

"No!" he shouted, as much to stop the infernal screams as to somehow bring himself back to himself. His breath felt hotter than it should, as if scorching him from the inside out.

"What's going on here? What's the trouble?"

It was a man's voice, a familiar voice.

Fletcher turned and saw a man behind the women. Though hatless and surprisingly bald, the marshal was still recognizable in part by his drooping mustaches.

"It's Millie!" shouted Hester. She looked

at Fletcher. "What have you done? Oh, Millie!" She rushed toward him, but the lawman had shoved his way forward and stepped before her, edging her back.

Fletcher noted the marshal was clad in only his long underwear, his boots, and, oddly, his vest, which hung from one shoulder, the silver star glinting in the lamplight. As soon as he saw the bloody mess that was Millie's body and bedclothes, his eyes widened and his breath hitched as he tried to speak. Finally he looked up at Fletcher.

"Apple didn't fall far from the tree," he said, his eyes narrowing on Fletcher. Then, without turning, he said, "Dominique, go fetch my gun belt. Hurry now."

That was when the situation finally resolved itself in Fletcher's mind. He was in a very bad position, found standing over a dead woman, freshly so from the looks of things, and his hand sticky with blood.

"What did you mean?" he said, looking at the lawman.

"I knew your father, and you're the only stranger we've seen around here for days. Nobody else came or went. Everybody in town liked Millie."

"But she was my . . . aunt!"

"Yeah, well, we all know the score on that. Besides, you busted on in here all angry-

115

like, and we all heard you shouting at her."

"You?"

"Yeah, I did. Me and Dom — Aw, hell, that is not the point!"

As if he'd had his head dunked in a cold mountain stream, Fletcher's thoughts sharpened. He saw how this looked, and he saw how this was going to play out. A beloved woman of the town was dead, and he, a stranger, was found standing over her with blood on himself. The marshal's gun belt, just arrived, was thrust through the gaggle of women by a fleshy unclad arm.

Fletcher saw all this as if time had slowed. The free man inside him, the innocent man, the clerk, the businessman who valued law and logic and decorum and decency above all else rebelled at what he could foresee was about to happen.

He bent, snatched up the loop handles of his satchel that sat by his right leg. As he stood, he blew out the lamp as the lawman grabbed for his gun belt.

Fletcher heard gasps as the room went all but dark in the gloaming of the dusk. He thrust the lamp clumsily aside atop the bedside table as he bent low and hoisted a leg up and over the windowsill.

"Hold! Hold there!"

But the young dandy had no intention of

holding or stopping or slowing or doing anything except getting the heck out of that room of death, a room filled with people who thought he had done something awful, perhaps the most horrific thing anybody had ever done or could ever do.

He managed to pull his second leg up and over the windowsill. It wasn't until that point that he remembered he was somewhere on the second floor of a tall house. And it was near dark. . . .

A thunderous noise sounded, echoing at his left ear, and another followed it, along with sizzling sounds and thunking close by. "Hold there, I say!"

That mad marshal was shooting at him!

Another boom and sizzle and the glass window-panes shattered; then the frame by his head blew apart. Slivers of wood and glass stabbed his face, and he gasped and stifled back a shriek as he shoved his way out the window.

He lost his balance, slipped too far to the right, and felt himself falling. *Here it is,* he thought. *I am going to die in a fall from a window, chased down as a killer. They'll find me collapsed and broken, bleeding out my last.* . . .

But that was all the time he had for fanciful thought, because he landed. Not on the hard-packed earth, but on something even less forgiving. The roof of a shed or shelter or lean-to of the house itself, he knew not which.

He slammed and clattered and rolled with it. Or tried to. The layered plank roofing bucked and sounded like thunder as it bounced beneath him. He heard a slight cracking and didn't know if it was his bones or the roof. He kept tumbling as though he might never come to a stop. And then he did — right at the edge.

He calculated he'd dropped a mighty distance, enough that the rest of his journey to the ground could not be that far below. He jammed the heels of his boots hard against the roof to find some footing.

But then he slid forward once more and felt the roof disappear beneath his legs, then his backside. Then his right side pulled down hard, careening him off the roof into nothing. He was falling again, and he hit hard once more, collapsing in a pile on the earth. His wind was knocked from him and he groaned, spitting sand and fighting to pull in a breath.

He saw flecks of bursting light before his eyes and thought for a moment he was seeing a town as if from on high. Then they disappeared as a ringing in his ears increased. The wood and glass pocking his face throbbed, and shouts grew louder with each moment.

Shouts? His plight came back to him in full and he shoved himself to his feet, wincing at new pains. His left ankle had most definitely felt sturdier mere minutes before. He also realized he still held the cursed satchel clutched in his right hand. Why hadn't he left it behind? It could only slow him down, laden as it was with guns and useless papers and a trinket with likenesses of people who hadn't cared enough for him to survive.

"Survive" — that last word struck him as though it were an open hand. There were the shouts, from the marshal, no doubt, and women, too, the women from the bordello. That would make them . . . prostitutes. And other voices, lights, lanterns flickering off to his left. From the shadows, it seemed he might be looking down an alleyway, perhaps between the buildings of the main street, such as it was.

Great, thought Fletcher as he spun, running away from the lights, away from what he guessed was the town proper. *I'm in this hellish, forsaken place for less than a day, and I'm to be set upon by a seething mob of locals. What did they call them? A posse? And*

119

all led by outraged, vengeance-seeking prosti-
tutes on the warpath.

As he stumbled, caroming off a rough-sawn plank fence, he saw the faces of the women in the room, in the dim light of that lamp, saw their pure confusion and sadness and anger and, yes, even fear. Of him!

He had caused that. Somehow he had caused all this; he was as sure of it as he was certain he was soon to be caught and lynched for something terrible, something terrible that he had not done.

Fletcher J. Ralston ran. Despite the blood streaking his face from the gashes and punctures of the wood and glass from the gunshot-ripped window frame, despite the swollen lump that was his left ankle, despite his cramped fingers, and despite the heavy satchel slamming his legs, he ran away from the little town of Promise.

Fletcher had no idea where he was headed, but he ran there just the same.

CHAPTER TWELVE

Skin had forgotten that he had always liked the way it felt to lay a blade to someone's throat and saw away. He'd done it to the old bird and it had indeed felt fine. Like a long pull of water after walking across a desert. It was a feeling he'd experienced several times on the trail since he left prison. Now he was here finally, the pit of the place, the center of the canker that had plagued him all this time.

He settled back against the wall, confident that the busted-down stagecoach beside him hid the glow of his cigarette from the crazy folk running back and forth down a ways from him on Main Street, Promise.

He hadn't expected them to pin his slicing job on somebody else, and quick, too. He'd no sooner slipped out of that old crow's bedroom window and made it to the roof when he heard some crazy man shouting in there how he wanted answers from her.

Why, it was all Skin could do to keep from sliding off the roof outside that window, he was laughing so hard into his hand! He felt like saying, *Sonny, you can shout all you want to, but that old whore's talking days are through!*

Now he stood back in the shadows well down the street, watching the commotion he'd caused, and wondering not a little who it was these fools thought had done the deed. He lit another cigarette and puffed with vigor. Tobacco had been something he'd missed in prison. It was rare he'd gotten a dose of it in that rathole.

Every sliver of every moment he'd spent in that hellish pit, Tin Falls Prison, welled up in him even as the first luscious drops of the old crow's blood pooled beneath the blade.

He'd relished that delicious moment when the old whore was still alive, still aware of who she was, where she was, and what was happening to her in that precious brief slice of time when her mind was still with her and the room still made sense to her.

Skin fancied he'd experienced it as she had, with her smells, her old, frail, failed body beneath the layers of quilting and

122

nightgown, and the ticking of her old mantel clock. The dim light of that dying afternoon cut in through the dusty, close air, through glass and the yellowed lacework curtains.

And when she realized what was happening to her, she tried to scream, but found it was too late for that, for her screams brought nothing but pink bubbles from the deep red welling gash — *pop, pop, pop.* That was the bit Skin Varney decided he had enjoyed most of all. The old woman's blinking eyes had given him the satisfaction he had long desired.

And yet he did not think the old bird knew who he was. And why should she? She had been but one of so many people in Promise who had wronged him, robbed him — that was rich, coming from the man who had robbed them, after all, and he chuckled at the thought. But then he grew grim once more. No, damn it, they would all pay, if they knew who he was or not.

He would let them know because he was their nightmare. He had been a man in his prime years, and they had locked him away, to rot and toil and sweat and eat bad food and fight rats for that very food and sometimes eat the rats, too, when the warden shoved you down in the Hole. The pit within the pit — that was what they called it.

No, these bastards deserved to know who he was and why he was there. He had nothing to lose. The entire time he was in that hellhole, he'd had one goal beyond wreaking his revenge on the town that had robbed him. This is where he would begin his hunt for Samuel Thorne, the real culprit in all this.

If they didn't know where he was, then he would take the town apart piece by piece, person by person. Promise was where he knew the double-crossing backstabber had spent all his time — with that witch who'd whelped his offspring, Rose something or other. A whore at Millie's Place. Lowest of the low.

And he knew all about whores. His own mother had been such, at a hog farm on the trail west, and he'd grown up scurrying like a rat from her diseased room whenever a team of drovers rumbled through.

He knew what whores did and what they were good for, and that was why he'd told Thorne back when they'd partnered up to stay clear of Rose. He'd wasted his breath. Might as well have talked to a stick.

Skin Varney shoved away from the east wall of the stage depot and scratched at his thick thatch of peppery beard, then gnawed a fingernail. He'd do well to play this game a little longer, tease it out and see how much of a knot these fools got themselves worked into.

"I got time." Varney chuckled low and walked back behind the empty depot to where his bone rack of a horse stood, hip-shot and dozing. "Skin Varney's got plenty of time now."

He smacked a hand on the saddle. "Wake up, horse. Let's us go make camp in the hills, then pay a visit to some old mine rats up thataway. Then we'll give thought to choosing our next visit to the pretty little town of Promise."

Within moments, the only sign of Skin Varney in town that night was the lingering smell of smoke and the last echoes of his low husky chuckling.

CHAPTER THIRTEEN

It was the deepest ink black night Fletcher had ever known. And yet, once he began to look around, really look into the darkness, he saw that it was not all black. The sky overhead was shot through with sprays of light, far off and high up. Starshine — and there was so much of it, he saw, now that he had slowed to a limping walk forward — was a sight he'd never beheld in such abundance before. Even if he had wanted to see such beauty, he had been nested in the sooty, cramped environs of Providence, his home, his town, his chosen place.

But had it really been his own chosen place? Or had he been forced into life there as a child to be kept tight and safe within it, schooled and sheltered?

He heard a far-off yipping. Coyotes, he was certain of it. He'd heard them several times on the journey west, and had been told of them by one of the stage drivers.

This one sounded too far away to do him any damage, or so he hoped. Yet he was now troubled with this notion that nothing, absolutely nothing in his life was as he had thought mere weeks before.

Before him, a soft sliding sound jerked him to a halt. It continued away from him. What could that have been? A rat? A snake? His toes curled in his boots at the thought.

He resumed walking, yet at a slower pace. His entire life so far had been a lie. And then he stopped trudging once again as a fresh and mighty notion came to him. Where had he come by the name Ralston? Neither from his father, this Samuel Thorne, nor from his mother, Rose McGuire.

Why should he have a name different from theirs? Unless this entire mess was some odd hoax. But why? To what end? To bilk him out of money he did not have? He coughed and sniffed as dust from his awkward steps tickled his nose. He was desperate for a drink, for food, for a bath, for clean clothing.

"If I thought closing my eyes would whisk me back to my home in Providence, I would already be there."

But that was not to be. And he knew it. It did not change the fact that he was in a predicament not of his making. In mere hours, he had become a stranger to himself. He was also not wealthy, as he had expected to be. Not only was he not the beneficiary of a substantial inheritance; he was penniless, save for a run-down bordello. He smiled in the dark, thinking of what the faces of his few friends back East would look like as he explained that he was now a whore-master.

He was also an orphan once again. Or perhaps not, as he had no way of knowing if his father was alive. And was this Samuel Thorne actually his father? To top it all off, he was now a man suspected of murder, a man who he guessed would now have a bounty price put on his head. All for something he had not done.

Fletcher sighed in disgust. He really was clueless as to the ways of the people out here on this savage, law-free frontier. What would they do to him once they caught him? He had little doubt that they would run him aground eventually. He'd run not so much to escape them as out of panic. He needed to give himself time to think.

"Think, Fletcher," he said to the night about him. "There must be a way to extricate yourself from this foolishness. What would Mr. Heep do?"

His supervisor was, after all, one of the

more clever people he'd ever met. "Mr. Heep," said Fletcher as he walked. He licked his swollen, cracked lips. "I know you are a busy man, but perhaps you could spare me a moment of your precious time. You see, I am in a bit of a fix — a bit of a pickle, as you might say."

In the dark of the Wyoming night, Fletcher waited for an answer, but the brilliant Mr. Heep did not respond. He searched his own cluttered, distracted mind, seeking reason and logic, even as he looked back toward the place he'd left, the angry little town where a woman lay dead, a woman who, it seemed, knew more about him than he himself knew.

After a fashion, he found he had been walking gradually, then steeply uphill. He had also begun with increasing frequency to walk into trees and low rocks. The trees grew thicker, and he recalled on the stage-coach ride into town that the slopes of the hills down which they'd rumbled had been treed, thick with them at times, what type he didn't know, but they hurt like the devil when he walked into them. He also recalled the town had been nested in a valley surrounded with foothills that led to mountains. He could be walking in any direction by now.

He wondered if he was leaving a trail. He'd read somewhere in his youth, at Swinton's School for Boys, about those larger-than-life frontier figures who could all read "sign," as they called it. One had made the boast that he could track a mouse across bare rock. If that were even half true, then Fletcher had surely left his own sign, a trail of dragging footprints, across the sparsely grassed, earthy countryside that led up into these hills.

No, "hills" was not the correct word. He recalled the size of the peaks toward which he'd roved. They were mountains. None of this helped him as he trudged on toward he knew not what. He might figure out what to do next if he found a quiet place to hole up, to hide away and think. Perhaps by a stream.

Oh, he would give his entire laughable inheritance for a drink in a clear, cold mountain stream. He giggled out loud. "Inheritance, indeed." He sighed. A brothel?

That his thoughts turned once again to the grisly, gruesome sight of poor old Millie, slain in her bed. Who had done such a brutal thing? And why?

Fletcher was also aware he had grown cold as the night thickened about him and the length of his strides had shortened. He'd shifted the satchel so many times from one hand to the other, he was no longer aware when he did so. He was aware only of the sore ache in his curled hands, the blisters on his palms, the throbbing in his face, the thudding pain in his left ankle. He hadn't dared to pay more attention to his face and neck than to pick out the largest of the slivers bristling from him like pins in a cushion.

You must keep moving, he told himself. *One step more and, after that, one step more. And so on and on until you reach . . . where, Fletcher? Where is it you hope to reach? Isn't one place as good as another when you are lost and alone in the mountains of Wyoming Territory?*

He put one dragging foot before the next, stumbling upslope, ever steeper in the darkness, cursing as he collided with unseen dangers. Eventually he groped a coarse-barked tree, bigger around than he could reach with his aching arms.

"Enough," he whispered, his breath clouding the darkness before him. He leaned, hugging the tree. "Enough for now, for tonight."

And Fletcher J. Ralston slumped, collapsing into a pile beneath the tree, half leaning against it as sleep overpowered him like a grizzly on a mule deer fawn.

131

CHAPTER FOURTEEN

What woke Fletcher wasn't apparent right away. He turned his head and dozens of hot needles poked his face and neck. He winced and groaned; his body fought the act of unfolding from the hunched, seated position he'd assumed the night before.

Exhaustion had draped over him, pressing down like a wet wool blanket, and he'd not moved in all the hours since. Muscles he hadn't used since romping on playing fields of his schoolboy youth had been exerted, stretched, pulled, twisted, and then dropped once more into disuse.

Through the fog of sleep and pain, Fletcher registered that the soundless thing that woke him and turned his head was the gaping black snout of a gun, the end of the barrel hovering two inches from his left temple. The barrel looked long and hollow and seemed to echo with the screams of everything it had ever laid low.

It was thick and made of gray-black steel and looked heavy, and though Fletcher had no idea if it was a shotgun or rifle, he did suspect it was the last thing he'd ever see with clarity.

Then something fuzzy-looking shifted some feet beyond it. The blurred thing was brownish and gray and wispy. Fletcher had trouble bringing whatever it was into focus. When he did, he saw a face, a man's face, an angry man's face. Silver bearded and bushy. And above the big mustaches, a long, narrow nose angled downward. It looked for the briefest of moments like a hawk's beak.

Above that sat two wet, flinty eyes the color of January river ice, surrounded with narrowed red lids. The eyes daggered into him as if he were something of extreme disgust to be killed, wiped out. Above the eyes, two brows, as amply furred as the mustaches, jutted at the outer corners like birds' wings about to take flight.

Atop the man's head sat a brimmed brown felt hat adorned with all manner of items. Tucked in and dangling from strips of rawhide were flopping feathers, multicolor beads, and bits of wood. The hat's band was of black and white hair from a creature Fletcher could not even guess at.

Fletcher tried to swallow. Despite the bone-numbing cold of the morning, a droplet of sweat slipped down his own nose and quivered at the tip, tickling him. Without much thought, he reached with his right hand to wipe it away.

The man with the gun grunted a quick, low sound, as if he was waiting for such an excuse. A gnarled hand, the one supporting the length of the barrel, adjusted its thick-fingered grip on the polished wood fore-stock.

Even through his fear, Fletcher smelled the sour stink of liquor wafting off the man.

"You . . ." The stranger's voice was as his grunt had been, low and even, like steel sliding slowly across steel.

"I —"

"Shut it."

Fletcher swallowed again and tried to stop shaking, but with no luck. The man continued to stare at him.

Fletcher let his eyes move away from the gun and the man's hard stare and saw, below the bushy gray beard, that the man wore a buckskin tunic, grease stained and adorned with tattered fringe and spotty beadwork. The whiskey stink mingled with other smells — stale sweat, woodsmoke, gun oil, a raw animal stink earthier than the rank odor of wet dog and undercut with a rancid-meat stench — that mingled to make Fletcher's eyes water and threatened to tease a sneeze from his dripping nose.

Finally, the man moved back from him a single step, but he held the gun as he had. Fletcher thought perhaps it was a shotgun, though his knowledge of such things began and ended at the marksman range back in his school days.

"What you doing here?"

"I . . . I don't know. I don't know where here is. I'm lost. I'm a stranger here. Turned around."

"Come from Promise?"

"Yes." Fletcher began to nod his head and the man prodded forward with the barrel once more. Fletcher held his head still.

"Yes," he said. "From town."

"That decides it then."

"What . . . decides what?"

"You're the one, the dandy."

"The dandy?"

The man nodded once. Then, without taking his eyes from Fletcher, he turned his head and spat a long rope of thick brown spittle to the earth. It looked to Fletcher as if he'd just deposited some of his meal. He wanted to ask if the man was ill, but then he recalled the shotgun rider's penchant for spitting, and he realized the man was chewing tobacco.

"The one who . . ." His bushy beard waggled slightly as he chewed and spoke. It was then Fletcher noticed that around the old man's mouth, his mustaches and beard were stained yellow and streaked with the darkest brown of the chaw juice dribbling from his mouth.

The teeth beneath the lips, what Fletcher could make out of them betwixt the flowing whiskers, were another surprise. Fletcher assumed, given the man's brusque demeanor, that his teeth would be rotted, jagged, painful little stumps. But they were whole, somewhat yellowed, and bared as a dog might do on seeing something it despised.

The other man let the spittle dribble from his lips, further staining the hair about his mouth. "The one who" — his voice rose in pitch and his words squeaked out as his eyes wrinkled — "killed and ran!"

"What?" Fletcher's eyes widened farther. "No! No!" He began to shake his head but the gun inched closer. "No, it wasn't me. I tell you I didn't do it. Let me up and I'll explain."

Once more, the man regained his voice. This time it was loud and thick with emotion. "You'll explain right where you are! And where you are is your death site, I tell you, varmint from hell itself!" He chewed violently for a moment. "Killing brute! I just come from town. I know what I know!"

"No, no, I only found her. I —"

This seemed to incite the man into a frenzy. His mouth chewed whatever god-awful thing was in there with a speed as though he were on the clock. His bushy brows rose higher and his blood-rimmed eyes bulged. His gun jammed tight, dimpling into Fletcher's temple, forcing his head sideways until his right ear nearly touched his shoulder.

It was time to explain, for his death, Fletcher felt, was nearly upon him. He also thought that perhaps he had urinated in his trousers.

"I couldn't kill her!"

"Why forever not?" The words were thick, loud, juiced with spittle and emotion.

Fletcher hesitated. *Think, man, think!* Indeed, why forever not? There was no logical reason he couldn't have killed Millie. He was a stranger here, after all, and he had more motivation to see her dead than most, he suspected. The property was his now and he had shown anger toward her. But he had to defend himself. *Think, fool! This old man is going to kill you!*

"She is . . . was my aunt, for pity's sake! I
—"

"Hey?" The old man turned his fiery red-rimmed eyes on Fletcher and he thought for a moment that the man had gained twice his stature, so frightening had he become. "What's this? Your aunt?"

All Fletcher could do was nod. He began to, then remembered that any movement elicited a near-death experience at the hands of this stinking, leather-clad mountain goat of a man.

"That makes you . . . ?"

The young dandy swallowed. "Fletcher. Fletcher J. Ralston." Out of introductory habit, he extended a hand slowly, then paused it in midair, wondering if the man would think in the dim light that he was trying to draw a gun on him.

That was when he thought of his guns. In his bag. Of no use to him at present, nor even afterward, for he had little practical knowledge of how to use such a thing. Still, they had looked to be in good repair, not rusted, but cleaned and oiled and shiny — almost new-looking, in fact.

The old man scowled at him, his face frosty and boiling with hate all at once. He looked to be considering the situation through his drunkenness. "Filth, is what I say. Filth and all . . ."

This made no sense to Fletcher, but he didn't dare speak. His news had somehow eased, if only slightly, the tension between them. Fletcher sagged, his muscles screaming. Despite his predicament, a thin groan leaked from his mouth.

The old man did not appear to notice. But he did ease back a step once more and Fletcher thought his grip on the gun had softened. The big knuckles were less white-looking.

"If you are who you say you are, I will give the matter thought before I touch the trigger on Ol' Bossy here and leave your head with a smoking hole where your brains ought to have been."

Fletcher had to think about this. Had he just been given a reprieve, however slight, from imminent death?

"Get on your feet and walk thataway!" The old man pointed uphill, to the right. "Now get on up there ahead of me."

"I . . . gaah!" Fletcher tried to stand and found he was paralyzed. Every minor movement twinged a lightning jag of hot pain, as if a knotted chain of razor blades was being dragged through his body up and down, side to side.

"What ails you, vermin?"

"No, not vermin. My body. I have not moved since falling asleep last night here in the dark."

"No wonder! Look at the clothes you're wearing! Layers of foolishness on top of foolishness. An onion of foolishness is what you are!"

Despite his predicament, Fletcher felt as though his ego had been thoroughly slapped. "I beg your" — he managed to straighten a leg and massaged a kneecap — "pardon, but I'm . . . gaah . . . clothed in the very latest wear available for a gentleman trending forth on an adventure westward."

"Sound like a fool who's experienced his life through a newspaper. Fools, all! Every damn thing ever come from a city is foolish, and no mistake." The wild man nodded, agreeing with himself.

It went on like this without cease as they walked, the once-near-silent, crazy old man berating him with unfounded accusations.

"Gunnar."

"Pardon?" Fletcher discovered that in addition to being deranged, the man was prone to mumbling to himself.

"My name!" He spat brown juice to the earth.

140

Did everybody in this fiendish place chew tobacco and spit upon the ground and half upon themselves?

"Gunnar. Gunnar Tibbs!"

"Ah, I see."

"No, you don't. You don't see nothing because you're from a city and city folks are all stupid. Blinded by what they think is their own importance and grandeur."

Fletcher almost said that he was impressed that the old man could use such a large and noble word, but he thought wiser of it.

"I will tell you what you can and can't see, and what you can and can't say. Far as I'm concerned, you're a dead man walking anyway. You're a killer and a thief and all."

"But I tell you —"

The crazy old man poked the gun's barrel into Fletcher's back once more. It hurt as much as it had the first four times and he responded again with an "Ow!"

It didn't matter to the man.

"And stop shuffling that sack of yours from one hand to the other. Pick one and stick with it! You don't stick with a thing in life, you'll never amount to nothing."

Great, thought Fletcher, trying to ignore the throbbing in his cramping hands. *I'm getting unsolicited advice on living from a lunatic.*

CHAPTER FIFTEEN

As they climbed higher into the mountains, the winding trail grew steeper and tighter and seemed to Fletcher to switchback into itself unnecessarily. He was so exhausted, he stumbled and fell into boulders and leaned, sagging, against trees.

"What ails you, killer? You got a case of the dropsy guilts?" This struck the crazy old man as humorous and he cackled.

Fletcher did not care much what this old fool thought of him. He risked showing the man, at least with his eyes, his displeasure at being treated with such callousness. The old man didn't notice.

At the next tree, Tibbs said, "You don't keep her moving, I'll give you what for!"

"As I don't know what that might entail, I will only say that I will risk it. I had a long night in the cold and I —"

"Oh, you had a long night? Ain't any longer than what my poor Millie has been through. And her night ain't never going to end! Now get on up the trail or I'll make meat of you!"

That got Fletcher's feet shuffling upslope once more.

Soon the trail wound around a cluster of boulders each taller than two men. Before them, in a glade somewhat stippled with trees, sat a cabin.

As unkempt and crusty as the old man was, his cabin, or "the homestead," as he called it, was a refreshing, surprising, and welcome sight. It seemed to appear before them as if it had been conjured.

The abode itself was a log structure, not a surprise given the preponderance of trees surrounding it. But it was also of a chalet design, wide and low with a center peak and colorful adornments, which surprised Fletcher. It looked not unlike those he'd seen illustrating the serialized adventures in *Cawley's Weekly Reader,* following adventurer Hans Sigridson's journeys into the high Alps of Switzerland.

Two windows flanked a plank front door, but it was the windows' shutters and flower boxes beneath, all painted a gay red and filled with yellow, blue, and green flowers and leaves, that most impressed Fletcher.

The front peak stood roughly eight feet,

though far out of the bent old man's reach. Adorning the end of the ridgepole was an impressive set of antlers.

Fletcher stood weaving and pulling hard breaths. His sight rested on the antlers and he closed his eyes to the bright blue morning sky above. As pretty as it was, it made his head ache. He opened them once more and noticed that something up on the antlers moved.

"That's Mort."

Fletcher squinted and realized the moving bit of the antlers was a black bird, a crow perhaps, though on the small side, but sleek and attentive. In fact, he looked to be watching the two men with as much attention as they were showing him.

"He looks . . . healthy," said Fletcher, noting the bird's shining wings and breast.

"He ought to. I feed him, so he don't work at all. Useless as birds go, but good fun to have around."

"Why Mort?"

"After my brother, another useless devil who relied on mooching and handouts to get by. Ended up marrying a rich widow, living out his life in high style in San Fran—Hey!"

The old man jerked the gun barrel to point at Fletcher once more. "I knowed you

144

were gifted with the silver tongue! That's how you got the better of Millie, and that would take some doing. . . ."

He pulled the gun's barrel back for another poke, but Fletcher shied away, spinning to face his captor. "I tell you, sir, I didn't kill anyone!"

He didn't care anymore what the old man thought or didn't think of him. He was fed up, beyond exhausted, and filthy with the grit and grime accumulated since the last decent bath he'd had, which had been in . . . St. Louis? *Oh, my,* he thought, *how long ago was that?* Weeks had passed since then. The very thought made him ill.

The two men regarded each other. To Fletcher, the old man, this Gunnar Tibbs, looked plenty potted and besotted with alcohol. He certainly exuded a drinker's stink, and his eyes were still bloodshot. He weaved on his feet, looking as unsteady as Fletcher felt.

A full minute passed before Tibbs spoke. "Could be I have read you wrong, dandy. Could be I am right, too. More than likely that is the case. I have yet to be wrong in this life, except for the times when I have been." He hiccupped and prodded the air between them with the gun's barrel once more, as if to emphasize the point.

"You saved your sorry skin, at least for a spell, by claiming to be Millie's nephew. It's possible you say you are him and that you are him. . . ." He hiccupped again.

Once more, Fletcher had no idea what to make of the man's blurry speech. He chose to keep his mouth shut.

"But you have presented me with a case of reasonable doubt" — here Gunnar smiled and nodded, anticipating Fletcher's surprised look at him uttering such an impressive phrase — "and I have been drinking to soothe the pangs of mourning that have draped themselves over me like an evil quilt."

"I had no idea an article of bedding could acquire traits of intent," Fletcher said in a low voice, even though he knew he should not have said anything at all.

Quick as a snake strike, Gunnar Tibbs jabbed him in the gut hard with the snout of the gun. "Don't test me, boy. I ain't stupid and I damn sure ain't deaf." He straightened and regarded the doubled-over dandy before him. "Now, I will forgive that fresh lipping of yours, at least for the moment. But I will tie you up while I cogitate on the situation."

Even in his freshened, wheezing state, Fletcher heard and understood what the crazy old man was about to do with him. "No, I can't . . . I won't take any more. No more!"

It pained him to hear himself wail like a fat child with no sweets, but there it was — the frontier had reduced him to savagery, just as it had all the people who had ventured west of the Mississippi River.

"Then I'll kill you where you stand, just in case I am right and you are the killer of my dear, sweet Millie!"

Fletcher hung his head, feeling the weight of futility and exhaustion once more.

"Walk on over to the front porch and drop that bag of yourn on the top step. No, to the right. Yes, that's the spot. Then walk over there where I'm pointing this death-dosing shotgun. You see that big rock yonder?"

"Yes."

"Good. Go over there and do your business. I'll keep a respectful distance. Then you get back here and get comfortable because I have some thinking to do."

When he'd returned, walking as if he were wading in knee-deep sand, Gunnar motioned him once more to the porch post. "Set down there and put your hands behind yourself. And no more of the city-boy, greenhorn, dandy whining, neither!"

Fletcher merely nodded and did as Tibbs

bade him.

The old man worked quickly, something for which Fletcher was grateful. Tibbs' breath close by him was a fetid wash of curdled air.

"Why should I not turn you in to Marshal McDoughty?"

"That man," said Fletcher, not trying to keep the sneer from his voice, "is a ruffian and a buffoon."

"I don't know I disagree with all that, as he's been a burr under my saddle for some time. Long time ago, he thought he'd slide on in ahead of me and get himself in Millie's good graces." Gunnar sipped from a bottle of amber liquid. "But she fooled him."

"How?" Fletcher would do anything, even perpetuate this inane conversation, to keep his mind off of the cramps and jags of hot pains he felt in his muscles and joints. He wondered if his knees and ankles and wrists would ever recover from this harsh treatment. *Why didn't I go into law instead of banking?* he thought. *I might then have known how to take this kidnapping ruffian to task once I am cleared of false accusations.*

"She saw his true colors, that's how. And she stuck with me through it all, as I did with her, too. Been sweet on each other a long time. Until last night, oh!" Tibbs' voice cracked and he wept once more into his outstretched grubby palms. " 'Twas the only night I hadn't made it into town before dark in a month. Had trouble at the mine."

"Then by your own logic," said Fletcher, "you are a suspect as well."

"Hey? What's that you say?"

Oh, no, thought Fletcher. *Why can't I learn to keep my mouth closed?*

The old man eyed him once more with that squinty gaze. He surprised him, though, by merely shaking his head. "Ain't polite to tell a fellow he's kilt the love of his life. Pray you never feel what I feel right now, boy." Tibbs stood and stretched. "Of course, as you'll likely only be alive for another few hours, it don't much matter what you pray for."

He swigged from his little bottle of amber liquid and nudged Fletcher's bag closer to his own feet.

"Those are my personal possessions, sir. I'll ask you kindly to leave them alone. You have no call to . . ."

Faster than Fletcher had ever seen any sleight-of-hand man, Gunnar Tibbs, drunk as he was, shucked a big-bladed hip knife, leaned forward, and shaved off two buttons from Fletcher's soiled gray waistcoat. The mother-of-pearl buttons spanged and popped upward before plinking to the worn floorboards of the porch.

"Hey!" said Fletcher, then stopped. The tip of the shining steel blade, a point as sharp as a snake's tongue, hovered before Fletcher's dirty, unshaven chin.

"What's that you was gonna say?"

Fletcher swallowed. "I . . . I believe you'll find a number of items of interest within my satchel."

Tibbs nodded and began lifting out the more recently acquired items. "Well, well." He unrolled the two-gun rig, hefting the pair of pearl-handled killing devices. He paused, admiring the gleaming black carved leather gun belt. "Oh, uh-huh," he said, nodding his head in silent agreement.

"What?"

"ST."

"Oh, yes. Those would be the initials of the former owner, one . . ."

Again, Gunnar nodded. "Samuel Thorne. Yep."

"How did you know?"

"Makes sense, as he was your pappy."

"I thought the jury's out on that particular verdict, Mr. Tibbs."

"Naw, no it ain't, neither." Gunnar set the revolvers aside. "You look just like him." He lifted out the box with the derringer, harrumphed. "Hideout gun. Hmmph, figures. Another of your papa's weapons."

Then he came to the locket, and even with his grubby, work-thickened fingers, the old man managed to pop it open. Fletcher half expected him to bite it to test for gold content, then stuff it in his pocket. Instead he squinted at the two pictures, smiled at one, frowned at the other, grunted, and clicked the locket shut once more before replacing it in the box.

Lastly there was the letter. He recognized the writing on the envelope as Millicent Jessup's and his face pinched a little.

"Oh, Millie," he whispered. He set the letter back in the bag, reached for his bottle, and glugged back a long swig.

"You may read it if you like," said Fletcher. "I have nothing to hide."

"Thank you, but I reckon I don't need to."

"Why not? In fact, if it will help to convince you I'm innocent of so ghastly a crime, I insist you read it, sir."

"Insist all you want, dandy. I ain't going to read that letter. I already know what it's got to offer."

"But how could you?"

"I was there when she wrote it. Asked my opinion of it all."

151

"From the look on your face, I'd say you disapproved of the course she took."

"Let's just say she didn't heed my advice on all of it. Or much of it, for that matter. Millie Jessup is . . . was . . . a woman who knew her own mind and to hell with anybody who disagreed." He smiled at the memory of his sweetie. "I think she asked me just to be polite, didn't have no interest in taking my advice from the start anyway."

He stood, rubbed his back, stretched, and yawned.

If his hands hadn't begun to throb like a month-old toothache, Fletcher might have felt more sympathy toward the quietly blubbering old man. As it was, he kept his peace and let Tibbs grieve.

Fletcher suspected he should feel worse than he did about her death. She was, after all, his aunt, of sorts. The fact that he hadn't known her did little to lessen his guilt.

Then the old man surprised him. "Time to eat," he said, and untied the rope he'd moments before wrapped tight about the porch post.

With his hands still tied, Fletcher struggled to a standing position once more. Tibbs poked him in the back and herded him into the cabin. "Set down there," said the old man, nodding toward a chair drawn up to a table. A few moments later, the old man had begun cooking breakfast.

"How come you dress as you do?" Fletcher asked.

Gunnar Tibbs looked up with bloodshot eyes from shoving bacon around in a cast-iron pan and regarded his guest. "I could ask the same of you."

He dished up the mad fried scramble of eggs, potatoes, and chunks of stale bread and draped the still-limp bacon atop. "Now let's us get down to the nub of it and we'll see if we can come to terms."

"Are you going to free me or should I just dine like a dog?"

"First off, who said anything about you eating? Could be I fixed up that second plate for myself, save me time walking to the stove to ladle up the last of the pan's offerings. Then there's this: Say I do untie you. What makes you think I can trust you? You're a city boy, and a rabbity sort at that. And I ain't yet convinced you didn't do the foul deed that laid Millie low. Hey?"

Even as he said this, he walked up beside Fletcher and slid the big hip knife out of its beaded and fringed sheath. The young man's breath hitched and he tensed. Gunnar laughed.

"Relax yourself, dandy. I wanted to kill

you, I'd have done it by now. Rummaging through your traps convinced me you likely didn't kill Millie. In fact, I got me an idea of who done it. It's a long shot, but then again, what else have I got, what with you innocent and all? Mostly anyway."

He sliced the rawhide binding Fletcher's wrists, and the young dandy's arms flopped down, hanging like wet ropes. Fletcher groaned as blood filled his hands once more, slowly rubbing them together, then his legs.

"Sorry to cause you such strife, but I didn't get to be an old crotchety mining mountain man by being carefree and citified."

"What have you got against cities, Mr. Tibbs?"

"Ain't nothing good ever happened in one, nor anything good ever come from one."

"I beg to differ. Innovations frequently arise from within so-called citified environs. And I myself am a product of the fair city of Providence."

"You ain't helping your argument, boy. Why, just look at them togs of yours. My word, who in their right mind wears spats? What's the point of such a getup?" The old man shook his head and stared in wonder at the begrimed, tattered gray thing hanging above Fletcher's right boot.

Fletcher's gaze followed and he noted with a sigh that his left spat had dropped off somewhere on the trail. They hadn't been cheap, but they had been, as the salesman at the haberdashery promised, "the very thing."

"Only thing worse than two spats is one."

"Are you going to be in your cups all day?"

"If you mean, am I going to suckle on the whiskey teat? You bet. Millie never much minded and she mattered to me. You, on the other hand, I ain't decided if you're annoying or if you're bold. You got spark. I'll give you that. Ain't nothing like Millie's, though."

He rubbed his chin and eyed the ceiling. "I tell you that woman was a tiger, but you got spine. That's your mama's doing. And Millie's, don't mind saying. Ain't nothing to do with that useless lump that was your father."

"What do you know about him? I want to know. Millie promised to tell me, promised to answer all my questions, but when I got there . . ."

The old man stared at him for a long while, then finally shook his head. "No, I don't know nothing that might help you. Nope."

"Okay, then. You mentioned something about someone else having done the deed." Fletcher nearly gulped down the plate of food the man had set before him. He'd not realized he was so hungry. Nor could he deny that the man, however crude, had proffered a truly toothsome repast, however crude.

Gunnar plunked a tin cup by Fletcher's elbow and drizzled steaming-hot coffee into it from a dented gray enamel pot. "I did, yep." He filled his own cup, then collapsed into his chair, uncorked the whiskey bottle with an audible *punk,* and dolloped some into his coffee.

"Man I'm thinking of is none other than Skin Varney." He looked at Fletcher with wide eyes and nodded his head. "Yep, none other than."

"Am I supposed to know who that is?"

"If you don't know who Skin Varney is, then you sure are from a city."

"I think we've already determined that I am. And proudly so. Who is he?"

"He's a notorious outlaw, an unsavory brute your father double-crossed . . . Oh, let's see. How old are you?"

"Twenty-four years of age."

"That's when it happened, then. I know folks who know folks, and I heard tell he was released from Tin Falls Prison not long ago. Why they would do such a thing is a mystery. He's a vicious, killing rogue wolf who should have been skinned out long ago."

"But surely he's aged, mellowed since then. I have read that prison will do that to a man. In fact, rehabilitation is the entire reason for imprisonment in the first place."

The sound that clawed up and out of Gunnar's throat was both a laugh and a gag.

"All right, then," said Fletcher. "Since you obviously disagree, why should we care that this brute has been set free on the world once more?"

Tibbs rolled his eyes. "Young people, all the answers and none of the smarts. Because, smart young dandy fella, Skin was double-crossed by your very own father all them years ago in this very town. Well, north of town, to be honest, on the old freight road that ran the Chillowaw Rim. Folks don't use it much now since mining tailed off. But back then, it was the quickest way to get from Talusville and the half dozen mines up back in the hills over to Promise way. Once Piker Holdings bought all those miners up and began ferrying ore and payroll back and forth, it was traveled regular."

"How does this . . . Samuel Thorne fit into all this?"

"Oh, you mean your very own pap?" Gunnar winked and sipped his coffee.

He seemed to take a sadistic pride in making Fletcher wince.

"Ol' Sammy Thorne, he was a piece of work, I tell you. Mined a bit here and there, but he was a dandy at heart. No big thinking going on to see where you got that fondness for frippery and all. He'd get into trouble now and again, lots of small-time stuff — things would happen away from town and he was the suspect. Couldn't necessarily explain himself or his whereabouts, but the law in them days was scant on the ground. Mostly it was vigilantes, citizen courts, and such.

"I remember that night of the big robbery. It was storming, vicious weather. When the thunder boomers come on in here to the valley, why, they savage us. Roll right down here from the north to the south, mostly in summer, sounding like a cannonball dropped onto a wooden floor. Anyway, one night we had all manner of weather happening hereabouts. And most of the town was crowded into Filbert's Dance Hall.

Don't look for it now, 'cause it ain't there, much to my lasting regret. Ain't no place finer a fellow could kick up a fuss and a fight and a dance, all rolled into one."

He nodded and sipped. "Your pap was in the dance hall, doing a solid job of winning more than he was losing to the baize goddesses. By the look on your face, you ain't a gambling man, eh, Mr. Dandy?"

"No, sir, Mr. Tibbs. It takes me long enough to make my money. The last thing I need is for some buffoon to take it all away from me due to an overreliance on liquor and chance. There is, to be certain, very little skill involved in thieving money from someone at a poker table."

"You'd think that, wouldn't you, bein' a greenhorn and all? I can tell by the way you run poker into the ground that you don't have any idea what goes into making a true gambler. Not like your old man and . . ." Gunnar shook his head. "Well, since Skin Varney's foul name has clouded my mind once again, I figure I might as well try to figure him out. See, I thought long and hard on this, and I come to the notion that Varney, he wants revenge. Sure, your father and him were pals once, but 'twas all of Promise who made him take to the high trails and go on the run, penniless and hounded by posses."

"How do you know all this?"

Gunnar's head whipped back as if Fletcher had smacked him with a dead fish. "How do I know? Why, boy, I was in on the posse. You got to understand: Nearly everybody in Promise and the surrounding mine camps hereabouts all had a stake in the money stolen that night. I was leaner then and could shoot the whiskers off a skeeter at a hundred paces. And I frequently did, too. Never was a skeeter in these parts who needed to own a razor. I was that good.

"Good as I was with my irons, your father was even better. I don't mind admitting it. Had himself a natural inclination, you might say, with those guns." He nodded toward Fletcher's satchel, in which the guns sat.

"Why would he steal from his own town mates, his own friends?"

"It's a solid question, but I think the answer's simply because he could. It was the challenge that intrigued him, not the notion of thieving from his fellows. Sam Thorne was a lot of things, but most of all he was a selfish young man who cared for his own comforts and happiness above all else."

"So where does that leave us, Mr. Tibbs?" Fletcher massaged his wrists where the rawhide bindings had trussed him tight.

"It leaves us at what they call an impasse. I reckon you're not the vicious bastard who laid Millie low. Could be it's Skin Varney coming back around for revenge. It's the best chance I've got for getting to the truth. And it's the only chance you've got to clear your name."

Gunnar let that hang in the air for a moment; then he said, "I'm not much for partnering, but" — he rasped a gnarled hand across his mouth — "I suppose if you don't get in my way, why, I could be persuaded to take you on, show you what I know. Maybe we can work together to free the ties that bind you. Same time, we can track Varney and lay him low, as he done to Millie."

Tibbs' olive branch was tempting, but Fletcher was still wary of the old rogue. "How do you know for certain it was Skin Varney?"

" 'Cause I don't believe in coincidence, that's why. He's released from prison and Millie's the one who . . . Well, you never mind that right now! Trust that I know what I know, is all. Too many questions. I knew it. This is going to be a big mistake. I knew it. I knew it. Should have blowed your head off while I had the chance. Now I got to put up with you."

"If this Skin Varney fellow is as bent on revenge as you say he is —"

"He is!"

"Okay, then, if that's the case, you really think he'll kill more people?"

"I don't think he will. I *know* he will."

"Until . . . ?"

"Until" — Gunnar shrugged — "the whole town's dead, I reckon. That's what he promised when they hauled him out of here in irons. And he can do it, too. That Skin, he's hellish with a knife and a gun. Always was, I don't reckon much has changed. If anything, I expect he's gotten meaner. Prison has a way of making a fellow curl in on himself, like a horn that keeps growing in a circle, until it grows right back in and poisons the body."

"That's a gruesome imagine, Mr. Tibbs."

"Yep," he said, nodding. "And that is what's happened with Varney. 'Gruesome' is the word for the likes of him, Mr. Thorne."

"Please don't call me that."

"What? Your name? Pshaw, I ain't about to call you something somebody made up when that's not who you are. Can't outrun your past, boy. It has long arms."

"I still don't understand how you've come to know all this. But perhaps you can tell me one more thing. For now."

"Just the one, eh? I'll count myself lucky if all you ask is one more thing and nothing else." Gunnar smoothed his mustaches with a gnarled hand and resettled his feather-bedecked hat on his shining dome.

Fletcher ignored him and plowed ahead. He reckoned that he knew the answer, given what Gunnar had told him all along about his father, but he asked anyway. "Is what you've told me the reason behind why Marshal McDoughty said the apple didn't fall far from the tree?"

Gunnar nodded. "Yep, pretty much what I've told you, boy. Your pap, Sam Thorne, he was a gunhand, a low-class gambler, and a thief. He was a scoundrel of the first order. He left a bunch of sore folks scattered all over the West who still, to this day, still feel ill-used by him, me included. The worst of them all was his old pard, Skin Varney."

"Why?"

Gunnar sighed, then nodded, as if he'd come to some agreement with himself. "Because your dear ol' papa made off with all the money from a big heist they pulled, left Skin holding the bag to take the blame. And for that, Skin got hisself sent to Tin Falls Prison. I for one, but not the only one, hoped that bastard would have died there

163

long ago. It ain't a forgiving place, from what I've heard. But as we know, he didn't. And now he's riding hard on the vengeance trail."

"What happened to Sam Thorne? I have his guns, left to me by Millie. She must have known him, met with him after the theft. I assume he's dead. That's what everybody seems to want me to think, isn't it? And the money, if she'd met with him then, perhaps she had the money? Maybe he left it to my mother? Surely if that had happened, perhaps she gave it to the authorities."

Gunnar looked at him for a long, quiet moment. His watery eyes didn't waver but held firm. Then in a quiet voice he said, "Could have worked out that way, yeah. But it didn't."

"What do you mean?"

Gunnar sighed. "I'll tell you this just the once. Then I'll never speak on it again. You hear?"

Fletcher nodded.

"Okay." Gunnar looked toward the ceiling. "So help me, Millie, I know I promised I'd never spill this sack of beans, but dang it, the boy has a right to know! And you didn't have any right telling me something like that in the first place. You know how I am with a secret."

He looked at Fletcher. "Your father, Samuel Thorne, that low-class gambler and thief, come back to the bordello that night you was born — same night as the heist. He had the money on him, and he demanded that Rose go with him. Millie wouldn't allow it. Wasn't possible anyways. You was not only coming. You was on the way. But that Sam, he was impatient.

"He told Rose if she didn't go with him right then, he was never coming back for her. He knew she couldn't, which made it all the worse. He didn't want to be stuck with a wife and a kid. Not a fella like him. Too stuck on himself, he was. But it broke Rose's heart to hear him say that. Millie, bless her, she was a spitfire. She leveled on him with her trusty sawed-off gut shredder — same one I carry now — and gave him an ultimatum. 'You will stay, and you will pay the piper,' said she.

" 'Or?' said Sam." Gunnar shook his head as if in disbelief at the memory. "Millie, she cocked both barrels. 'Or I will kill you.' "

"Well, that Sam, he licked his lips, looked at the struggling, failing Rose, about to have his baby, and said, 'But . . . the money, the law. I can't go to jail!' Then he smiled. He was a waffler, old Sam was. Even then he tried to make a deal with Millie. 'I'll tell

165

you what,' he said. 'I'll split the money with you.'

"Millie shook her head no. 'Tell *you* what. You will take your leave right now, or I will kill you where you stand.' "

"What happened then, Mr. Tibbs?"

Gunnar sighed, blew out a breath. "Well, Millie ran him off into the night. But oddly enough for him, he was true to his word. Mostly."

"Mostly?" said Fletcher. "What's that mean?"

"Millie did see him one more time. At Rose's funeral, Millie swore he was there, overlooking the proceedings from a small rocky rise. Then she never saw him again."

Fletcher was silent for long moments, sipped his cold coffee, then said, "Were they in love?"

"She loved him, yes."

Fletcher offered a wry smile. "That's not what I asked, Mr. Tibbs."

"Oh, I know that. I'm no expert on such foofaraw, boy. If I was, I'd likely have married Millie a hundred years ago and had a passel of squallerin' brats."

Again, there was silence. Then Gunnar said, "Look, boy, I can't tell you what I don't know. And I won't make up something just so you can feel good. That would be a lie, and while I'm not above working up a windy tale now and again, it doesn't sit right to lie about that to you.

"But your mama, Rosie McGuire, now she was something else. Don't know much about her past. Millie told me some years ago that she was an orphan girl ended up making her way out West from back East somewhere. Was poorly treated by folks on the trail and Millie found her near starved here in Promise. Took her in and the girl sort of fell into the way of life natural-like.

"But Millie was no demon madam like you will hear about now and again. She was a mother to them girls. She run a clean operation, wouldn't brook no badness from the men who visited. Millie was hellish with that shotgun of hers. That one there. She give it to me when she took too ill to heft it well. The other women there, Hester and Delia and Dominique and the rest, they all have weapons of their own. I wouldn't cross them.

"But your mama, she was a peach. Kind-hearted and always smiling, no matter what foul things she'd been through before she got to Promise. Never spoke of them except to say the past was always something you could learn from. It was your duty to learn from the past, that sort of thing. Good egg, that's what she was. And devoted to Millie. Never was a cross word betwixt them. Not until she fell in love with your pap anyway. Then she went against the grain with Millie, got crosswise with her a bit. Never enough so they'd fall out, nothing like that, but there were hot words tossed back and forth. Millie saw Samuel for what he was, you know, but couldn't convince Rose to keep clear of him. Love is like that."

He stopped talking long enough that Fletcher, who'd been tracing a pine knot on the tabletop with his fingertip, looked over at the old man. Gunnar was wet eyed and gazing out a front window.

"Fine, I'll take you on. I'm going to need you to work with me, no question, so we can lay low ol' Skin Varney. I can't let that man get away with this madness of his, killin' folks and all."

"And you'll help me clear my name."

"Yeah, that, too."

Fletcher nodded, but decided he'd need to keep a close eye on Gunnar Tibbs. Not because he didn't trust the old man. In the short time he'd come to know Gunnar, he felt certain he could trust him, but he also knew the old buck's hatred for Varney and his own father was so deep — and for good reason — that it might cloud him when a critical moment showed itself. What that should be and when, Fletcher had no idea. But he had to be ready.

"Did my mother really love this Samuel Thorne?"

Gunnar sighed and sipped his coffee. "This again?"

"Yes, this again."

"You mean did she love your namesake?" Gunnar cackled and smacked his buckskin leggings with a gnarled old hand. "You bet she did."

"But how could she love so unsavory a character?"

The old man looked at him for a long moment, his head tilted to one side. "You ain't never been in love. Else you'd know the how of it."

"I most certainly have," said Fletcher, reddening.

"No, no, you ain't, neither."

"Well, maybe I have and maybe I haven't. I really don't see where that's any concern of yours."

"You're right. None of my affair, but it explains a whole lot about you, boy."

"Such as?"

"Such as how you make a snorting sound anytime anybody mentions their fondness for somebody else."

"I do not."

Gunnar nodded. "Yeah, you do, too. I mentioned how I felt about Millie, and you did it. And a couple of times since when your mama's name come up and Thorne was mentioned."

"Oh. Well, I had no idea."

Gunnar waved a paw at him. "I'm not bothered. But you ought to figure out a thing before you go trying to knock it off its feet. Besides, you can see the reason in that locket of yours. Your pap was a handsome fellow, and your mama, she was a looker. Sweet girl, too. Very kind, always laughing. Thorne fell for her. Shame his heart was already occupied by somebody else."

"Who else? Was he already married?" Fletcher had thought that his newfound life story could not possibly become more complicated.

"No, I meant him. He was in love with himself. Thought he was God's gift to the world."

"Everybody speaks of him in the past tense, as if he were dead. Do you think he is?"

The old man shrugged. "No idea. Wouldn't surprise me none, though. Fellows like that usually don't last long. I expect he'll have met his end since leaving

Promise in the night. The only thing you have to keep in mind is that Millie kept her vow to Rose. Your mama wanted you to get an education. I'm not certain why Millie sent you back East for such, but I've thought on it some over the years."

"And did you come up with any reasonable hypothesis?"

"There you go again, lobbing two-dollar words at me. Thing you should be asking yourself is how she could afford to pay your way all these years."

"I was told it was an anonymous party that wished to remain so. After a while I gave up trying to find out."

"Even after you got to an age where you could think for yourself?"

Fletcher nodded. "Even then, yes. But you know the truth behind it, I can tell. Otherwise, you'd not have brought it up."

"I'm guessing Millie knew that all the good schools were back East, so she set you up there, give you a new name so nobody'd ever know you were . . . Well, in case anybody ever went snooping, they'd not find you so easy."

"So that's the beginning and ending of how I got my name?"

Gunnar shrugged. "Might be she mentioned an uncle or some such back in the family woodpile with the name of Fletcher or Ralston."

"Hm." Fletcher grunted. "But why would Millie do all that?"

"Shows you how much she thought of your mama. That Rose, she was like a daughter or a baby sister to Millie."

"And so that made me a nephew of sorts to Millie."

"Yep," said Gunnar.

"It's ironic."

"How so?"

"Millie did so much for me, yet she was nothing to me."

Gunnar turned on him, fire in his blood-shot eyes. "Nothing? Maybe she wasn't nothing to you, but you were something to her. She was always going on and on about you. Like to never shut up about how well you were doing in school and such."

"How would she know that?"

"Oh" — smiled Gunnar — "she had her ways. When Millie took a notion, there wasn't a thing she couldn't figure out. She was like time itself, was Millie. Unstoppable."

It was a long while before Fletcher said, "My name, my real name. I'm not really Fletcher J. Ralston."

The old man leveled his gaze on Fletcher

once more. "Your mama named you herself before she passed on. About the last thing she did, according to Millie."

"Then it's true?"

Gunnar smiled and nodded. "Good enough for your pap, good enough for his squallerin' bairn, I reckon." He sipped his coffee and said, "Junior."

CHAPTER SIXTEEN

Horton Meader woke to the sound of a bell gonging somewhere deep in his head. There were no bells anywhere near his hillside hidey-hole. Heck, he didn't know of any bells within a hundred miles of these mountains. It took several long minutes before it dawned on him that the bell was the god-awful sound of his hangover tormenting him, nothing more.

It also took him that long to crack an eye. He'd have cracked open two, but he had lost use of one a long time ago — twenty-four years back, to be exact. It had been on that cursed posse ride tracking that stink-hided Skin Varney and thieving Sam Thorne, though they all suspected ol' Thorne had blown on out of town that night of the heist, near a week before.

Still, they'd reasoned, it would have been worth their efforts to catch up with Varney, who several folks swore they saw lingering in the region. Why? Likely he was on the scout for Thorne, too.

Maybe he suspected Thorne had stashed the haul somewhere local. The Piker brothers, owners of the mine company who had the biggest share of the stolen money, as well as the dozen or so independent miners who had had their shares filched, estimated the take at more thousands of dollars than Horton had ever seen to that point in his life.

Had he known that that was going to remain the case for all his days and that he'd end up living out those days in Promise, Wyoming Territory, he'd have slit his own stringy throat right then and there on that hellish posse ride. Or he'd have worked harder to track Thorne and relieve him of the money — and kept on riding himself.

That annoying thing called hindsight told him he'd made a mighty poor choice in staying on at his diggings near Promise after the big gun down in the hills north of town. There hadn't been a week that went by since that he hadn't cursed that posse ride and the gruesome theft it had spawned.

"Should have gone away and stayed there," Horton Meader murmured, the words echoing in his hungover, cottonmouthed, throbbing, bell-clanging head.

And as he lay there on his sag-rope cot hoping for a second dose of morning sleep to drop on him of its own accord, his mind dragged back to that cursed time when everything in his life had turned to muck.

Back to that morning twenty-four years before when his pard, a fellow on a claim but two ravines west of his, wiry Gunnar Tibbs, had dropped in on him all in a lather. Should have known something was stirring. Should have said no to him, should have not even answered the door when Gunnar knocked. But he had.

"Curse me for a fool," murmured Horton as memory and not sleep smothered him. . . .

Twenty-Four Years Earlier
"Horty, you in there? Horton?"

"Yeah, yeah, door's open. I'm frying up a mess of bacon before it goes south on me. It's been greenin' earlier and earlier with this heat wave."

"Heat wave?" said Gunnar. "Why, it's November! We got one day last week that nibbled up into the forties and you're ready to shed your clothes, which ain't something I care to look upon."

"Why are you here, Tibbs? If it's to insult me, I hear that all the time anyhow. Not

176

like you to make the trip over here this early, less you're out of whiskey and looking for a few swigs of the dog's hair."

"Nope, not this time. This time, I'm here on official business. Of a sort. You and me, we're some of the few miners in these hills who ain't sold out to Piker Holdings, right?"

"Yeah, so what? Don't mean we didn't lose money, just the same." Horton stuffed another log into his stove and rattled the door closed. Tibbs always took forever to get to the point.

"So what? I've a good mind not to tell you, that's what!"

"Good. Then leave me be so I can cook my old bacon in peace." Meader had known that would rattle Tibbs and he'd come out with it. He forked the sizzling slabs of pink-and-tan meat and waited.

Sure enough, Tibbs growled, "They still ain't caught Skin Varney for his part in the robbery."

"No? Not a surprise, I guess. Been a week or more. He's likely long gone by now."

"That's just the thing. He ain't!"

"What? Why on earth would he still be around these parts? You steal from folks, you don't linger. I mean, I don't much like Varney, never did, but that don't mean he's stupid."

Gunnar nodded. "Sure enough, but something's keeping him hereabouts. Spinelli and Crawford saw him. They swear to it."

"That don't explain why you're here. Unless you think I'm hiding the rascal."

"Deputy McDoughty and a few of the boys are spreading out into the hills looking for him."

"A posse?" Meader slowed his prodding of the spitting, crackling bacon. He wanted it good and dead before he'd consider tucking into it. He reckoned he'd have to share it with Gunnar, too. That story of it greening wasn't but half the truth and Gunnar's nose worked as well as any man's.

"Yeah, a posse." Tibbs nodded his head, eyeing the bacon. "I was sent to fetch you."

"Fetch me? I am not a parcel, Gunnar. I won't be fetched."

"Don't you want to see that rascal caught?"

"Sure, though I'd rather see him and Thorne caught, along with the money."

"Me, too, Horton. So would everybody. That's how come there's a posse."

Meader prodded the crispy bacon curls about the pan a bit longer, then shoved it off the hot spot. "I reckon I'll go along."

He didn't really want to, but he wanted to dig for color even less on that particular morning. Fire just wasn't in him yet. Not that he'd admit that to Gunnar Tibbs. "But I haven't eaten my breakfast yet."

"Now you mention it, neither have I," said Tibbs, still staring at the pan much as a dog would do when shown forbidden goods.

Horton closed his eyes a moment, then sighed. "Pull up a chair, then, you rascal, and you can tell me all about it."

A half hour later, the two men, well-fed and sloshing with coffee, rode back down the trail toward Promise proper. Halfway to town, they met up with the rest of the cobbled-together posse.

"Where have you two been?" growled Mc-Doughty. "We been setting here for far too long, waiting on you slowpokes!"

"Well, now, McDoughty." Gunnar eyed the man with a cool level gaze.

Horton kept quiet and watched the two butt heads, a common enough occurrence betwixt them. The rest of the men did the same. They were all fellows Gunnar and Horton knew — some townsmen, some rock hounds such as themselves, all sitting their horses and trying not to look as uncomfortable as they felt.

"I told you, Mr. McDoughty, that me and Horton wouldn't need you all to hold our hands. I expect we can track a man in these hills about as good as anyone here."

"Yeah, but I have to deputize you first."

"Why?" said Gunnar.

"Because then whatever you do will be legal."

"You saying that whatever I get up to in a day's time ain't legal?"

"Nope, never said that, Tibbs. Now just raise your right hand. . . ."

"Why?"

The lawman sighed and dragged a hand down his face, same thing he always did when he conversed with Gunnar Tibbs. If that was what you could call this chatter.

Gunnar raised his hand anyway, surprising everybody, and let Reg McDoughty proceed with the oath. The other men had already been sworn in. Before the lawman could finish with his instructions, Gunnar and Horton wheeled their horses around and departed in a choking cloud of grit.

"Didn't want to say anything back there," said Gunnar, "but I saw a strange track on the way down. Figured you and me could follow it up."

"Hold on now. Just what are we supposed to do should we find Skin?"

Gunnar shrugged. "Ain't worked that out yet. But I will, now that I've had bacon and coffee." He winked and led the way higher into the foothills northeast of town, keeping his eyes on the trail and his ears perked.

He didn't doubt Skin Varney could lay them low at any moment. The thought was humbling, and not a little exciting, too.

CHAPTER SEVENTEEN

A bullet spanged off a granite ledge crusted with pine duff, a front porch for a squirrel that wasn't certain what to make of the proceedings unfolding before his house.

Gunnar had only just heard howling beyond, erupting from a copse of trees to his right. He had thought it might be where Horton was holed up, but he wasn't certain — they'd split apart when they got closer and smelled a campfire some minutes before.

Despite the bacon of earlier, the scent of grease-popping, pan-frying ham slabs had set Gunnar's gut growling once more. He'd nodded toward Horton to dismount so they might advance on foot.

Horton, however, who was prone to bouts of stupidity or deafness — Gunnar didn't know which it ever was — began talking in the loud, dumb voice of a fellow who spends his time pounding steel against rocks. That was all it took for Skin Varney, or whoever was holed up in the rocks hereabouts, to open up on them. Gunnar and Horton had scattered.

With the tumbledown boulders all about the place, trekking in a straight line wasn't possible, and now he had no time to find out where his pard had gotten to. The howling ceased and Gunnar nibbled his lip hair. What to do?

"Skin Varney!" he finally shouted, and then paused, hoping the fool would give up a clue as to his whereabouts. He didn't hear anything, which worried him because if Horton had been shot but was still among the living, he'd likely be howling some more, yelping, running around and cursing, or something. He was a fidgety sort anyway.

"Come on out! I'll make it easy on you!"

"Ha!"

That did it. Gunnar jerked his head to his left. Maybe those three boulders, the topmost looking almost as if a giant had placed it to balance for eternity on the others. Or at least until some doughhead with a stick of dynamite chose to ruin the setting.

Just then another shot cracked the silence. Gunnar heard a whistling and a buzzing and felt a slight breeze, then something soft drifted down past his face. It was the top half of a feather. A large feather.

"Hey!" he shouted. "That was my prize eagle feather, you bastard!"

What he got in reply was another bark of laughter. "That's a taste of what you'll get if you keep hounding me, Tibbs! I already did for your idiot friend!"

"Like hell you did!" came a wheezing shout from Gunnar's right. It was Horton, alive. *Good,* thought Gunnar. If Horton was swearing, he was in decent enough shape to throw lead at Varney.

Gunnar cranked off a shot toward the rock stack. Nothing happened: no screams of pain, no yelps of surprise. It was too much to hope for that he'd laid the varmint low with a single shot.

High above them stretched a long white cloud like a misshapen ox yoke being pulled apart against the blue slate sky. Not for the last time did Gunnar Tibbs wish he was up there, on the wing, soaring where the eagles took a notion to do so any old time they chose.

The silence was unnerving, since Gunnar knew how cruel Varney had been back before he was wanted for a big daring theft. The fact that he had been seen at the crime with Sam Thorne linked him enough in the eyes of the town, a town that all but depended on the income from the mines. You took that away, and there wouldn't be a chance of keeping the bars open or the mercantile, the whorehouse, any of it. So the townsfolk were suitably dandered up. And Skin knew it.

"I didn't do nothing wrong, you know!"

"Technically," said Gunnar, shifting position so he might get a better view of the rock pile and maybe Varney with it. "That means you did do something wrong."

"Huh?"

Gunnar scooched his hinder parts to his left, but kept his head tucked low. "You said you did not do nothing wrong. So that means you did something that was wrong." The logic of his words had sounded solid when they first popped into his head, but Gunnar wasn't so certain anymore.

"You ain't making sense, you dirty woodchuck!"

"Names, Skin? You of all people want to go and call me names? You dress like you found your clothes in a hole in the ground, and you smell like you ain't washed in a year of Sundays!"

Again, there was silence, then a chuckle. "Gonna have to work harder than that, Tibbs, you want to rile me!"

"Wasn't trying to, Skin. Just making

185

conversation, stating the truth." Gunnar pictured the big, dark-haired, rangy brute sniffing his shirt, his pits, beginning to doubt his hygiene.

"No wonder the women run from you! And you're bowlegged, to boot!" Gunnar nibbled his knuckles to keep from giggling.

"I ain't, neither! And I never heard the ladies complain!"

"Not the ones you got to pay for — money makes a liar out of all of us, Skin Varney! Now quit this and come out. The whole posse's here, and while you've been yammering in them rocks, we got you surrounded!"

"Like hell, Tibbs." Skin peeled off another shot that scored rock and plowed a finger-length furrow inches from Gunnar's face. Flecks of granite drove into his right cheek like tiny fists.

He bit back a yelp and a snarl and clapped a hand to his face. Blood welled from what felt like a hundred tiny rat bites. Gunnar heard Skin's chuckle pinch off as the sound of horses drifted closer, carried up trail to them from below, from the south, where Gunnar and Horton had ridden up. He gave brief thought to their own horses, but no — this wasn't the sound of a horse or two walking aimless with no riders.

This was the sound of several mounts, snorting, being ridden with purpose, huffing up that last steep bit of trail. They'd break through any second. And then they'd be visible to everybody up here — Skin included.

"Get back!" Gunnar shouted. "You on the trail! Take cover!"

That was all he had time for, because Varney opened up and cranked a volley of shots at the newcomers. Gunnar guessed it was the other men from the posse.

The horses stopped. They were close enough, though, that Gunnar heard low, growled words and whispers.

"What's going on up there?" It was the deputy.

Gunnar wiped at his cheek a last time, checked his palm — it was bloody, but nothing serious. He'd live. He could still hear and see, so he reckoned he'd survive. He wanted to live long enough to back Mc-Doughty into a corner and beat on the man something fierce. He'd rarely felt that way about anyone in his life, but something about the smarmy lawdog annoyed him to no end.

But right then there was no room for that pettiness. They were all treading water in this river together.

Then Reg McDoughty's black hat worked into view. "Get down, you fool!" shouted Gunnar.

The man did, ducking down behind a rock, for all of two or three seconds. Then he popped up from behind the rock once more. "Skin Varney! Don't shoot — I'm unarmed!"

"What in hell are you playing at, Reg?" growled Gunnar, not twelve feet from the man. "He's crazy with that gun, and you know it!"

If the lawdog heard him, he didn't respond. "Skin! It's Reg McDoughty, the acting marshal!"

Now he's taking over the entire department, thought Gunnar. *Just because Joe Pooler's laid up again with the gout.*

"Skin, now look. My hands are up. I only want to talk!"

For long moments, no sound could be heard, save for a quick breeze rustling through the big tips of the ponderosas. Then Varney said, "What you want?"

"We all know what I want, Skin. For you to lay down that gun of yours and give yourself up. This ain't no way to end your days, mister! Because that's what will happen. And for what? For some money?"

"Nope! For revenge! I want Sam Thorne's

head on a pole, damn it!"

"We all want that, Skin. Now look. If you give yourself up and we talk this all through, I expect it will go a whole lot easier on you with the judge than if you were to try to kill any of us here. Big ol' difference between killing a man and stealing his money. One's a stint in the jail. One's a quick jerk on a short rope. You ever heard what a neck snapping sounds like, Skin? Like you was snapping up sticks to start a fire. Only there's but the one snap. Then that's it."

As he spoke, Gunnar saw that McDoughty held his hands up still, yet they were slowly creeping back down, either out of laziness or else he had some strange idea of drawing down on Varney, a man who could see him but whom the daft lawman could not see.

That was when the oddness began — Skin started talking. "I never wanted trouble from this!" he shouted as if his statement was an accusation leveled at them all. Gunnar heard a scuffing sound and peered to his right, past the boulders where he hoped Horton was still holed up and doing okay.

Beyond that he saw a fawn-color hat moving slowly along. It was one of the posse men, slinking, cutting wide. He'd better keep himself quiet. Then Gunnar saw another cutting to his left, far and wide. How many were there?

If all of them had come with McDoughty, that meant ten men were right now trying to surround Skin Varney. Gunnar hoped for his and Horton's sake that the fools held their trigger fingers stiff and straight and not trembling.

"Hell, it was all Thorne's fault."

"What was?" said the deputy.

"The robbery, you fool!" Skin stopped talking then, for he realized at about the same time all the rest of the men did that McDoughty had tricked him into admitting for the first time that he'd had a hand in the robbery.

Up until then, it had been the word of two people at the crime scene who'd sworn on a Bible as to the identities of both thieves. Now they had genuine proof from Skin's mouth.

Thorne had been identified by lots more folks because he'd thundered on out of town that night, looking strangely bereft of any load of cash. And that left a whole lot of folks wondering where he'd buried the loot. In town or just outside of it? In the coming months, everybody in town had become suspicious of everyone else. Lots of folks had been seen at odd hours wandering around with shovels.

The only one who seemed to keep herself above the childish behavior in Promise had been Millie Jessup. Gunnar couldn't understand it, but he respected her all the more for it.

Something irked Skin, for they heard a growling sound and he spat in disgust. Then he opened up once more. Bullets spanged off rocks; a fresh volley of moans arose from over Horton's way behind the far boulders to Gunnar's right.

Through this all, the acting top lawdog, Reg McDoughty, quickly lost his nerve, tucked low, and flopped to his left. He collapsed down onto his shoulder as if he'd been shot, then sort of rolled himself behind cover. Trouble was, he was still a good five to six feet from the rock when he popped upright again.

Somehow, it worked, because instead of seeing a bleeding fool in the dirt, Gunnar watched as Reg popped up, realized he was still a couple of feet shy of his goal, and finished scooching to his left, where he hid behind the safety of the near boulder.

That was when the shooting from both sides ceased. For long minutes, nobody heard a thing. Finally, Horton shouted, "Help! My eye!"

Several of the men prairie-dogged up and

showed their heads as they scouted. No shots — which would have been easy as pie for Skin to make — were taken. He was gone, had to be. But where and how?

He'd slipped by, no doubt, between the posse men before they could close in on him. All that palaver had been a ruse to allow him to skedaddle. And it had worked. McDoughty began shouting orders while Gunnar slipped away and followed Skin's path.

Meanwhile, back at the rock pile, Horton tried to stanch the blood oozing from the wound Skin had delivered to him. He was a mess, as Gunnar would later find out — Horton had been shot in the eye.

One of the men, Jasper Winkins, fancied himself a bit of a doctor, as he wasn't squeamish once the blood spilled. The other men had been more than happy to have him tend to the yowler's ills. They held him down and Jasper, not a light man, knelt on Horton's wiry if muscled chest.

"What you gonna do to me with those?"

Winkins had fashioned a pair of tweezers, whittled from a springy forked pine branch, and they descended on the thrashing man's face with not a little smile. "Tighten up, Horton! I'm about to cure your ills."

"I ain't got no ills!"

"That's rich, coming from a man covered in his own blood."

To the surprise of them all, not the least of whom was Horton himself, Jasper's remedy worked. Sort of. He probed the whimpering man's eyeball, the lids of which had been pulled wide by the grubby hands of Stanislaus Corrs, farrier and amateur taxidermist.

Winkins plucked from the corner of Horton's eye a lead slug big as a navy bean, though not quite as long, and held it up between two bloody fingertips. He looked down at Horton. "I expect you can see now."

But the slug had done some sort of damage to something stringy, and apparently vital, behind the eyeball. The eye, once it had stopped bleeding and had healed as much as it ever would, never regained its true purpose.

In fact, its former deep brown coloring would soon turn a shocking milky gray, and Delia, one of the women at Millie's, claimed it was "interesting," while the eyeball gave the rest of them the willies. Horton soon thereafter took to wearing a patch he fashioned out of scrap leather.

He fancied it gave him a daring look, but few others thought so. Delia showed less interest in him. Eventually she took up with a limping drummer of millinery and left town in the night some years after the eyeball incident. She returned in the night less than a year later.

Horton secretly cursed Jasper Winkins, the self-styled medical man, but only for two years, because Jasper, having treated a family traveling through for what he called "some minor pox or other" came down himself with it shortly after the four-member family (a mother, a father, an old woman, and a young boy) all died.

No one could be certain whether the family's skinny ox and two bony chickens might not also be carriers of the dread pox, so they, too, were dispatched and buried alongside the family, along with all their possessions.

Miss Houlihan, a musical-minded schoolmarm, had lamented the pretty parlor organ that the poxy family had actually found on the trail west of St. Louis. It had been set carefully by the side of the trail, as if someone might come back for it at any time.

Unfortunately, by the time the poxy family came along, the organ was far from playable. Dust and rain had sprung the hide-glued stops, keys, and hammers. In the end, Miss Houlihan decided against attempting a rescue of the organ, but nonetheless wept as dirt covered it over.

Frustrated medical man Jasper Winkins died alone mere days later, racked with chills and hallucinating he was a distant cousin of St. Jerome. At the man's service, Horton secretly vowed to stop blaming Jasper for the loss of sight in that eye. Sure, Winkins had been a blowhard and a fake doctor, so it had been easy to fix blame on him, but Horton knew Skin Varney was the real culprit.

Though they'd been friends for several years before the Skin Varney incident, Horton Meader and Gunnar Tibbs became better friends in the weeks and months following, and so Horton learned of Gunnar's experiences that afternoon with such detail that he felt as though he had been there. In later years, he came to think he had.

Of the immediate proceedings at the little rocky knob northwest of town that day of the posse ride, Gunnar was ignorant, as he'd taken off silently after Skin himself. He resented the notion that the big, gun-handy lummox was making a fool of him and the rest of them, and he vowed to apprehend Skin himself or lay him low in the effort. Mostly he lit out after Skin to show up Reg McDoughty, the annoying lawdog who'd of late taken to spending time with Millie

Jessup. This sat poorly in the craw of Gunnar Tibbs.

On that day, Gunnar hoped Horton wasn't injured too badly, but as Reg had been slow in assessing the situation and dithering to figure out how best to proceed, Gunnar did what he felt he did best — he worked alone.

Skin was on foot and so Gunnar would be, too. He'd retrieve his horse later. Skin was an idiot and didn't know it, and Gunnar reasoned he could use this knowledge to his advantage.

The man didn't have much of a start on him, but since Skin had been out there living rough, at least for the week or so since the robbery, perhaps longer, he had the advantage over Gunnar. He had not roved that particular parcel of the woods and high places in several years, and then only in pursuit of a mule deer he'd failed to drop with his first shot.

They were high up, lost and nested in these piney foothills. Now and again he'd come across scout rummagings where miners such as himself had sunk test holes to search for color. That there were a number of them and none of them bore recent sign of the usual occupants, all elbows and backsides as they dug away for gold, told Gunnar this hill wasn't likely to offer up a living wage, let alone a sudden fortune.

Every fifty feet or so, Gunnar stopped and cocked an ear. From behind, he heard no sound of the townsmen, a fact for which he was grateful. As to the trail ahead, though Skin was attempting to disguise his trail, he left behind boot prints pressed into the dry earth here and there, enough that any dolt could follow.

Getting reckless, thought Gunnar. That was when he heard a hammer being pulled back.

"You ease off, Tibbs. I want to be left alone and that's all. But it's possible I've killed men before, and it don't trouble me none to do it again."

Gunnar cursed himself for paying such close attention to sign. He should have known it had been too simple.

"I admire your sand, Skin, but if you didn't have anything to do with the robbery, as you been saying, then why not go back to town with us and tell the judge?"

"Ha! All they'd do is string me up anyway. They're fixing for a fight."

"Nah, Skin. Ain't none of us on the posse wants to see your neck stretched. We just want our money back."

"I don't know what you are talking about, Gunnar. I'm innocent as a lamb."

It took much of Gunnar's strength to not laugh out loud. Skin was a lot of things, but lamblike was at the bottom of that list. And Gunnar suspected Skin was not a man who tolerated laughter in his face, not when he had a sight line on you.

"Then why are you running, Varney?" As he said it, Gunnar turned, his rifle held by the forestock in his left hand, arms ready to jerk down, tuck in, and lever a round while he spun.

He dropped low and a shot knocked his hat off. He cursed and dropped lower and scurried on his belly to a nearby pine. "You're giving yourself away again by shooting, Skin. Why don't we talk about this?"

"I see you, Tibbs. Next shot will part your hair."

"You kill me and they'll surely hang you. Right now there's no killing on your plate! There's even the chance you can convince them you didn't have nothing to do with that robbery."

"You heard McDoughty. He tricked me into saying I was there. Talking's over with. I'm going now! You stay put and don't tail me, or you're done!"

Gunnar heard his rapid boot steps clunking across rock, crunching sticks, then a peculiar hollow sound . . . then a shout, a curse, an "Oh, no!" then a thud.

Gunnar held his spot hugging the earth, his chin hairs resting on pine duff. "Skin!"

No reply.

"Skin? You hurt?"

No reply.

Gunnar lay there a few more long moments, then sighed. He pushed up to his knees, still clutching the rifle, and eyeballed the terrain. Beyond, from where Skin had been yammering, the earth appeared to drop off, angled downhill.

Gunnar crept closer to the drop-off and peered over.

As drops went, it wasn't much of one. The slope could have been traversed to the gravelly bottom some fifteen to twenty feet below by switchbacking. But Skin Varney had instead tried to tempt fate by scampering across the ravine, a mere thirty or thirty-five feet, aboard an old, long-fallen ponderosa pine that had felt the prickly bites of thousands of pine beetles.

Though he guessed that any strength the old fallen tree once possessed had long since been gnawed away, it wasn't a sudden, sickening crack that Gunnar had heard.

By the time Skin had clambered aboard, the trunk's bark had loosened such that his frantic boot steps had shoved it this way and that, sloughing it apart like the shell off a hard-boiled egg.

The bark came away in great smeared-off rafts, dropping a dozen feet to the dry wash below. Skin had no doubt crab-walked too far out to turn or lunge back when his smooth leather boot soles began to slide.

From the position of his body down below, he'd likely spent his few last seconds upright windmilling atop the log, hence the curse Gunnar had heard. Then the outlaw had slipped and fallen, landing in a sprawl at the bottom between boulders.

He would no doubt have smacked his head open like a raw egg, but he'd found the best possible spot on which to drop: an earthy, dusty patch, home of a handful of stray grasses gone brown in the late season. His rifle lay snapped in half some feet beyond his reaching yet still right hand. The outlaw's dust-caked black hat had popped off and lay crown up an impressive dozen feet away.

From his vantage point, Gunnar Tibbs thought perhaps Skin had broken an ankle, given the unintended jut of the lower half of his left boot. That the man had also not broken his neck was not yet known.

Gunnar grunted and scrambled and slid down to the bottom of the ravine. "Simple as that, you stupid bastard," he muttered as he approached the unmoving man with his rifle at the ready.

He prodded Skin's shoulder. The man jostled from the touch but did not respond with his own effort. Gunnar grew bolder and stepped to within easy snatching distance of Skin's left hand. It did not snatch at him.

"Hey," said the bearded miner. "Wake up, Varney!"

Nothing.

"You dead?"

A sound came to him then — a groan.

"Hey!" shouted Gunnar once more.

A wheeze rose up from the prone man.

"Damn," said Gunnar. "Too much to hope you'd ended yourself with good grace. Now you're just plain stupid again." He sighed and kicked the gasping man on the shoulder. "Get up and face your fate, Varney."

The big man shoved up slowly to his shaking elbows and even more slowly shook his curly black-haired mess of hair. He groaned again, and when he tried to drag his legs into a useful position, he cut loose with a volley of sounds he'd intended as words, but came out as the whimpers of an animal in pain.

"Serves you right for being dumb enough to try to cross this ravine like a squirrel instead of thinking like a man."

"Huh?"

Gunnar sighed. "Hm. I reckon you've taken a nasty knock to the bean."

The dazed, ground-bound man shook his head slowly once more, as if he were a grizzly waking from a long winter's nap. Despite his obvious confusion and discomfort, Gunnar noticed Skin's right hand slithering from the ground to his hip, toward the sheath knife that rode there.

Gunnar thumbed back the rifle to the deadly position and pointed its snout at Skin's head, three feet away. "No, sir! No, sir, I say! My word, but you are a piece of lamentable work, Skin Varney. You hold right there and don't even think of touching that knife or I will pop a hole in that thick skull of yours."

"Aw, Gunnar Tibbs, just let me go. I tell you true: So help me, you won't never see me nor hear from me again."

Gunnar hated to admit it even to himself, but the ease of such a task, simply doing nothing, was mighty tempting. He mulled it over for several seconds. It was pause enough that Skin thought perhaps he'd gotten a boot in the door, so he opened his mouth again.

"I'm not funning you, Gunnar. I won't make a peep around these parts ever again."

Watching Skin Varney mewl on the ground before him repulsed Gunnar, made him think of all the times when he'd seen Varney slobbering about Promise. He was usually half in his cups, harassing folks in Chalkey's Saloon or talking rough to one of the women at Millie's.

Once, Gunnar had seen the girl Skin had been with sporting a bright red cheek, just the one side, and a downcast look in her eyes and Gunnar knew Skin had smacked her for some imagined offense. Varney was not a man to be trusted, to be forgiven, or to be negotiated with. He was the roughest cob going and he needed to be served up his dish of just deserts.

"No, sir, I say again. You're going to make hard acquaintance with your earned come-uppance." Keeping his eyes fixed on the surly outlaw, Gunnar jerked his rifle skyward and cranked off one, two shots before leveling it on Skin once more. "They'll be here before long." He was less certain of Mc-Doughty's tracking skills than he sounded, however.

"Tibbs! I'm telling you!"

"And I'm telling you, Skin Varney, you

keep up this whining and groveling and I'll shoot you in the forehead. Now shut up."

The man tried once more, got out the first half of a word, and Gunnar moved the rifle an inch to the left and squeezed off a shot. The bullet whizzed so close to Varney's big knot head, Gunnar swore he saw a sweaty black curl waggle in the breeze.

Skin yelped and leaned back, eyeing Gunnar hard and rubbing his leg, as if he'd just realized his ankle was a sore mess. The look he leveled on Gunnar was enough to make a tough man widen his eyes.

"I won't forget this, Gunnar Tibbs. Wherever you go, I will find you. And I won't let you go, no matter how much moaning and crying you do."

Gunnar swallowed, then offered back his own level stare. "Lucky for you I ain't planning on going nowhere, so you won't have to track me far. And I'm not prone to belittling myself before another fellow, so it'll be a sore disappointment to you, I reckon, to find out I'll not be whining. But I will be waiting. Do come on back. Anytime if you're still able."

The unspoken message he'd sent was plain — *if you're still among the living.*

It didn't surprise Gunnar to know he had to wait longer than he would have liked with the glaring, bull-headed man. McDoughty's posse took longer than it ought to find them.

The men who finally arrived did so on horseback, which meant they'd been forced off the trail, slowing them. Reg looked down on them from the edge of the ravine. "Heard your shots."

"I never would have known."

"What's that?" The acting marshal chewed his quid of tobacco with more vigor, color already rising in his ruddy cheeks.

Normally, Gunnar was of a mind to let troubles waft over him, but he was sore and tired and annoyed all at once. "I'm just sure glad I wasn't hanging by my thumbs!"

"You'd best keep in mind who you're addressing, Tibbs."

"Same to you, McDoughty. Now get down here and deal with your prisoner. I'll collect my reward accordingly. How's Horton?"

"He'll live. Sent him back with Winkins to get himself doctored further. And there ain't no reward."

"There will be."

And Gunnar was right. He pressed the head of Piker Holdings and made vague mention of some point regarding questionable mining practices being dragged into the light of day. From a deep-pocketed outfit such as Piker, Gunnar Tibbs had little problem resorting to blackmail for cash. However meager the reward, it would be enough to help him limp along at the diggings.

The slow trip back to Promise, on which Skin Varney had to ride aboard Reg's horse while McDoughty walked, leading the beast by the reins, allowed all parties involved to stew and fester over their individual plights.

McDoughty, as the lawman whose posse had captured the villain, should have been pleased. And yet because he had once more been personally bested by Gunnar Tibbs, Reg strode back to town in a dark mood. None dared bother him, save for Gunnar.

As for Gunnar, he appeared to enjoy himself too much for everyone's taste. He cracked wise and giggled a time or two, as well.

Skin Varney was found guilty of the theft, despite the lack of sober witnesses and the definite lack of stolen money and gold nuggets and dust. Despite his insistence of cluelessness when questioned by the judge as to the whereabouts of Samuel Thorne, Varney was not believed.

As for the attempted murder charge, Horton made the mistake of mentioning while under oath he still had hopes of regaining his vision in his bedeviled eye. The judge gave this serious consideration and decided that Meader hadn't suffered a grievous enough wounding, and thus, the man who'd committed the act shouldn't suffer for such. Only for the theft.

That Horton would soon enough learn he'd never again see out of that eye came as news too late. The judge had sentenced Skin to five years of incarceration for his part in the crime of robbing the good citizens of Promise.

While Skin Varney was jailed in Promise, awaiting transport to Tin Falls Prison, word came that he was also wanted in Oregon Territory for the probable killing of a man and his dog over a spilled beer, and in California for kidnapping a prostitute and abandoning her, naked and abused, in a dry wash that had then filled in a flash flood.

The irate woman had been able to cling to a log and thus make it to the safety of a Mexican village, where she was rescued by a humble shepherd who had but two days before prayed for a woman to marry him and mother his six children.

Despite this amicable ending, the law looked on the capture of Skin Varney with grim satisfaction, and he was sentenced to twenty-four years of hard labor for his known and assumed yet unproven shenanigans.

And thus, the town of Promise, Wyoming Territory, celebrated in grand style the day they carted Skin Varney off in chains, howling his rage and swearing revenge. He rolled away in a barred wagon bound for Tin Falls Prison, a hellish place no one had actually seen, but all had heard of, a fitting hole for Varney.

Horton Meader recalled all this through the long view of time, twenty-four years after the events, as he lay supine with a forearm draped over his face on his sag-rope bed in his old cabin at the diggings. But now Skin Varney, as Gunnar had told him, was out on the warpath and howling once more for blood.

Well, hell, thought Horton. He had never done much to harm the fellow back then. Just gone along on the posse because they had told him to. And of all the men who had been involved that day, he had been of little value to Skin. True, Gunnar had shared with him the reward takings he'd gotten from threatening the Piker company, but that cash had worn out long ago.

"And still I'm here," Horton said with a groan.

"Not for long."

Horton stiffened. *I never even heard the door open,* he thought as he slid his hand from his face. He knew that voice.

"Skin," he said in a trembling voice no louder than a whisper. "Skin Varney."

"Yep."

Horton looked up and, even with the other man skylined against the morning light filling the doorway, he could tell it was indeed Varney.

"Twenty-four years late, but I'm here." Then Skin Varney laughed, a low, grating sound like chains dragging over rock.

CHAPTER EIGHTEEN

Some days into his stay at the cabin, Fletcher asked Gunnar how he'd know if he made Skin Varney's acquaintance. The old man merely said, "You'll know."

"Perhaps a more specific description might be useful."

Gunnar sighed. "He's big and mean and homely. Least he was all them years ago. I can't imagine time has softened his edges none."

That was all Fletcher could get out of the man, so he decided to let it rest for the time being. Gunnar mumbled something about visiting a tree and walked outside. It was obvious something was bothering the crusty old miner.

Fletcher decided a surprise might soften Gunnar's edges. He'd try something at which he'd not had much experience — cookery. He'd seen Tibbs make biscuits enough these past days that he felt confident he could master the menial task with little effort.

He set about the job with zeal, and as luck would have it, Gunnar stayed away until Fletcher had amassed a small, towel-covered pile of his efforts on the table.

When he returned, Gunnar held one up to inspect it. "I don't know, boy. I just don't know. I ain't never seen anybody torture a living thing like sourdough in such a way before. It ain't a biscuit, and it ain't a cracker, and it ain't hardtack."

He looked at Fletcher, not working very hard to suppress a grin. "I don't know what it is. I can tell you one more thing it ain't, though: It ain't natural — that's what it ain't. What it is, I don't know yet." He bit one and shrugged. "Flavor's there, but that's the power of the sourdough, not your skill. I appreciate the effort, I surely do, but I'm sorry, boy. You'd best stick to whatever it is you're good at. What is it you're good at anyway?"

Fletcher shrugged. "If you had asked me that a month ago I might have replied that I was most excellent at tallying the books at Rhodes and Son, the banking firm in Providence at which I am employed. Now . . ." He shrugged again. "Now I have no idea who I am and what I am doing, let alone what I may or may not be good at."

"Well, never mind about all that. Since we've established that you aren't much of a cook, I expect we'd best explore some other way you might prove yourself useful, at least to me. Rummage in that bag of wonders of yours and retrieve those fancy irons and we'll see." Gunnar ambled out the cabin's back door. He returned a moment later. "I had hoped you'd take that as a cue to follow me, boy."

"Yes, well . . . about those 'irons' . . ." Fletcher's cheeks and ears had reddened.

Gunnar sighed. "Guns, revolvers, pistols, irons — same thing in any lingo. Now let's get cracking. I have ammunition enough for a spell."

Within minutes, they were out back behind the cabin, where Fletcher had strapped on his father's ornate double-gun rig at the behest of Gunnar.

"First off, that ain't how a man goes about holding a gun."

"It ain't . . . I mean, it isn't?" Fletcher looked down at the revolver in his left hand. His fingers were wrapped about the middle of the spinning round bit the crusty old man had called the "wheel."

"Second off, give me that thing." Gunnar snatched the pearl-handled gun from the

214

youth. "Liable to kill me before we commence!" He shook his head. "Now, which hand do you favor?"

Fletcher looked down at his once-spotless hands, the long fingers now slightly callused, the nails mildly begrimed, despite his attentions. He shrugged. "I am, in most matters, of the left-handed persuasion."

"Well, now, if I were to hold this pistol like so, betwixt your hands, which one are you inclined to reach for it with?"

Again the young man shrugged and moved toward the firearm with both hands. "Either, really. This is often the case with me. I am of neither one mind nor another in certain situations, and thus equally adept with either appendage at the task at hand."

"Uh-huh," said Gunnar, sighing and shaking his head. "That about figures right."

"How so?"

"Because your pap, now I think on it, was the same. 'Ambivalent,' I believe that's called."

Fletcher smiled. "You mean, 'ambidextrous.' "

"That's what I said." Gunnar reddened. "Now stop interrupting me or we'll get nowhere fast! For now, make like you're a left-hander. Muckle onto that grip like so, and hold it firm like you're a man and you mean it."

Three hours later and many spent cartridges littering the earth at their feet, Fletcher and Gunnar stood side by side, watching blue smoke clear away as the last of the young man's shots echoed.

A line of mismatched green, clear, and brown glass bottles stood whole and glinting in the sun, as if in proud defiance of the insults thrown at them for hours. Fletcher wanted nothing more than to run at them, knock them off their roost, and smash the smug vessels with a big rock. He settled for a groan and a growl of disgust.

"Aw, don't take it so hard, son. I reckon you're just not inclined to gunplay. Goes against reason, but maybe it didn't run in your family. You'd best stick to those books and figures and such."

Fletcher's eyes smarted from the gun smoke, and his ears buzzed and rang so everything the old man said sounded as if he'd spoken to him through a long tube.

He slid the pretty pistol back into its handsome leather holster. He'd grown fond of holding the two revolvers, of feeling their solid heft in his hand, first one, then the other, though he'd been a poor shot at best with either hand. "I may as well do something useful with them," he said, and made to unbuckle the gun belt.

"What are you doing?"

"Taking them off. I would like you to have them, Gunnar. It's little enough, and they should be owned by someone who can appreciate their obvious quality."

"No, no, no, you don't, boy. Them guns are Sam Thorne's and you are Sam Thorne, whether you like it or not. Didn't they never teach you nothing in all those years of fancy educatin' you got yourself? Such as how heaven wasn't cobbled together in a day? No?"

Fletcher felt chastised as if he were about eight years old. He reddened and looked at the mountainous horizon.

"Besides" — Gunnar looked at his moccasins — "I appreciate the gesture, but I can't shoot with one of those like I used to. Eyes are leaving me. That's why I tote Millie's sawed-off. Don't need skill with that snarlin' demon. Just a general direction and a finger." He cackled and hunched over, slapping his knees.

Fletcher rubbed at his ears to dampen the ringing, and Gunnar said, "Tomorrow we'll stuff tufts of sheep's wool in our ears. It helps a little. Not as much as hitting the target now and again, but it helps." He winked. "But before we pack it in for the

215

day, you got to give it one last go."

"Why? We've already seen I'm not the gun sort."

"Naw, could be I was wrong. Ain't happened much in my time, but I'll allow as it has happened here and there. But a wise old man once told me that when you feel like you've done all you can on a thing, give it one last go. It will often surprise you."

Gunnar nodded toward the line of as-yet-unharmed bottles perched atop the firewood chunks and rocks standing on end at the edge of the cabin clearing. "This time, don't think about it at all. Just close your eyes, pull a deep breath, relax those slumped, bookish shoulders, and see what happens."

Fletcher fought down another sigh. *Might as well play along with him,* he thought. *It's not as if I have tickets to the theater or a game of snooker at the club.*

He let out the long breath in an easy stream, relaxed his bookish shoulders, and thought of a most pleasant thing to him — a long, rainy afternoon at the Algernon Davies Memorial Library, lost in the stacks, making his way slowly up and down the aisles, sampling from poetry, architecture, medicine, philosophy, novels.

He never quite felt his hands reach, his long fingers seat themselves with practiced

216

ease about the pearl grips, never felt his long thumbs peel back on the stiff little bird-head-shaped hammers, never felt his pointer fingers squeeze the triggers. He only came to as the two centermost liquor bottles, one green and one brown, exploded at the same time in clouds of powdered glass.

Fletcher stood, wide-eyed, looking at the impossible. He glanced over at the old man beside him.

"Sweet Lord above," whispered Gunnar Tibbs. "I never seen nothing like it. Whatever you did, son, you just keep on doing it."

"That advice was from a wise man, indeed. Who was he?"

Gunnar offered a wistful smile. "My own pap."

Then he reached up and smacked Fletcher on the shoulder. "End the day on that high note. Come on. I'll treat you to a slab of charred cow and a shot of something that'll burn your gullet."

CHAPTER NINETEEN

Horton's headache drifted away like gale-driven smoke. He squinted through his good eye again at his uninvited guest. "How you been keeping, Skin?"

"Oh." The big man stepped into the room, the motion uneven. "So you want to talk over old times, huh?" Skin dragged a chair backward across the floor to a corner where he could see the open door and the rest of the cabin, including Horton. "First, I'm going to need you to brew up a pot of coffee. That is, if you are all still civilized enough in these parts to offer a guest such niceties."

"Oh, yeah, sure, Skin. Sure." Despite his fear and conviction that he was about to meet his end, Horton Meader couldn't help but be curious about Skin's appearance here.

As he shoved up out of the bunk, he did his best not to take his eye from the big man, who groaned in accompaniment to the wooden chair's pops and creaks.

"You're surprised to see me, I expect," said Skin, readying a cigarette.

"Oh, well, not really, no. You see, Gunnar told me a couple of days back he heard in town you'd been let out of Tin Falls —" He shut his mouth and prodded the stove's innards for coals to revive. He wasn't about to mention that Gunnar also said that he suspected it was Skin and not the dandy greenhorn who'd killed Millie.

Skin chuckled. "Okay, that answers that question. I expected that bastard would still be hereabouts."

Horton cursed himself, and in doing so, the leading edge of a thin squeak escaped his tight-shut mouth.

"Aw, don't go blaming yourself, Meader. I would have found him anyway. That's why I'm here, after all. Looking up old pals — don't you know? What do they call it?" He looked up at the ceiling toward which he blew his smoke. "Yeah, getting reacquainted and all."

"Oh?" Horton fumbled with the stove's door and it clunked with a harsh metallic bang. "You . . . you still know many folks hereabouts, Skin?"

"Why, you bet I do. Some of them are the same folks you recall, too. You know, from the posse."

"Yeah, look, Skin. That was a long ol' time ago. Ain't many of us left, I expect. I mean, I wasn't . . . I didn't never do nothing to . . . I didn't want to go on that ride!"

Skin nodded and puffed. "Yeah, I know that, Horton."

The man at the stove sagged a little in relief as he filled the pot with a dipper from his water bucket, which sat atop a stump beside the stove.

Long minutes passed and neither man spoke. Skin watched Horton and Horton fretted and didn't look at Skin.

Finally, Skin broke the silence. "But you did, Horton. You did ride along. Rode right along with them others with but the one thing on your mind: to capture me so I could be hauled back to town to swing in the middle of Promise proper."

"No, no . . ."

"No? You mean all this time I thought it was you whose eyeball I shot out, but it wasn't?"

"No, no . . . I mean it was, but I didn't lose the eye. I still got it, see?" He flipped up the patch and pointed to the milky eye beneath.

Skin leaned forward. "So you have. Don't look worth much, but I expect it's some small comfort to you to have it instead of a puckered hole in your face, huh?"

"That wasn't called for and I don't care who you are." Horton's words spilled out much bolder than he felt.

"Uh-huh. Well, I expect you know what we're going to get up to here this morning. I can't make it an all-day chinwag because I have a pile of folks to visit, you see." He sipped the coffee Horton set before him. "This is mighty fine. Ain't sure I've had its like since before I was sent away. It's one of the things I'll surely miss about Promise. Folks around here know how to brew up a pot of coffee, yes, sir." He nodded, agreeing with himself, and sucked his teeth.

"What do you mean, you'll 'miss about Promise'? You going away?"

Skin chuckled. "Don't sound so hopeful, man. I ain't going anywhere, but you might say that Promise is. You see" — he leaned forward, his voice sliding out low and cold — "I will let you in on my little secret. I have big plans. Been thinking about this for a whole lot of time and I've concluded that it's only right that in life we should pay in kind for the misdeeds we've done.

"A fellow I shared my cell with taught me that lesson. He was in many ways a savage, even worse than me, but he had a head on

221

his shoulders. And what he said rang true with me like a big brass church bell tolling way down yonder in Mexico on a still, hot day."

"Why, Skin, you're a poet," said Horton, cringing at this paltry effort to suck up, yet still hoping he might somehow wheedle himself into the man's graces, if he had any. The outlook was bleak.

"Thank you, Meader. Coming from you, that don't mean much, but I'll take my praise where I can."

Horton ignored the dig and tried to hold his cup steady with shaking hands. The coffee sloshed onto his knuckles. He knew he should be thinking of some way to save himself, to do something — cut loose with a gun or a knife or a club or some such. But the only thing he felt sure he might do was keep the man talking.

Hadn't it been Gunnar who said Horton could do that better than he could do almost anything? He was a born talker, and he didn't mind admitting it. Though when he was on the far side of a drunken evening, Horton admitted he was less inclined to chatter. That didn't help him much now. But he had to try.

"So what's your secret, Skin? You said . . ."

"Oh, yeah. Well, as I was saying, the folks

of Promise have got to behave, you see. Got to do the right thing in life. Folks can't expect to ruin a fellow's life and then sit back, fat and happy, as if nothing has happened."

"What . . . what are you planning, Skin?" The notion of Skin hunting down a whole town struck Horton as frightening, yet humorous, as if the man was having one over on him. *Got to be my swollen head,* thought Horton, *to make me think that any of this is funny.*

"Why, Horton. I'm planning revenge." Skin stood up, stretched, clunking his knuckles on the wall, and rested his big hands on his waist. He looked down at the still-seated Horton.

"And I would like you to know you hold an honorable position, Horton. You get to be first — Well, no, that's not quite true. There was that pesky old whore. She wouldn't tell me what I wanted to know, so I had to let her have the honor. She didn't deserve it — the honor of being first blood on my tour of vengeance. The treatment she got, however, she surely did earn."

By now Horton's head was swimming. Had he heard the man right? Was he going to take some sort of revenge out on him? The other person must have been Millie

Jessup. So Gunnar was right. Skin Varney had murdered Millie. Had to be. What other "old whores" were there about the town?

And from what Gunnar had told him, the old girl had ended up in a bad way, a very bad way. Throat cut in her own bed. She was going to die soon anyway, but still, that was too brutal for words.

"Okay, Horton. Get up and come on. No sense making a mess of things in here. Might be I'll want to use it for a spell and I don't fancy having to clean up after myself if I can help it."

"Oh, no, not me," said Meader, shaking his head and melting into the chair. "I'll sit right here and I won't say a word, Skin. You can leave me be. I swear I'll keep shut of ever seeing you. If it helps, I'll skedaddle from here and you'll never see me again."

"Well, it don't help, and no, you'll not skedaddle. You'll take this like a man."

Horton sat still a moment, thinking. Then he finally said, "At least let me fight like a man, damn your homely hide!"

He always remembered Varney as a big, ugly lout who got only homelier and nastier whenever he'd drink at Chalkey's, which was most nights of the week.

Then Skin and Sam Thorne had become chums, and the whole thing had gotten worse. They drank together all the time, pulled a handful of small-coin thefts, enough to keep them in whiskey, and next thing you knew, there was the robbery. Thorne came up missing and Skin was pinned to the crime.

Quick as a rattler strike, Skin's big right fist reached out and snatched the front of Horton's green work shirt, balled it in his fist, and dragged the groggy little one-eyed miner out the door.

"What? What . . . ?"

"Time for talk is over," said Skin, barely huffing at the effort. His left hand rested on his revolver. Beside that, saw Horton, hung a big wide-blade knife, a Bowie if ever there was one. He recalled Skin had earned his name as a trapper in the high places back in his youth.

Horton was towed along, his moccasins drumming against the planked floor that led to his front door. A door, he realized as Skin's fist drew tighter around his neck, that he'd never again walk through. So this was how it was going to end?

No, curse him! Shake off the fuzziness! Horton commanded himself. *This man is not your friend. This man is a killer and a thief and a jailbird and who knows what else?*

Anger finally roused Horton's dragging

body, and he growled, spat, and windmilled his arms. He managed to land a shot to Skin's crotch, which brought up a groan and slowed the big brute a moment.

Skin swung his left hand around and snatched at the shirt on Horton's back and hefted him higher. "Don't make this harder than it needs to be."

Then a funny thing happened. The big man caught the toe of his boot on one of the crooked planks. It was his left boot, the foot he limped on; Horton recalled something about Skin injuring himself when Gunnar had previously tracked him down.

Skin's left leg buckled at the knee and he went down, letting go of Horton on the way and thudding hard face-first to the ground. Horton did his best to roll out of the way. He scampered as quickly to the door and outside as his addled mind would allow. His headache came back with the force of a hammerblow, and he groaned and made odd noises that might have been embarrassing, had he not been fleeing for his life.

Somehow he found himself up on his feet and running, and still making a weird whining sound. *At least,* he thought as he ran, *if I'm making any sound, that means I'm still alive.* Behind him, he heard shouts from Skin, words he couldn't make out, but they didn't sound friendly.

Horton stumbled on, his breathing coming harder now. Still he kept moving, over and then off the trails he'd made over the years, past his various test holes and false starts.

There was the spot he thought he'd build his cabin, until he found a hunk of promising ore. He'd mined the spot and built his cabin elsewhere in the meantime. Then he found that the spot wasn't promising, so he built his latrine over it. As it had that lovely view, he didn't build a door for it. Just three walls so he could have privacy from the rear while he was doing his morning business and not get ambushed by Gunnar or somebody else looking for coffee and flapjacks.

If there was one thing Horton always reckoned he could do right, it was fix a morning feed. He was a fair hand at that. Never had interest in baking breads or anything else, but folks liked his breakfast.

More than once, after he'd lost the use of his eye, folks, mostly Gunnar and one of the ladies at Millie's, Connie, had told him he ought to give up on the gold seeking and move on into town, open up a little diner, and serve breakfast all day long.

It was an idea he'd considered with seriousness for a spell. But the notion of having to get up even earlier than the rest of the folks and make all manner of food and then serve them — well, that was distasteful.

At least with a mine, you knew where you were going to be all day long and what you were going to do. You were going to wake up, eat, visit your outhouse with a fine view, then peck a deep hole deeper in the ground for a few hours, stop, drink coffee and water, and eat a few cold biscuits, maybe some god-awful beans, then get back to it.

Now that was a sight easier than rising before the cock's crow and forking over food for other folks. All for money? No, sir.

That stream of thoughts rabbited through Horton's fevered mind as he ran. Just past the outhouse, the trail angled and he glanced back to see Skin not nearly as far back as he thought he should be. And worst of all, the big bastard was standing still and aiming a rifle at him — where'd he get a rifle? — and smiling. The man was about to kill him and he was smiling about it, as if he finally saw a present he had long been expecting.

Horton set to squealing again and dove in time to feel air sizzle a course where his head had been a scant moment before. From a sprawling seated position, he gulped and saw dirt furrow up by his outstretched right leg. He pulled it back with a yelp and saw blood welling up where the tip of the moccasin had once been.

Now there was a ragged hole, as if a puppy had worried it, and blood leached into the rawhide. He wondered if maybe he'd lost a toe. Good thing it didn't hurt yet, because he had to keep moving. He had a notion he could lose Skin by hiding in a deep shaft he'd sunk some years before when he had more ambition.

It went into the hillside for quite a way and angled left and right at odd intervals. It wasn't his favorite place because he'd once heard a rattler somewhere in there when he'd gone back in to poke around. He'd not dug in there for several years since.

But it was still there, as he'd left it, and now he felt his foot throbbing. He knew he wouldn't be able to outrun Skin, even with the brute's own limp.

There came another shout, something of a cackle, mismatched with his own frenzied sounds.

"Got you now, Horton! All this time and I got you where I want you! Open that eye wide, man, because it's about to see something it ain't never seen before!"

Skin's husky, raw-edged bellow chased Horton as he scrabbled in his moccasins, slipping and sliding on scree, looking for the mine hole. Where was it? And still the big man's voice chased him.

"You guess what it is you're about to get a good look at, Meader?"

Another shot whistled by, parting his hair and sending his head lower, as if he were a startled pond turtle.

"It's death, man! Death! And it'll be the last thing your one good eye ever sees!"

Varney's vicious howling sounded as if it were dropping behind. Maybe Horton was losing him back there in the twists and switchbacks he'd taken.

Then Horton saw the partially caved-in black maw of his old mine diggings. He noted that the path to it was rubble, so he wouldn't leave footprints behind. He gulped but once as he ducked low, knelt, and crabbed his way in. If there were critters lying in wait, he'd as soon die of a bite in his own diggings than shot in the back by Skin Varney.

As soon as he thought that, he knew it wasn't true. He'd seen a man die of a snakebite once. It had been back in Paso Canyon years and years ago, long before he'd come to Promise and stayed.

He'd been on a crew hired out to a big mining firm hauling in timbers and shoring up tunnels. Rough work but honest. A snake had emerged amongst them at the noontime meal when they'd sought what meager shade was available among a boulder tumbledown.

That vicious viper had doled out at least three fast strikes to the man's neck, one to the jaw, and his entire head had swelled up like a pig's bladder blown full of air. He thought it might pop but instead it had purpled, then blackened.

All the while, the man's howls rose higher in pitch, while his eyes bugged and bled, and his breath whistled and wheezed. Then his screeches pinched off and his eyes were lost inside the bulbous, doughy mess that was his head. His limbs trembled and his body spasmed, fingers scrabbling and flicking, and then he stiffened. Finally, he sagged in on himself and died.

No, I'd sooner take a bullet, thought Horton, but he continued forward, holding his breath with each step he took, leading him deeper into the low tunnel. He'd ventured only about a dozen feet when he heard a rattling behind him. He froze, certain it was snakes. Then he heard a raspy chuckle.

"You think you could hide in that there hole and escape from me, Horton Meader?"

Horton held his breath and shook his head

as if he'd been stricken with palsy. How could he ever live through this? Oh, no, no, no . . .

Skin sighed long and deep, as if he were in a stage production. "All right, then. You've left me no choice, Horton. If you won't drag on out of there under your own steam, I'll send in my friend. Maybe you've met one of his cousins sometime in the past, being a mining man and all, used to playing with rocks."

What? thought Horton. *Cousin?* He heard a match flare, then a snapping, hissing sound. "Horton, you're about to meet my friend, Mr. Dynamite Stick. Mr. Dynamite Stick, meet an old chum of mine, ol' Horton Meader. Okay, here we go. . . ."

"No!" Horton shouted, and clawed back toward the light, falling on his knees, scrabbling at the rocks with his hands. One of the greatest fears he'd ever come to know was not just being underground. No, he'd never had trouble with that, especially not in a hole he'd dug himself. He had always been careful about shoring up his efforts.

But stuck in a collapsing tunnel? Now that was something he could not abide. What a hellish thought, to have rock and earth and dust and timbers collapse down on a man, crushing him to death with no hope of ever breathing good, fresh air again. No, not that. Anything but that. Anything . . .

He reached the edge of the hole, gulping and gasping at the fresh air, knowing he had better dive to one side. Surely that dynamite would be smacking into him at any second. His eyes adjusted to the day's light, and he looked up at Skin not ten feet before him.

Horton shoved out from the awkward black hole in the hillside and stood, half crouching, his mouth sagged open and his eyes — one milky gray, one brown — wide. He was vaguely aware he'd lost his eye patch somewhere.

Skin laughed and held up a finger-thick stick as long as his hand. His other hand held a smoking match. With his mouth, he made a hissing sound, as if a flame had livened a wick.

"That . . . that's not . . ."

"Dynamite?" said Skin. "Nah, I ain't got no dynamite." He tossed the stick into the rocks beside him and, slick as you please, shucked his revolver. "But I do have bullets."

He thumbed back the hammer, and as Horton watched, the snout of the gun's barrel, itself a neat black hole, swung slightly so that he felt he could see straight into it.

And so Death was not the last thing Horton would ever see. The last thing his one good eye would ever see was that little black hole as it spat hot lead venom in his face.

The last thing he would ever feel was not the deadly, crushing weight of timbers and rock and earth and dust, but clean, fresh mountain air. *At least there was that,* he thought, closing both his eyes. *At least there's fresh air.*

CHAPTER TWENTY

Gaw, but Edna could snore!

Sounded like a bucksaw blade being dragged across shale. And she kept up for hours on end. Then she'd stop, as if the snoring got to be too much and her body gave out, and Reg would think maybe that was it. She'd not breathe for a good fifteen seconds, maybe longer, and he'd find himself wondering if he should prod her to get her going again, or should he let her go? Maybe this time she'd just stop breathing, as if the snoring got to be too much and her body gave out. But every time, the air would return to her chest with a low snort.

Such thoughts had nested in Marshal Reginald McDoughty's brain since he'd been snagged awake by the god-awful rasp of his wife's snoring. Edna wasn't a particularly large woman, but she made up for it in the wee hours with a ferocity in her slumberous breathing that, at one time, many years before, she'd reserved for other nocturnal pursuits. That had been all right, of course. Nowadays, he'd have gladly traded such amorous intent for a half night's solid rest.

Those had been heady times, back when, despite the fact that Gunnar Tibbs had actually been the one to lay hands on Skin Varney, Reg McDoughty had been deputy marshal, the lawman in charge of that posse, and with ten men under his command.

Joe Pooler, his boss, had been laid up with gout when the robbery took place. They never snared Sam Thorne and the money, but as a consolation prize, they sure as heck were able to catch Skin Varney.

That had been a couple of dozen years back, back when he'd been younger, had had more hair on his head than on his chin and less meat around his gut and more on his arms. He'd been, he didn't mind admitting, a solid sort of fellow. He liked to think he still was.

Back then, maybe he'd been a little over-eager to show what he could do. But he believed — and he still felt this way — that was how a fellow should behave when he was in his prime years. And he was proof it worked.

Hadn't he landed himself a pretty young firebrand for a wife? Hadn't he gotten ol'

Joe Pooler, after hemming and hawing and shuffling cards and kicking dirt, to retire as marshal of Promise so he could take over? Hadn't most of the town rallied for him? Not everybody had, though, and that stuck in his craw. Gunnar didn't like him, and then there was Millie, the very woman he'd tried to court for so long. She hadn't supported his efforts much at all.

That had been a big ol' disappointment, despite the fact he'd still won in the end. Edna had come along, a roving school-teacher. He reckoned she really did love him, and he her, but it had been something else when she'd all but proposed marriage to him.

"That's my job," he'd said.

"Well, seems to me you're sleeping at work, then," she said. "And when I see something that needs doing and nobody else around doing it, I tuck in and get it done. So how about it?"

He had reckoned he didn't have much choice in the matter. And then, by and by, they'd had two children, though neither lived long. Little Elmer, named after Edna's favored grandfather back in Illinois, drowned at the age of four in a freak flood that swelled up the Chalk River behind town.

And then little Adeline, named after Edna's favored granny, also back in Illinois. She had taken ill with a chesty croup at the age of nine months and died within two days. Edna had never forgiven herself and had never been quite the same toward him since.

And now here he was, twenty-some years since they'd wed, married to the same woman, not sharing much in their bed other than time, him awake, her asleep.

That was why he sought the soft comforts of one of Millie's girls, Delia, a couple of times a week. Mostly they'd talk and then he'd nap. Doze right off without giving thought to the how or why or where.

Delia never once said a thing about it, never judged him. He was grateful for that. Truth was, he needed the sleep, and unlike his old boss, Pooler, he'd never felt right about locking the door and dozing on a cot in one of the cells. He had a lingering mortal fear that somehow the cell would lock. He always kept the spare key on his person anyway, but you never knew.

So he snailed his way to Millie's every few days, always through the back door. It was a small town, though, and he suspected Edna had gotten wind of what he was doing. But nothing was ever said about it, and so life had gone on like that for a number of years now.

And that was how Reg had wound up at Millie's that night of her death, half dressed in his long underwear and boots, when he shoved his way into Millie's room to see the spitting image of Samuel Thorne in a murderous pose.

That pesky lawyer Millie had hired, Chisley DeMaurier, claimed the kid was Thorne's long-lost son, which made sense to Reg, as the young dandy's looks had puzzled him in the street. But no matter who he ended up being, he'd sure looked guilty, standing over Millie with her throat all gashed wide and deep. Then he'd rabbited out the window, carrying his own sack of luggage, same one they'd dealt with earlier in the street.

Sure, he was a stranger in town, and it didn't seem like Millie was a threat to him at all; in fact, another thing he'd learned from the lawyer was that the kid would inherit Millie's building and the business, such as it was. So why would he kill a woman who'd been so kind to him? And if he had, where was the knife he'd used?

None of it added up to much, but Reg had been out scouting the region, looking for the young man. He needed answers, and he figured the young man had some. But even before the kid showed up in town, he'd heard that Skin Varney had been cut loose from Tin Falls Prison.

Varney's last words as they'd hauled him off to prison in that barred wagon were that he'd be damned sure to live through it all so he could return to Promise and kill them all — lay everybody in town low, and then lay the town low, too. Could it be he was keeping that gruesome promise, starting with Millie? Could it be that Sam Thorne's long-lost young son had been telling the truth when Reg had found him over Millie's dead body?

Reg shuddered in the dark and shifted to his right side, dragged the top of the blanket over his left ear and tried to think of something else. He could still hear Edna's snoring. But at that moment, even that sounded okay to him. Anything was better than his thoughts about Skin Varney and his quest for vengeance.

CHAPTER TWENTY-ONE

The faint sweet tang of sage wafted through the darkness of the small hours as Skin rode through Promise, not caring if anybody saw him, not bothering to hide his face. He'd reacquaint himself with every damn one of the townsfolk before too long anyway. Just now, though, he had to get to the lawdog's place. He had a special something he'd like to try out on him.

It didn't take long before he approached the tidy abode of Promise's boss lawdog, Marshal Reginald McDoughty. Good fortune was with Skin, for the marshal and his wife lived on a well-tended plot of land at the east end of town, not square in the middle of the business stretch, which suited Skin just fine, particularly for what he had in mind for the tin badge and his woman.

In many ways, Reg McDoughty was the one Skin most wanted to kill. He represented the filth of the law, the unfairness of

241

it all, the very reason he had lost so many years of his life.

Gunnar Tibbs was high on the short list, too, as Gunnar was the one who'd caught up with him, but Skin was saving him for last. Gunnar was the man who'd earned the most hate Skin could muster on those long, hot — or freezing, depending on the season — nights in his cell, when he lay awake in the dark, vowing his revenge, yet deliciously uncertain how exactly he was going to go about it.

He imagined, in much detail, how each citizen of Promise would react. Mostly they begged him and promised him anything and everything, all at once. In his dreams, he'd say, "Why, yes, as a matter of fact, there is one thing you could do for me."

"Anything!" they'd shout, tears soaking their faces, their heads nodding, desperation making their lips tremble.

"I could use two dozen years of my life, bundled up tidy, and topped with a pretty bow. If you could hand me that, I believe we could come to some arrangement."

Their faces would slump and they'd cringe and cry harder than ever. That was about when Skin would wake up, smiling every time. Sometimes giggling, too.

As he approached the lawman's place, he

saw that it was a pretty little thing. The two-story clapboard house was painted white. Storm shutters flanked the windows and a brick walkway led to the front door. Where would a lowly town marshal come by the money for such a dandy home?

Skin felt he was not a front-door sort of guest, so he decided to skirt around to the back door, tied the bony old horse to the white slat-rail fence, and left him to doze. It was about the only thing the horse did with any dedication.

Skin's fingertips checked the revolver and his wide-bladed hip knife, riding on each side of his waist. He walked quietly up to the back porch, a small affair that served as a place for the lawdog and his woman to store firewood out of the weather.

Skin seized in place halfway to the house when he heard a slow, low sliding sound. He wondered if they might have a dog. *No,* he told himself almost at once. He'd have seen it, or sign of it, when he'd spied on the place earlier in the daytime.

Maybe it was the old woman's ghost come back to torment him. He smiled wide. Nah, he didn't believe in such foofaraw. At least not until a spirit interfered with his mission. Then they'd have words.

He proceeded on up the three steps,

across the small roofed porch, and paused, standing to the left side of the door. He tried the knob, a wooden deal in contrast to the seldom-used brass affair on the front door. The door wasn't locked. Didn't mean Skin was going to stand in front of it yet.

He bet a dollar to himself that nobody was awake. He eased the door open. It squeaked, so Skin put pressure on the knob, pinching off the sound, and opened it enough to step into the dark, still room that smelled of past meals, of meat and gravy and coffee too long on the boil. He closed the door behind him, mindful of the squeak, and crossed the room, waiting for a plan to come to him.

He didn't have to wait too long. A quick, sharp sound, as of a floorboard popping under sudden weight, came to him from the darkness upstairs, somewhere to his right. After a few moments, similar sounds, soft sounds, followed, drawing closer. Down the stairs, across the dark room beyond a half-closed door that led to the kitchen. Then they paused.

"Who's there?"

The voice was a man's and it was scared, cold, and tight in the throat. Skin was close to busting with giddy excitement in his shadowed hidey-hole spot by the pie safe.

"I say, who's there? I know someone's

244

here. I heard the boots, heard the door." He walked, sock footed, nudged the door open and took one, two steps farther into the kitchen. Skin watched the man's profile in the dark, silhouetted against the window in night blue light. The man had a turkey wattle hanging below his chin — not much of one, but it sure showed sign of a fellow who didn't get up to a whole lot of labor in a day's time.

There were a few chin hairs there, too, and mustaches. From what Skin had seen of the marshal's wife — not a bad-looking little critter, and not prone to fatness — she had a shade of lip hair, too. Odd that. He'd never understood how women could have such. *The fickle ways of nature,* guessed Skin.

He waited another moment, one more step; then Reg McDoughty would be in the center of the room, likely armed — no right-thinking man would be caught otherwise when rousted in the middle of the night by a strange noise. There, he'd be the same number of strides from the back door, which Skin had closed behind himself, and the door behind the lawman, which he himself closed, that led to the rest of the house proper.

Since McDoughty was sock footed, he was a silent beast. He was also used to his own house, so he had that advantage. But what he didn't have was Skin's big knife, the edge honed keener than a spinster's tongue.

"How you feeling tonight, Marshal?" Varney said low and even, a couple notches above a whisper.

Marshal Reg McDoughty didn't react as Skin had expected — the man didn't yelp, barely hitched his breath, and from what he could see in the scant moonlight, didn't but half turn to face Skin behind him.

"Skin Varney. I suspected as much."

Oh, man, thought Skin. He hadn't seen McDoughty in twenty-four years, but already he was talking as if he knew the situation inside out. Irksome.

"Glad to hear I didn't disappoint you, lawdog. It's been a while, so I thought we could catch up, chat a little, see what each of us has been up to."

"I know what you've been up to, Varney. You've been in Tin Falls Prison. At least until a couple of weeks ago. That's about a week's easy ride southward of here. I figure you took your time, committed a few crimes along the way, and then showed up here to seek that revenge you howled about all those years ago. That about right?"

Skin stepped out of the shadowed corner, gun in one hand, his other hand resting on the butt of the knife's handle. "Why, Marshal, it's almost as if you was with me the entire trip. Yes, sir, it's uncanny how you knew just what I've been up to."

"Crimes and all, eh?"

"Oh, you bet, McDoughty. You bet. You can't expect a little ol' thing like two dozen years in prison to change a man, can you?" Skin chuckled, long and low. "I'll keep my voice down so as not to disturb your pretty little sleeping missus."

CHAPTER TWENTY-TWO

Skin watched as the marshal stood taller and pulled in a breath. *That got the man,* he thought. But a fellow could only look so menacing standing in his long handles and socks.

"You even think of harming a hair on my wife's head and I'll —"

"What is it you'll do, Marshal? Hmm? Ain't a thing I can think of that you could do to me that ain't already been done. You humiliated me, you locked me away, you robbed me of my prime years, you stole my rightful fortune, you bumbled finding Sam Thorne, and to top it all off, you took away my favorite pigsticker knife — you ain't still got that about this foul little town, have you?"

"Huh, you know what? That knife could well be at the office. I rarely throw away such items. Trouble is, that has resulted in two shelves in the storage closet full of other people's junk."

"Ain't junk, Marshal."

"Fair enough. What'd it look like?"

"You tell me," said Varney.

"I can't. As I said, I've stacked up twenty or more years of such goods from all manner of folks. You want to walk down there with me, I'm happy to look it all over. You know, Skin, so far as I know, you haven't committed any crime I can't overlook since you've returned."

McDoughty had been hoping he might be able to butter up the man, get him out of the house. It didn't work.

Skin snorted, obviously not afraid of waking Tully's wife. "You must think me a fool, Marshal. You and I both know that I cut the throat out of that old crow Millie. You going to forgive me for that? Tell me it's okay for me to kill a person? Shoot, I've laid low a handful of them on the road from Tin Falls Hell House to Promise. That old whore come next, then Horton Meader."

Reg groaned. "Not Horton, too?" His voice came out as a wheeze. "Why him?"

Varney's brazen admittance of murder caught the marshal like a plank to the head. His thoughts swam and he snatched for the back of a kitchen chair. *This job,* Reg thought, *it's getting to me. Hell, it caught me a long time ago.*

"What's the matter, Marshal? You ain't going to give up the ghost before I get to do it for you, are you?"

"You aren't going to do a damn thing, mister!"

Both men turned to see a wraith in a white nightgown glowing in the doorway. The wraith held a shotgun at gut level, aimed at Skin Varney.

"Edna!" shouted Reg. "No! Go back! Get out of here!"

"Like hell I will, Reg. This is the vermin you told me of?" She readjusted her grip on the heavy gun.

From the way she braced her feet, Skin could tell it was an effort for her to hold the thing.

"Now, now, Edna. That's what he called you, ain't it?" Skin tried to make his voice smooth and soothing. He should have been mortally afraid, he knew, but something about her appealed to him — she was a witchy little thing. And he liked it.

"I'd like to get you to calm down, but we ain't going to get far in knowing each other if you keep calling me such hurtful names. Vermin? Why, that's downright unfriendly."

"Good."

"Edna, back away. Now!" Reg barked that

250

last word, and she flinched, glanced at him. It was what he'd wanted. Had to break her spell. She could be as dedicated to a thing as a dog on a bloody bone.

Skin's gaze jerked toward him, and the marshal raised his revolver. He pulled the trigger at the same time Skin did. Both men jerked as their bullets burrowed into flesh.

Skin growled and snatched at his left side, mashing a fist hard into the spot. Right away he knew it was not an immediate mortal wound. Might be later if he didn't tend to it, but unless McDoughty or the devil woman dosed him with another shot, he'd live through it.

Reg spun from the punch of the bullet deep in his right side. He braced his back-swept right leg to keep himself upright and fought to raise the revolver again. At the same time, he shouted at his wife.

"Get gone, Edna! Go!"

Like always, she didn't do a damn thing he said. Never had.

She dropped the shotgun in the doorway and rushed to him.

Skin retreated back a pace, closer to the shadows, and held the revolver steady before him. His position was perfect to level on either of them.

"Reginald!" She nearly knocked him over

as she reached him. Her feet slid on something wet and slick on the floor. Even in the scant light, they saw and smelled the rank, curdled sweetness of blood, a whole lot of it.

She clapped a hand to her husband's belly and he groaned and staggered backward, his revolver held weakly in his left hand. He staggered and she guided him backward.

They clunked against the wall, and his head knocked into a small round of needlework of two flowers leaning together she'd done years before on their fourth wedding anniversary. He'd made a cute frame of twigs and twine and hide glue. The small remembrance slipped off the tack and came to rest on his left shoulder as he sagged against the wall.

"Oh, Edna," he whispered as he squinted at her face, inches from his. "So sorry, all of it. Love you, girl . . ."

"Hush now, Reg. You're going to be just fine." But her voice was a trembling thing, not sounding a bit like the voice either of them had known all those years together.

With her left hand, she reached to her wheezing husband's chest and laced her fingers tight among those of his own bloodied right hand. With her right hand, she pried the revolver from the fingers of his weak left hand where it sat atop his bloodied rising and falling belly.

She sat against the wall tight beside him, her head close to his, and said, "I love you, Reginald McDoughty. Always have, always will."

Then that little nightgown-wearing woman thumbed back the hammer.

"No!" Skin shoved away from the wall and worked around the table, fouling up on an overturned chair.

Edna raised the revolver to her right temple.

"Don't do that, lady!"

She let out a quick, stuttering breath and pulled the trigger. Her head slammed into her husband's as the bullet passed through her skull and into his.

Once more, thunderous sound and blue smoke filled the room, swirling and choking everything with its bitter stink. The force of the close-fired bullet smeared blood and bone together in a grisly collision.

"Aww, hell," said Skin, too close to have looked away, but too far to prevent Edna from firing.

Skin regarded the two dead folks laid out before him. "Huh."

Voices from down the street drew closer. He let out a low sigh and winced at the pain in his side. "Well, here are two they can't say I had a hand in. Plain to see they done for each other."

His voice echoed in the otherwise still kitchen. As he walked to the door, holding his side, the revolver hanging from a hand, he looked down at the woman. "Now that's a damn shame. Could have had us a time, darling."

He nodded to the dead pair, then stepped over their legs and out the back door as fists thundered on the front door.

Chapter Twenty-Three

"What's the matter, boy?" Gunnar's question reached Fletcher from his corner where his broad bunk sat, heaped with skins and blankets. The man's voice filled the midnight air of the cabin.

There was something about the crude mountain man and miner that, try as he might, Fletcher could not help but like. He was honest and not prone to playing games with words or deeds. That was a big difference from the folks Fletcher had known his entire life back in Providence.

Maybe it was city folks' way of protecting themselves, arming themselves with words since they couldn't rightly go around all day wearing guns strapped to their waists. Out here on the raw frontier, however, it seemed as if everyone wore a gun or a knife, or two guns and a knife, or a small ax on their belt, or all of them at once. Did that make him feel any safer? No, but he'd found that a good number of the folks on his travels westward were as Gunnar was, kinder somehow, perhaps more honest.

"I expect you can't sleep either," said the old-timer. He yawned, a loud, drawn-out sound that ended in a growl. Fletcher smiled despite himself.

"I might as well head out," said Gunnar.

"Head out? Where are we going?"

"We ain't going nowhere." Gunnar shook his head. "I am. You go anywhere, it'll ruin everything. I have to get back to town. I stay away too long, folks are going to suspect something's foul, like I'm hiding a fugitive from the law or some such. Besides . . ." He looked out the window at the darkness.

He faced Fletcher. "I didn't scrape the dirt off myself down at the creek last night for nothing. Figured I'd sniff around some, see if I can learn anything while I'm there. I expect folks will have all manner of opinion about you, though few of them will know anything close to the truth, nor even who you are."

"The ladies at Millie's will have told all, I'm sure."

"Don't be surprised. Millie's gals ain't stayed in business this long by blabbering what they know. Elsewise, a certain lawman would have been run out of town long ago. At least by his wife."

"The marshal is married?"

"Course."

"But he was at Millie's, and when I saw him, he was half dressed."

"Yeah."

"Oh."

"Yeah."

Fletcher thought for a moment. "If I talk with the marshal, he'll understand. I'll tell him I ran because I was afraid. I'll explain that I'm currently low on funds, so I won't go anywhere while he investigates."

"Nah, even if he wasn't inclined to see you hang, he'd only arrest you for vagrancy or some such. But once we get this resolved, you can live at the brothel."

"Live there? I can't live there! It's full of . . . well . . ."

"Fallen women?"

"Yes."

"Well, hell, son, your mother was one and you didn't turn out too bad. Awful taste in clothes, though."

Gunnar rummaged in a wooden chest and tugged out clothes that to Fletcher didn't look much different from what he was wearing.

"I really should be there," said the young

man, reviving coals in the stove.

"Nope. No, you should not. You can pay your respects later. Right now that fool Reg would arrest you because you're the easy answer, and the town would praise him, and that would be that. Meanwhile, Skin Varney would still be running around these hills, not shouldering any blame for laying Millie low."

"What'll I do while you're gone?" Fletcher almost hated to ask. Gunnar wasn't the most reasonable old fellow at the best of times. He was likely to saddle Fletcher with all types of domestic chores.

"Oh, I figured you'd ask that. I'm not sure working on your aim is a good idea while I'm away. I have to buy more bullets as it is. Speaking of buying things, you got any money? I can't expect to keep you in flapjacks and coffee and bullets on my meager takings from the diggings."

Fletcher nodded and rummaged in his pocket, then turned to his satchel. He pulled out his wallet and offered Gunnar what he had — seven dollars.

"That's all you had on you when you landed out here?"

"I don't live in the upper echelons of refinement back in Providence, contrary to what you've been told."

"I'm sure the folks of Promise would appreciate knowing that, seeing as how they paid for your lifestyle as it is."

Fletcher let the comment go. He still wasn't convinced that all the stolen money had been used to fund his life.

"Speaking of money," he said as he tested the tepid, revived coffee, "maybe I could work the claim for you."

Gunnar snorted. "You know anything about digging for silver and gold?"

"Well, no, but I watched you the other day. All you did was dig and pick and scratch around and mutter a considerable amount."

"Yeah, well, everybody has their own methods."

"Do your diggings still earn?"

Gunnar puffed up and eyed Fletcher as if he'd insulted a little old lady. "Course they have promise! I wouldn't waste my time on 'em otherwise. I just can't do all the labor it all requires anymore."

"Have you ever thought about liquidating your assets and —"

"And what? Move? Why would I do that? This here's my home." Gunnar stomped a moccasin. It echoed in the little cabin. "Besides, I wouldn't get anything for it."

"Then you have thought of it."

"Course I thought of it, but I wouldn't get anything for it anyway."

"How do you know it's still a worthy claim?"

"Got me a feeling." Gunnar winked and tapped his nose. "Either that or it's my rheumatics playing up on me."

They sipped coffee in silence while the morning's first rays of sunlight glowed through the small windows' wavy panes.

"Best time of day," said Gunnar.

Fletcher nodded but didn't say anything.

"If you really are interested in learning about the diggings, and you ain't just whistling, I could show you a spot to dig later. I got a feeling about it, a fresh spot I never touched with shovel nor pick before."

"Yeah? I'd like that. Will you show me before you leave?"

"Well, now, there's a certain way of commencing a hole. We'll do that when I get back. But I will show you where I've been digging for now. Get yourself some practice."

A little while later, Gunnar led Fletcher over a low rise behind the cabin and pointed to a shored-up hole in the steepest slope of the rise. It stood perhaps four feet tall and three feet wide. The entry was squared off by bark-on timbers and hewn at the corners.

Fletcher bent and looked in. It wasn't a deep tunnel. Barely seven, perhaps eight feet in, but the old man had done a decent job of chipping the gravelly, loose-looking innards smooth sided and hauling the debris out, one bucket at a time.

"This here's a hole I've been working on and off again for a handful of years now."

Fletcher backed out. "I assume that pile of detritus is what has been removed from there?"

"You assume right, mister."

"And how does one go about, um, removing said debris?"

"Huh? Oh, well, you use this here." Gunnar held up a steel bar half as long as Fletcher's leg. "And this with it." Gunnar held up a hand sledge. "And once you've loosened up what you're after, you fill that wooden bucket and drag it out and dump it yonder. You don't know enough to know what you're looking for, but I do. So leave the takings and I'll rummage through the pile when I get back from town."

"How will I know where to dig? Surely one spot in there holds more appeal than another."

"Yeah," said Gunnar, nodding. "There's a jag of ledge in there, just to the left — center of it has color running through her. Or at least it smells of it enough that I remain hopeful. Millie used to say that if me and Horton didn't have no hope, we'd blow away on a stiff breeze."

Fletcher looked to where Gunnar pointed and saw a yellowish smear that appeared to continue behind a shelf of brittle-looking rock.

"You chip all that odd-colored gray stuff out to get at that promising color back there." Gunnar rubbed his big old-fingered hands together as if he were freezing. "Wish I was staying here with you. There's promise in there, I can tell." His eyes glinted with possibility.

"Yes," said Fletcher, keeping his own eyes wide and forcing a smile. "I can hardly wait to engage in this most exciting task."

Gunnar squinted at him, uncertain if he was fooling or if his wordy remarks were genuine. "Okay, then. Well, I'd best be off. You get ambitious, and you can keep on going. That hillside's pretty sound. Ain't had a cave-in up here in a couple of years."

As he walked away, he heard Fletcher say, "Cave-in? You mean the dirt collapses inward and fills the tunnel? Mr. Tibbs? Mr. Tibbs!"

Mr. Tibbs kept walking, a smile riding

wide behind his freshly combed, voluminous beard and mustaches.

CHAPTER TWENTY-FOUR

As he switchbacked down the last length of trail to the town proper, it occurred to Gunnar he'd not need to visit the settlement near as often anymore now that Millie was gone.

Visits to town had been a rare thing for him as time wore on. His age was the culprit mostly. It was a long walk. But he'd long ago given up beasts of burden. Felt bad about them having to lug him and his gear and goods. When his last donkey, ol' Nedley, died eight . . . no, nine years back, he'd not sought a replacement, though he'd been urged plenty of times to do so.

In truth, life had been easier since then — he didn't have to figure out how to feed the beast, which left more of his meager income for him to survive on. He put that toward tobacco, whiskey, and vittles, and with what little else was left over, he often bought Millie gewgaws and fancies and useful items, too, for her sewing.

That woman had loved to sew quilts and such and had been a dab hand at it, too, as the handsome and warm quilt on his bed back at the cabin proved.

Sometime later found him in the kitchen at Millie's, talking with Hester, the woman who'd run the place for a year or more now, since Millie had taken ill and, so, to the bed. Millie could not have chosen a more capable — and intimidating, Gunnar didn't mind saying — woman.

Hester was a mulatto from Virginia or some such place back East, born into slavery, but she'd fought and bought her way west years before, all on her own. How Millie had managed to accumulate such a household of tough women, Gunnar had no idea. He'd asked Millie once, and she'd only said, in true Millie fashion, "What makes you think all women aren't that tough?"

And now Gunnar was facing the most frightening of the lot. Coming down out of the hills toward town, he'd made up his mind to tell Hester he had Fletcher J. Ralston bunking under his cabin's roof with him, and what was more, he knew him to be innocent of Millie's killing.

The instant fire that rose in Hester's eyes

forced Gunnar back a step, and he gulped a time or two. His throat was suddenly craving a glass of cool beer. And he'd take it in hell itself — anywhere but that kitchen.

"You come here and tell me he's living with you? And you think he's innocent? After what he did to Millie?" Hester's eyes narrowed as she looked at Gunnar.

"Thought you'd feel that way," said the crusty old miner, pooching out his bottom lip. "Oh, well, not much I can do about how you feel. Even if you're wrong." He glanced sideways at her.

"What do you know?" she said. "You have some sort of proof? Because I was there and he was standing over her . . ." She turned back to punching her bread dough.

"You sound as if you know your mind so well, there's no way you'd ever change it. That right?" Gunnar had known the woman for nearly the same amount of time he'd known Millie. And now that Millie was gone, he reckoned he'd soon know Hester longer than he had Millie. But never as well.

"Have you ever known me to lie, Hester? You forget how much I . . . how very fond I was of Millie?" He wiped at his leaking eyes and found he didn't much care if Hester saw him weep or not.

Without looking at him, she said, "Never

266

have known you to lie, Gunnar. But this time . . ." She shook her head as she worked the dough.

"Trust me," he said.

Eventually she nodded, then wiped her own eyes and changed the subject. "How long you figure we'll be allowed to stay on here?"

"Stay?" Gunnar pulled a thoughtful frown. That was something that had not come to him. He assumed Millie's would always be where it was and what it was — same went for the women who lived and worked there.

"I don't see why you can't hole up here until you go on, as Millie used to say, to meet your eternal reward. Why do you ask?"

"That nephew character you're so fond of," she said, wringing out a cloth she'd used to wipe down the flour-dusted table. Her thick fingers were wet, the knuckles red. "He worries me."

"He shouldn't. I tell you, he's a greenhorn with a hard shell, that's all. Between you and me, he ain't got the sense God gave a squirrel. But he does have a way with words, perfumes the air with enough of them. It's of tallies and such he tells me he's most proud. Numbers! I never heard the like. I told him the only numbers I like are the ones I get for my diggings in the form of cash money. Elsewise, I don't care much."

There was another long silence and Gunnar knew Hester well enough to see that she'd mull over what he told her, and it still might not make any difference. It was all he could do. "I got to pay a visit to McDoughty, see if I can convince him of the same thing I hope I've convinced you of."

Hester stopped pinching biscuit dollops off the big wad of dough and looked at him.

"What'd I say now?" Gunnar settled his hat on his head and laid a hand on the back door's latch.

"You haven't heard, then."

Even before he replied, Gunnar knew something awful had happened. "What ain't I heard, Hester?" he said in a low voice.

"He's dead," she said, going back to pinching off lumps of dough and laying them on the cutting board.

"Dead? Reg?"

She nodded. "Yeah. Edna, too."

"Oh, no. When? How?"

"A day since. Figured that's why you were here." She sighed. "It looks like she did it and then shot herself. Finally got tired of him coming here, I guess."

For once, Gunnar didn't know what to say. "But . . ."

"No buts about it, Gunnar. Just that it

happened so close to Millie's murder." She turned on him, picking dough off her fingers. "Unless you're wrong, and your back-East city boy did this, too."

He finally looked at her and shook his head, frowning. "Couldn't have."

"How's that?" she said.

"Like I said before, he's been with me. Since the night Millie died."

She nearly dove for him, knocking aside a chair. Jamming herself between him and the door, her back to the door handle, she said, "You listen to me and you listen good, Gunnar Tibbs. Millie was my friend, too. Best one I ever had. A mama, a sister, and a best friend all in one. Just what is this game you're playing?"

"What game would that be, Hester?" Lordy, he thought he'd gotten through to her. Gunnar Tibbs didn't scare off easy, but Hester was a formidable woman.

She stared at him a long time, then walked back to the counter. "You really saying he's been with you?"

"That's right."

"Never slipped out and made his way back to town last night?"

"Nope. Getting so he hardly leaves my sight, save for visits to the necessary house. It's a little annoying. He's so green he can't find his own feet without a map."

"Hmm," she said.

Gunnar didn't think she sounded convinced yet of Fletcher Ralston's innocence, but at least she wasn't throwing dishes at him. But that was of little concern just then. What he really wanted to know was more about Reg and Edna. He didn't believe in coincidences such as this. He asked Hester a few more questions about the circumstances of their deaths, and then there was a long moment of quiet.

He left through the kitchen's back door and made his way eastward along the rough track that paralleled Promise's Main Street. It would lead him to Reg's house eventually, and he wouldn't have to worry about bumping into folks back here. He wasn't in any mood to listen to their townie whisperings, but he had to see for himself what had happened at the marshal's place.

Varney was around Promise. Gunnar could feel it. That vicious brute was as close as close could be. He had done for Millie, and Gunnar was sure he'd downed the marshal and his wife. Who was next? Varney had said all those years ago that he was going to find his way back to Promise and make them all pay.

But nobody had believed he'd ever survive

prison. Hell, most folks, Gunnar included, thought the law would come to its senses and hang the bastard, if only as a safety measure.

He kept up a brisk pace, walking toward the McDoughty home. Hester had said the killings took place in the kitchen. He'd never been in their house, but he figured there was a back door that led to the kitchen, same as most other houses in town. He'd forgotten to ask Hester who was the law now but guessed it was the Dover boy. He regularly acted as deputy and filled in when Reg wanted a day off, usually Sunday.

He wasn't certain what shape he'd find the house in — it could have been scrubbed clean, knowing some of the biddies in town, or it might still be a bloodied mess.

Hester had told him that the couple had been buried together in a single box. Odd that, given how they seemed to feel about each other. But then who was Gunnar Tibbs to judge them? They'd been laid to rest the very next day, as the reason for the killings seemed obvious to one and all. But that didn't sit right with Gunnar. Again, it was far too coincidental, given that he felt sure Skin Varney was on the loose and around Promise once more.

Gunnar glanced about, and while he saw

no one, that didn't mean somebody wasn't spying on him from afar through grimy windows. He stepped up onto the small back porch and looked in through a glass pane. He did not expect to see anyone, and in that, he wasn't disappointed. They'd had no children who lived, and so he assumed the couple would be laid to rest alongside the graves of their dead offspring.

He tried the knob. It gave, and he pushed open the door. A stale, thick smell wafted into his face. The house hadn't been aired; no windows had been left open that he could see. He shoved the door open and had a moment of uncertainty. Several fat bluebottles roved the space, and one thumped against a pane of wavy glass in the thin sunlight. He saw dark brown and red stains along the floor to his immediate left, and more of the same farther in.

The wall, low and close to the floor, and the cabinet front beneath the dry sink were spattered with the same age-crusted gore. Gunnar held his breath. He took one step inside, but kept his hand on the door.

The scene, hastily cleaned at best, was still awful. There seemed little he could learn from the mess, but something deep down in Gunnar's gut — what his old mama called a person's "witchy sense" — roiled and flopped in his belly like a head-caught snake. And it told him he was right — Skin Varney was guilty of this. Sure as day and night didn't come at the same time.

He left the room and closed the kitchen door behind him quietly, not because anyone out there might hear him, but because it seemed the thing to do. He might not have liked ol' Reg McDoughty, not as a marshal nor as a man, but that didn't mean others didn't, least of all his wife. Nobody should die in such a manner. And especially not at the hands of the likes of Varney.

Gunnar stood at the bottom of the steps and stroked his beard and mustaches in thought. He had intended, while in town, to buy more victuals, more pipe tobacco and chaw, but he was put off the notion of shopping.

After seeing the blood in that house, poorly cleaned up by the townsfolk, and knowing the personal possessions of that couple would likely be frittered out among them all, he wanted to get out of Promise. Sure, they would show no outward judgment of one another as folks filched the goods of the couple and squirreled them away in their own burrows, but they were townies, and as such, there would always be talk.

Gunnar had lost any desire to mingle with them, to pretend he was interested in their questions, to listen to the gossiping at the mercantile. No, not today, and maybe not for a long time to come. He felt an urgency to get back on the trail homeward. He was confused and needed time to think.

He reckoned he and the kid could wiggle by for a while yet. Coffee, beans, and flour were all in decent stock at home, too, even with two of them eating off the supplies instead of one.

Gunnar ambled along the same backyard route, avoiding the eyes of people he knew too well and had known for so long. When had he become so settled? As a younger man, he'd rambled and roved all over the vast Shining Mountains, trapped beaver and traded with the natives. Heck, he'd once blown half a winter's fur earnings at a single trappers' rendezvous.

Then he'd sniffed for gold and silver throughout the same hills even farther southward, on the trail of lost Spanish gold, though he never found much. That changed when he came to Promise, however, back when it was little more than a dugout trading post by the now-dry Chalk River.

He'd detected color on his claim in the hills and grabbed rights to two adjacent claims. He knew his life there in Promise, Wyoming Territory, would be short-lived, for he would soon make his fortune. But it had taken a little longer than he anticipated, so he built a cabin and told himself he might as well live in some bit of comfort, at least until his fortune was made. That had been thirty-one years ago.

Gunnar sighed, then winced as a rock twisted under his moccasin and a hot jag of pain lanced up his gammy right leg. "Damn rheumatics," he mumbled, and kept walking, shifting his rucksack to his other shoulder.

He wasn't keen on leaving the kid alone at the cabin. If what he suspected about Skin was true, he needed to get back and make certain the kid was where he had left him — hopefully digging away at finding color in the rocks — and then they'd make for Horton's place. He had to warn his old pard.

When he'd found out a month or more back in town from the Dover kid that Skin Varney was soon to be let out of Tin Falls Prison, Gunnar had told Horton that the snaky man might well make his way back to Promise.

"Why on earth would he do that?" Horton had asked, shaking his head. "Seems to me a man who lived that long closed up tighter than a bull's backside would find better things to do than wander back to the place where his life wobbled off the rails."

"You're thinking like a man who has sense — not much but some." Gunnar had smiled, then said, "Thing with Skin Varney is he's a man who'll spend his last penny to make certain you don't get it."

"What's that mean? How come you know so much about Skin Varney? And why would he want anything to do with Promise anymore? Was a posse of us townsfolk who ran him aground, a whole crew."

"Was a posse of folks from Promise who helped, as you'll recall. Me and you, though, we did more than any of them others to get to him."

Horton had nodded. "I'll allow, as how I lost an eye in the effort."

"And I caught him in the end. I didn't lose much, but I had to put up with his godawful palaver waiting on the rest of the posse. He swore me up one side and down the other, said he'd get me and everybody else in town if it was the very last thing he ever did."

Pulled from his memories, Gunnar offered the cold afternoon a grim chuckle as he walked back alone to his cabin from Promise. "When did I ever get to be an old-timer?" he asked the trail, squinting up at the hills ahead. "Me and Horton. Old. Huh, who'd have thought it? As much as can kill a man out here in the wilds, and we two fools managed to live through it. So far anyway."

His words hung in the still air. The urge to let Horton know of the danger, warn him once more that Skin Varney was amongst them, suddenly became overwhelming.

Gunnar Tibbs quickened his pace homeward.

CHAPTER TWENTY-FIVE

"Horton!" Gunnar ambled closer to the shack. "Horton Meader! You got company, and I brought somebody! Don't answer your door wearing nothing but a drunk smile, you rascal. This here's a gentleman. We got to give him a decent impression or we'll be embarrassed."

They stood at the edge of the clearing. Fifty feet before them, Fletcher saw a squat cabin, not unlike Gunnar's in basic size, but in appearance, the two small abodes couldn't be more different.

Where Gunnar's home was tidy and resembled a handsome chalet with a clean front yard and tidy trails leading around the place to an outhouse, a woodpile, and shade trees overhead, this one looked to have been carved out of raw rock and trees and earth by a distracted giant many long years before.

Gunnar yelled again. "Come on, Horton, wake up! Got news for you — good, bad, and otherwise."

They waited a moment longer.

"Either he's hungover from drinking too much alone last night, or he's got his head stuck underground, sniffing around for gold. Happens. Why, I recall a time not long ago I come bumbling back out of my own diggings and was surprised to see I'd worked clean through all the daylight hours of that day."

As they advanced toward the cabin, Fletcher noticed that Gunnar held back a bit, peered left and right as if expecting somebody to jump out at him. They came to a halt behind the half cover of a pair of ponderosa pines, each trunk thick as a man's head.

"What's wrong?"

"Don't know yet." Gunnar's voice was low and he held out a hand to keep Fletcher back behind him, as he pulled out his revolver. "Something ain't right.

"Stay here." He gave Fletcher the hard eye, but Fletcher shook his head and, without taking his eyes from Gunnar's stern gaze, pulled out one of his father's revolvers and set it at half cock.

"Together, right? That was the whole point."

Gunnar stared at him a moment longer,

then growled low. "Do what I say and stay behind me. We get to the door, you take the right side. I'll shove in through the left. And always watch behind."

Fletcher nodded agreement.

They continued to advance toward the cabin. Nothing moved.

"Camp robbers," said Gunnar, "should be squawkin', but they ain't."

It took a few moments before Fletcher realized the old-timer was referring to the gray jaybirds that always seemed to yammer away at Gunnar's place.

They reached the cabin and took up their positions flanking the door.

Gunnar shouted, "Horton! You in there, you old reprobate?"

Again, there was no reply. Gunnar licked his lips, fluffed his beard, and with the knuckles of his left hand shoved the door inward. Only the top half of the Dutch door swung. He waited a moment longer, then peered in.

Fletcher craned his neck a few inches to his left to see. The room was dark, and a thin light from a window somewhere out of sight shone on a tabletop. He spied a lone gray tin cup on what part of the table he could see.

Without warning, Gunnar jerked the

handle on the bottom half of the door and shoved his way in, revolver rigid before him.

In their brief time of acquaintance, Fletcher had never seen Gunnar move so quickly or fluidly. It was as if he'd shed twenty years.

"Okay" came his voice from inside.

Fletcher followed him in.

"You stay in here, keep an eye, see what you can find. I'm going to scout out the back door."

It was then that Fletcher noticed another Dutch door in the back wall. Gunnar opened it with his same caution, then disappeared outside. Fletcher waited to hear signs of distress from outside. After a few moments of silence had passed, he stalked the room, eyeing the contents without touching anything.

It appeared much as Gunnar's cabin had to Fletcher on first notice — the unclean home of a man long used to living alone. But on closer scrutiny, he realized that Gunnar lived a much tidier existence than his friend did.

Where Gunnar's home was merely cluttered and heaped with all manner of items, from pine cones and rocks and half-finished whittling projects and clothes, Horton's was a crusty jumble of many of the same items, but tinged with dust and the accumulated dirt and grime of someone who didn't give much thought to cleanliness.

The clothing was stained, soiled, and torn; the socks reeked a vicious odor all their own. The low tabletop alongside the wood-stove bore sigs of rodent droppings, un-washed spoons, and a crusty bowl and plate.

The floor, where Gunnar's was planked and worn smooth from years of being trod upon, here was dirty and crusted with curls of wood shavings and bark bits, especially by the woodstove. The room smelled of sweat and greasy food poorly cooked and woodsmoke and dust.

The man's bed sat, as did Gunnar's, in the farthest corner. Though it was dark there, the mass of blankets and fur scraps was arranged such that even when Fletcher prodded it with a long stick that looked to be a walking staff he'd found leaning against the wall, nothing moved. There was no body, sleeping or otherwise, within it, he discovered as he flipped the blankets.

"Well," said Gunnar, sighing as he clumped back into the room. "Maybe ol' Horton is off at his diggin's. But the place sure don't smell good. He's usually fresher than this." He waved an arm and let it drop. "And look at them bottles. I'd say he's been sipping more than usual, even for him. Oh, boy. Got to have a talk with that fella one of these days."

Fletcher thought that perhaps Gunnar could follow his own impending advice regarding the excessive consumption of alcohol, but he held his tongue.

"Maybe we should visit him at his diggings, just to be sure?" said Fletcher, not quite certain that was what he wanted to do. The man he'd not yet met seemed as uncouth a brute as he'd likely yet encountered on his adventures in the West.

"That's where we're headed next. You see anything odd in here?"

"Nothing save for the obvious," said Fletcher, then winced as Gunnar gave him more of that hard stare.

"Follow me, boy. And keep your eyes on our back trail. I won't feel cozy about any of this until we find Horton."

As they walked up a well-worn trail, Gunnar grew more lively. "You'll like ol' Horton. He's a good fellow. Known him a long time. Yonder's his outhouse. Take a peek. See if you can see what's different about it."

"Must I?" said Fletcher.

"Yep. You're getting a schooling, and I'm the teacher — don't forget."

Fletcher sighed and walked over to the

small structure. "It looks surprisingly well-built." He reached the far corner and looked up at the view, uninterrupted from the rim of a most impressive vista. Then he looked back at the outhouse. "There's no door."

"Yep," said Gunnar, smiling.

"Oh. Huh, your friend is a fellow who knows how to enjoy a view, I take it."

"He does, indeed. Ol' Horton likes most everything. Except for the things he don't."

They walked on, passing several mounds of chippings, scatters of timbers, and the beginnings of shafts in the graveled slope leading to nothing but a shallow hole.

"What happened here?" said Fletcher.

"Diggin's. Horton gets bored easy. He'll no sooner commence a new hole than he'll get to be convinced that the spot next to it is the mother lode of all mother lodes. Can't never teach him that you got to stick with a thing in life. He's fiddle-footed and per-snickety, is Horton."

"He's stuck with mining all these years. And with you as a friend." Fletcher suppressed a grin. "That alone takes persever-ance, I imagine."

It took a couple of steps before Gunnar's eyebrows rose. "Well, now, if the greenhorn ain't gone and dug himself up a sense of humor!" He cackled and walked on up an incline and rounded a bend. His laughing jerked to a stop along with his walking.

He stood staring at something Fletcher could not yet see. He huffed to a stop beside Gunnar. "What's the matter?"

There before them, not twenty-five feet up trail, next to the black opening of a mine, lay a man's body, slack stony face staring up at the sky. A bubbled black clot of gore marked the center of his forehead.

"Oh . . . oh, no. Horton . . ." Gunnar's voice wheezed out, a hoarse, low whisper. He rushed forward and stood looking down at his friend's body.

Fletcher kept back, his stomach bubbling, his scalp prickling. He raised his revolver and looked around, turning in a circle. Was the killer close by? "Is he . . . ?"

By then Gunnar had knelt beside Horton's shoulders and rested a hand on his chest. "Course he is. Head shot." His voice cracked as he spoke. He looked at the pistol in his hand and, as if it were a writhing rattler, Gunnar flung the gun from himself.

Fletcher noted the spot where it landed, intending to retrieve it later. He kept watch, turning slowly in place, looking for sign of anything that might indicate they were being watched. The sounds coming from Gunnar, though low and muffled, were those of raw mourning, and Fletcher felt a great wash of sadness in sympathy for the mountain man.

Fletcher gulped back a hard knot in his throat and turned around once more. As he faced the grisly scene, he noted something odd about the face of the broad slab of rock beside Horton's body.

Something on the broad face, as long as a man and half as high, looked not unlike symbols, letters, manmade scratchings.

Had Horton done this in his final moments? As quickly as Fletcher thought it, though, he knew this was not the case. Horton had been shot in the head, after all. How many men could function in such a state? *None,* he wagered.

Fletcher stepped closer and eyed the rock face. Yes, there were letters, but they weren't from some language of old, nor from the dead man.

The message, scratched in jagged, hand-height letters, read:

GUNNAR, WHERE ARE YOU?
FIND ME OR I WILL FIND YOU.

Fletcher thought about the message a moment, stepped closer, and read it a second, third time. There was no getting it wrong. It had to be Skin Varney. Who else? And that meant he was after Gunnar.

"Gunnar."

The old man didn't respond, just sat hunched like a small old vulture beside his friend, one old horned hand atop the dead man's chest, same as it had been minutes before.

"Gunnar."

"What?"

"The rock, to your left."

Tibbs didn't even look up.

"Gunnar, I . . . I think it's a message from Skin Varney."

That got the old buck's attention. His gray head swiveled around and his eyes squinted. Fletcher almost asked Gunnar if he wanted him to read the note to him. But then he recalled the two filled bookshelves in Gunnar's cabin and his occasional lapses into something akin to literary discourse, and Fletcher knew it would be a mighty insulting thing to ask. And yet not but a week before he would surely have done just that without thinking.

Maybe I am changing, he thought. *Maybe Gunnar is right and there is hope for me, after all.* The notion almost made him smile, for he thought he'd been just fine before he discovered the peculiarity that was Promise and all it had revealed itself to be to him.

"You're damn straight it's from Skin Varney." Gunnar shoved up from his knees to stand glaring at the message scratched in the rock.

Fletcher looked around them. "How worried should we be?"

Gunnar shrugged. "Varney's a game player. Used to be anyways. Seems like he ain't changed." He gestured at the message.

"What if you're wrong?"

Gunnar shrugged. "Then he'll shoot us anytime now."

Fletcher retrieved the old man's revolver. "Here." He handed it back to Gunnar. "I'd feel safer if you kept this close at hand."

"Thanks, boy. I was overcome with a fit of disgust for the violence men do to one another. Plumb tired of it, I am." He sighed. "Come on, boy." Gunnar dragged a rawhide cuff across his face beneath his nose and didn't disguise the sodden look his eyes had taken on.

"Where to?" said Fletcher.

"Got to get a pick and shovel." Then Gunnar stopped. "On second thought, no, I'm not thinking right. Help me with Horton." He moved up toward his friend's head. "You take his feet. We'll bring him back to his favorite spot, bury him there."

"Where was that?"

"Take a guess."

They stopped, as Fletcher had suspected, close by the open-fronted outhouse.

"Now we need a shovel and pick," Gunnar said.

"I'll go back to the cabin. I saw his tools in that lean-to off to the side. It'll give you time to spend with him," said Fletcher.

"Appreciate that, boy. I surely do. And if I knew ol' Horton — and I guess I alone knew him about as good as a fellow can know a friend who was like a brother — why, he'd be thankful, too."

Fletcher offered a quick nod. "Of course," he said, and lifted out his revolver and walked away.

"Boy," said Gunnar, "keep an eye." He pointed to his own eye, then to the landscape surrounding them.

It was as if Fletcher were seeing it for the first time. All the same gray and tan boulders, the towering Ponderosas, the beaten trail. It all looked suddenly filled with shadowed nooks and outright hiding spots large enough for a big leering grown man to hide in and level his revolver and rifle and shotgun on them, on him. Then the brute would squeeze the trigger. . . .

"Stop it, Fletcher," he told himself as he

hustled along the trail back toward the cabin. Gunnar seemed to think Varney wouldn't still be around, so he had to take that as a fact and keep moving. Otherwise he'd work himself into a frenzy of foolish behavior — good for no one.

As he walked, eyeing the terrain, it came to him that he did not know what Varney looked like. Gunnar had never given him a satisfactory answer.

CHAPTER TWENTY-SIX

They buried Horton Meader and Gunnar mumbled low words over the rocked-over mound. Then Fletcher followed in silence as the old man trudged back to his cabin. Later, over coffee gone cold, Gunnar growled, then spoke to the ceiling. "That's twice now when I wasn't where I should have been. Well, it ain't gonna happen a third time." Gunnar looked to Fletcher to be holding back a gush of rage.

"I'm sorry, Mr. Tibbs. I don't understand."

"Happened first when I wasn't there for Millie, and again when poor ol' Horton met his end with nary a friendly face in sight."

"What can you do about that now?"

"Retribution for my friends, boy! Payback, revenge, a reckoning. Call it what you will — it's what I had in mind when you first came stumbling up my mountainside. I let training you lull me too much. Now, I ain't blaming you, but it's high time I get back to the plan. Now . . . out of my way."

Gunnar shoved past Fletcher, knocking the table and flinging scraps of firewood, half-whittled spoons, stray socks, and stale biscuits.

"I'll take out after him," said the grim-faced old man to himself as if he'd forgotten Fletcher was there with him. "It's down to me and him now. I'm the one he wants next. He's bound to continue on his vengeance ride and he won't be happy until he kills everyone in Promise. I got to stop him."

Fletcher shook his head at the old man. He was impressed with the old-timer's anger and eagerness, but he knew this was likely a short-lived spur-of-the-moment decision fueled by the quick flame of raw hate. And that was exactly what Varney wanted.

"You can't do it alone."

"Huh?" said Gunnar.

Fletcher knew he wasn't listening. Still, he tried to explain his logic to the old-timer, but Gunnar shook his head and continued storming about the cabin, selecting items and tossing others over his shoulder.

After a few moments of no response, Fletcher tried once more. "At least let me go with you. To back you up, if nothing else."

"No, sir. No, I say. Don't you see? Can't be that way. Just can't. Don't ask me why." Gunnar stood in the middle of the rubble of his usually tidy cabin. In the past few minutes, he'd pulled everything in sight from hooks on the walls, cleared entire shelves, and rummaged in his clothing chest, upending everything in the cabin in the process.

"What are you looking for anyway?" said Fletcher, flummoxed because Gunnar wouldn't stop and talk with him, let alone listen to reason.

"I'm looking for my lucky socks. You ain't seen them, have you?" It was the first time he'd looked at Fletcher in many long minutes.

"What? Socks? No, I don't think so." Fletcher stared at the old man, whose head was ringed by a frazzled nest of long gray twiglike hair, his beard and mustaches a dervish-twisted nest, his eyes wide and wet and red. Gunnar stood in the midst of the cabin, a torn old undershirt in his right hand, now more rag than shirt, and a moccasin with holes in his left.

"Don't you throw anything out?" said Fletcher.

"Course not. I work for my money. Ain't had nobody ever send me money nor much else but a letter now and then from a sister of mine back in Maine. She's passed now. Oh, I see what you're up to — changing the topic so I'll forget myself! No, sir, won't work this time." He pointed the floppy old moccasin at the young man. "Now where are those socks?"

"What do they look like?"

"Look like? Oh, they're green with red about the toe."

"Like those?" said Fletcher, nodding at Gunnar's feet.

The old man looked down, wiggled his toes. "Yep, them's the ones. Phew."

"Why are you worried about socks?"

"Worried? Why, boy, these socks are filled to the brim with luck, that's why."

"I thought they were filled with your bony legs."

"Don't mock things you don't understand."

"I'm sorry. What makes them so lucky, then?"

"Why, I was wearing them when I captured Varney so long ago. I give up wearing them for years. Then when I heard Varney was released from prison and would be among us once more, I dragged them out of the storage trunk. They're about worn through, though. No heels to speak of. I darned them so often, they're mostly new all over, but it's the spirit of the originals, the ghost of them that's important."

"I see."

"Don't care if you see or not. Point is, I was wearing them then and the cards fell in my favor, so why change a thing? In life, if you are successful doing something a certain way, why, it only makes good sense that a man keeps on the same path if he wants that success to continue, right?"

Fletcher nodded. "I admit it's not a thread of logic I'd ever have thought to follow, but it makes sense when you put it that way. Nothing in my life has worked out lately as I expected, so I might as well defer to alternative ways of considering my situation."

"Well, whatever you said, I'm sure it makes sense to you. Best leave it at that."

"Now that your socks have been found, let's get back to the initial point of the discussion, which is that I should go with you."

"No, that's your thinking, not mine. You stay here. I can't be nursemaiding you and track that vicious killer at the same time. No, no, and no!"

"But . . ."

"Look, boy. Varney's a brute. He don't know no other way but to kill. He's already laid low my Millie. He's killed off the biggest pain in my ass, Reg, and his poor wife, Edna."

"Oh, my word!" said Fletcher.

"Yep. And now he's kilt my best and only friend, ol' Horton Meader. We come to these hills about the same time. We been scratching out a living out here so long, you'd think we were brothers — twins! And sometimes I ain't so sure we wasn't one and the same person. I reckon I knew him longer than most anybody else I know."

"I understand, Mr. Tibbs, and I am sorry, truly, but you said we were going to do this together to clear my name and to avenge Millie's death."

"I did. But that was before Varney went on a killing rampage. Now I know I'm next. He's drawing me out, boy, and I don't want you to get caught on accident — you hear me?"

Fletcher opened his mouth and the old man shook his head and held up a callused palm. "Enough talking. Now leave me be."

Twenty minutes later, Gunnar was packed with the barest of essentials, light enough to travel easy on foot: matches, a hip knife, a revolver, a tomahawk, a shoulder pack slung bandolier-style across his back with jerky enough to last a week, a dozen flat hard biscuits — holdouts from Fletcher's first attempt at biscuit making — plus a waterskin. Last, he hefted Millie's shotgun and filled a leather pouch full of shells.

"No coffeepot?"

Gunnar shook his head. "I'll be camping dry, dark, and light. No fires."

"But . . . no coffee? No offense, Gunnar, but I've seen you without your coffee."

The old buck held up another pouch. "Full of coffee beans. I chew them. Serve me fine. But I appreciate your concern, Mr. Ralston."

"What about me?" said Fletcher. "What'll I do?"

"I been thinking on that, and I think you should go to town."

"What? But . . ."

Gunnar nodded. "I know. But I think you should ride back into Promise. Tell them about Horton, and tell them . . . oh, hell, tell them whatever you like. I'm through with the palaver." He turned and walked out the door, leaving Fletcher staring wide-eyed after him, standing in the midst of the old man's cabin, confused and unsure of what he was supposed to do.

He ran outside shouting, "Hey! Mr. Tibbs!"

Gunnar stopped in the trail that led toward Horton's and beyond. He didn't turn around.

"Good luck, Mr. Tibbs. It's been . . . interesting getting to know you. And thank you."

Gunnar stood still a moment. Fletcher expected him to turn back, say he was wrong, that Fletcher should accompany him. Anything at all, but instead, Gunnar raised the blunt sawed-off shotgun over his head, shook it once, and walked on.

Fletcher didn't know what to make of that. He figured the man was so far into his grief that he might never come out. He also figured that it would get the old man killed.

He didn't know whether to follow him or to take his advice and go to town. If he followed Gunnar into the mountains, he'd be ill-equipped and outmatched in any skill he needed, from feeding himself to defending himself to navigating. And Gunnar would surely know he was being followed.

Or he could go into Promise and . . . what? Nobody there thought him anything other than the killer of an old woman and likely that, too, of the marshal and his wife. He might be set upon by the angry townsfolk themselves. Wasn't that how people in small towns on the frontier operated?

Was there a third alternative? Yes, he realized with surprise. Without saying so, the old man had given him an unspoken third option. He could leave it all behind, get away from the madness that was Promise.

But that would mean never knowing if Varney had succeeded in killing Gunnar Tibbs and exacting his revenge on the town. It would mean throwing away everything that Millicent Jessup and his own mother, Rose, and even his father, Samuel Thorne, had done for him.

No, that was not an option; he realized that now. If only because he could not let down his friend. Odd as it sounded to Fletcher, Gunnar Tibbs, that crusty old mountain goat of a man, was indeed his friend, the truest friend he had ever really known in his entire life. And the only one.

Fletcher stared at the empty trail's forked paths. The left led sharply away toward Horton's cabin and into the wooded hills, where his only friend had ventured off with purpose. And where a killer lurked.

The right trail led back toward town, the town of Promise, the place of his birth, the place where the only people who had ever really known him, known who he really, truly was, had lived and died. The place where so much treachery, some of it on his behalf, had taken place.

And right then he made his decision. He ducked back into the low door of the cabin and gathered what he needed of his things. He tucked the letter from Millie into his inner coat pocket, pulled on his battered bowler, tugged on his one remaining spat and his ridiculous holey gloves, and swatted away the dust from his dirt-shiny vest and trousers.

Next, he filled the bullet loops on his father's gun belt and strapped it and its shiny nickel-plated guns with the pearl grips about his waist. He noted with surprise once more that it fit to perfection in the one worn hole in the belt. Perhaps he was more like Samuel Thorne the elder than he knew.

Fletcher slid the little derringer — what Gunnar called a hideout gun — inside his coat's inner pocket. Last, he pulled out the locket by its slender gold chain, fastened it about his neck, tucked it beneath his collar and shirtfront, and patted his chest once to ensure it rode there. Then he strode out of the cabin.

A squawking sound pulled his gaze back toward the cabin. Mort the crow sat atop the old antlers at the roof's peak. He bobbed twice and cawed once more.

"If you're wishing me good luck, Mort, I'll take it." Fletcher saluted the bird once and resumed walking toward Promise, hoping the presence of a crow meant good fortune and not anything else.

Chapter Twenty-Seven

Skin hadn't intended to kill Horton Meader as quick as he had. The moment had caught him by surprise. There was a flicker of time when he saw Meader standing there before his silly little tunnel where Skin could have sworn the man was Gunnar Tibbs, the bastard he really wanted to lay low. The sight had made him giddy.

But he hadn't wanted to do it in haste. No, he'd wanted to make it last, draw out the juice of it, like biting into a bloody, hardly cooked slice of meat off the flank of a young deer, so young it ain't had time enough to work its muscles into something tougher than a boot sole. Skin envisioned himself taking a bite, the blood squirting hot into his mouth, running down over his chin. . . . That was how he wanted killing Gunnar Tibbs to feel. Slow and enjoyable.

He'd had long enough to think on it. His biggest fear for the last few years while jammed up in Tin Falls Prison was that Tibbs would somehow give up the ghost before he could get out of prison and track him down.

He wasn't a fool — he realized that his anger had shifted from finding that fiend Sam Thorne and the money to tracking down Gunnar Tibbs and making him squeal out his last as if he were being crushed slowly by a boulder, from the toes up.

In fact, that had been one of his most cherished dreams, a way to help himself fall asleep in the wee hours, as his gran used to call the darkest minutes between nightfall and dawn. He wanted to crush Tibbs slowly until his squeals were drowned in a gush of his own blood. Or maybe slice him apart with a dull knife, one little hack at a time, until he was nothing more than a bleeding, screaming mess of meat and bone, topped with two eyeballs watching the whole thing happen to him. Such thoughts had brought Skin Varney much pleasure over the years.

It hadn't taken him long to find out where Tibbs lived. He'd never really known all those years back, had no more notion of the spot than a general direction. But first he'd had to find out if he was still about.

He'd asked a youngish-looking fellow outside of town the first day he'd reached it on his stolen nag if a fellow by the name of Tibbs ("Gunnar, was it?") still lived around these parts. Been a long while, Skin had said, but he was an old friend, from years and years before, and he wanted to pay him a visit, say hello, and catch up on old times.

The kid looked to be one of a hundred other farm kids, dragged from Kansas or such to the mountains with his family a few years before. His pap likely thought he was going to strike it big in the gold fields. Instead, his family came to naught but misery.

Women fared the worst — each worked like a demon, came from living in a snake-infested soddy on the plains to a rathole of a dugout on some forsaken hillside in the mountains, all the while struggling to care for her brood of ribby children with snot noses and runny eyes and one or two still dragging on the teat.

If she didn't kill herself with work, she crawled into a bottle beside her husband as she watched her brood die off from some sickness or other. And if she outlived them all, she wandered off, crazed, on her own.

And sometimes, if she was unlucky enough and didn't end up starving in the wilds and ravaged by wolves or bears or mountain lions, she ended up at a hog farm, selling her disease for a few pennies a throw.

Skin Varney knew of what he spoke, as he'd been one such a boy himself. His pathetic father and addlepated mother had had too many kids, and he'd survived somehow to be tall and broad of shoulder, if not handsome.

He'd also been born smart, as he liked to think. Smart enough, at least, to walk away one day when he was fourteen and as tall as his father; he left the doomed family before they could ruin him any more than they already had.

That was the reason Skin had never taken a wife nor stooped so low as to heft a pick or shovel and scratch in a rocky hillside himself for ore. He'd reckoned himself smarter than that. He'd mined the miners instead. One slow squeeze at a time. When it came time for more money, he'd steal from someone too far from the law to do much of anything about it.

And if he got caught, he'd kill them. Threats, he knew, did nothing once your back was turned and you were walking away. People weren't smart enough to realize he'd given them a chance to live. Soon enough, he had taken to gutting the fools and leaving an untraceable trail of dead behind.

Despite his caution, it had always surprised him that he'd not been caught. But then again, that had also served to show him he was right — people were dumber than you had any right to expect of them.

So when he'd been riding toward Promise and came upon that hollow-eyed farm boy, he'd taken a chance, wondering if the youth had been around the town long enough to know who was local. But he had, and he did.

"Tibbs? Uh, yeah, there's an old man name of Tibbs yonder in the hills someplace. He's sweet on the woman runs the house of fancy. Mama told me that. Told me never to talk of others, then goes and tells me that." The kid had swung his head and smiled. "Mama, she ain't one for taking her own advice none."

"You lived in these parts long?" said Skin, a little bit curious about the boy now.

"Some. Since before I was growed big as I am now. Four, five years, I reckon."

"Is your papa a miner?"

"You could say that." Again the kid grinned and shook his head again as if at some inner joke. "He's rootin' in the dirt, but if he finds gold, it'll be a miracle. Not only will it be the first gold he ever did find, but it'll be impossible, on account of him being dead and all. That's how I come to say he was rootin' in the dirt."

"You're a funny kid," said Skin, feeling smug at having proven once more that he was correct. The kid was doomed to dirt, digging and dying with nothing to show for it, just like his own papa.

He supposed the thing to do would be to pay the kid for the information. After all, the kid was dressed in shabby togs — trousers too short for him, shirt-sleeves the same. Skin could see more dirt and holes than cloth.

Trouble was, if he gave the kid a few coins, the kid might remember him easier than if he just rode off now. But the kid did remind him of himself as a penniless fool. He reached in his saddlebag and tugged out an apple, one of several he'd taken from the crazy man and his gimpy daughter some days before.

He tossed the apple to the kid, touched his hat brim, then rode off toward Promise, assured Gunnar Tibbs was well alive off yonder. Had to be. He'd choose to believe so. *Because,* Skin thought, *if you believe something hard enough in life, you make it so.* That had to be true; otherwise, he'd not have lived through twenty-four years at Tin Falls Prison.

And now here he was, a minor but pesky bullet wound in his side from that jackass marshal. But he'd left the man and his harpy of a wife dead, and Horton Meader dead, and that bossy old crow of a whore, Millie, dead, too. Now, if he could lure Gunnar Tibbs out, he'd have killed off everybody left over from that posse that had wronged him personally. Then he could finish off the rest of Promise, maybe with a match or two.

The old woman had said Samuel Thorne — his old pard on several robberies and, most important, on the big one from that fateful night — was long gone, had left town right after the robbery.

She had no idea where he was or where his money was hidden. "Rosie's dead, dead as dead can be. And Samuel Thorne, good riddance." She'd made a sound in her throat as if she might spit. "Hopefully he's dead by now, too."

"You don't know if he is or not?"

"You fool," she'd said, looking up at him. "I see it in your eyes that you're looking for revenge, nothing more. Just hollow revenge. Well, good luck, for if he is alive, he's far from here," she'd said, and then she had done a very funny thing.

She'd looked right at him, up from her

pillows, on her very own deathbed. She'd stared into his eyes in a solid, serious way like nobody had ever done to him before, and then she'd laughed at him.

"Why is that funny?" he'd asked her, his voice thick. He'd barely been able to ask, since all he'd really wanted to do was peel her nasty old putrid head from her wrinkly neck stalk.

"The way you look so hopeful, Skin Varney!" she'd said, coughing. "It's as if you expected Samuel Thorne to be here waiting for you, cash in hand. Begging for your forgiveness. You fool!"

She'd cackled then, and he'd done the thing he had intended to do to her anyway. He dragged his big Dag blade across her wrinkled old throat. She'd jerked, her eyes wide.

Skin had gotten a warm feeling down deep at seeing her face sag, at hearing her cackle snag and stutter into a wet cough, then a gagging and finally a gurgling sound. He hoped the old bird was in terrible pain, for she'd earned every second of it, laughing at him like that. Laid up there in her whorehouse, pretending she was something she wasn't. Well, he'd taught her a lesson.

He would have kept on, too, maybe made the rest of her bedridden, feeble old body pay, too, but he'd heard sounds outside the room. Somebody had been on the stairs, so he'd made for the window, the same route he'd taken to get in. At the bottom, he'd pulled the ladder away from the shed roof and leaned it where he'd found it, in the dirt against the rear of the building. Then he'd hotfooted it on out of town.

He'd pushed his luck by visiting the old bird in town, but he'd had a hunch she knew something. She'd been like a mother to Sam's girl, Rose, after all. Treated Sam like he was dirt just because he was Skin's friend — he just knew it. So it stood to reason that Sam would have taken his girl with him that night, and he bet the old girl knew something about them, some clue about where they'd be. Which would lead him to the money.

It was only later that Skin realized that he could have played it quieter with the old woman, could have gone in through the front door and made up some story about how he was a changed man, free of prison and looking to make amends. Might be he could have gotten more information that way. But he would have been seen too soon by too many folks in Promise.

CHAPTER TWENTY-EIGHT

The walk back to the town of Promise, Wyoming Territory, was one of much rumination on Fletcher Ralston's part. He wasn't certain in the least that he was doing the right thing.

He wasn't sure the townies, as Gunnar called them, not without a whiff of curled-lip contempt, would believe him when he told them . . . what? What, exactly, he asked himself over and over again as he trudged, was he going to tell them?

Before he left Gunnar's cabin, he had felt certain he could convince the townsfolk that forming a posse to track down Skin was the best thing they could do. After all, he was possessed of a solid intellect due to a fine education.

But now he wasn't so sure he would be able to convince a collective of townies that not only was he innocent of the charges they no doubt had laid against him, but they had darn well better follow his advice and help him track the killer.

He nodded in agreement with himself. "Yes, that's the stuff, Fletcher Ralston." Yet even that name was a lie, if what Gunnar Tibbs and the lawyer had told him was true, and he had no reason to doubt them, most certainly not Gunnar. And if that were true, then he, Fletcher Ralston, or perhaps Samuel Thorne II, was no more than one of them — a townie, a product of Promise, Wyoming Territory.

Nay, not just that. He himself was a product of the basest desires of such a base place. As if to bolster his dour mood, a large dark cloud slid slowly before the sun, shading the day and casting shadow where moments before sunlight had prevailed.

Fletcher passed a number of landmarks, boulders mostly, that he hoped appeared familiar. The last time he'd come this way, he'd been an animal on the run, hounded, he imagined, by enraged locals with burning brands in the night, armed with all manner of weapons, from blade to gun. Had that been the case? Perhaps.

Were he in their shoes, he might well feel as he suspected they did. The thought did not help his mood.

He spent his walk waffling in this manner,

fluttering from one conviction to another. After he'd corrected his course twice, not certain at times of the path — after all, few people used the trails out to the wilderness, as Fletcher had come to think of the location of Gunnar's and Horton's cabins in the hills — he smelled woodsmoke and saw the barest haze of it through a ragged edge of leafless aspens ahead.

The town? Another cabin? He walked on, uncertain and hesitant in his steps. Then he spied a roofline and another of tall buildings, too tall to be cabins or homesteads. Finally, he found himself there above the western end of town, looking down on the cluster of buildings from a ragged spit of rock.

From the looks of it, it was a spot at which Gunnar Tibbs had stopped, too, in his comings and goings on his regular visits to Millie Jessup.

Fletcher rested a foot on a rise of reddish rock with black flecks. *Granite?* He didn't know his rocks well at all. But the height was perfect for a bent knee to accommodate an elbow. He took a breather — smiling, as it sounded like a phrase the odd old man would have used — and admired the scene below.

There was much more to the town than

he had remembered from the last time he'd been there. He'd never seen it from this vantage point. Along the southern edge of the main street, which ran east to west, or as he was viewing it west to east, there sat the lawyer's office.

Chisley DeMaurier had been an interesting man, cultivated and cool in how he regarded Fletcher, kind but always assessing. He, of course, knew Fletcher's business, the details of his life. In a way, he knew more than Fletcher did, long before Fletcher had strolled in, acting imperious and aloof.

Fletcher felt himself redden at the memory. What an oaf he'd been — demanding as if he owned the town. Instead he'd come to learn he was, in some ways, one of its baser citizens, the product of lust.

No, that was unfair; at least from his mother's point of view, if Millie and Gunnar were to be believed, it had been love. But she had still been a prostitute. And his father had been an unscrupulous, thieving gunhand who'd robbed the very people of this town. And apparently had done so without remorse. That left Fletcher as the beneficiary to the head prostitute's legacy, such as it was. A run-down bordello, threadbare and quaint in its way.

Fletcher sighed and sighted along the

northern edge of town. There it sat, Millie's Place, the fourth building from this end, not the tallest nor the best maintained, but solid-looking nonetheless.

As he knew the builders were wont to say, it looked to have good bones. Certainly it was finished inside to a decent degree and furnished to a certain level of finery. That had surprised him. Perhaps Millie had come from refinement back East? He would ask Gunnar.

Thought of the man and of his mission in returning to town gripped Fletcher inside and he hastened once more down the trail. Come what might, he had to help Gunnar Tibbs. No more doubts about it, he'd do whatever he had to, short of getting caught and held in town, to help his friend. But letting himself be caught would never do. He'd escaped from these people once before, had he not? He would employ the same wits to do so again. If he could not enlist help, he would take to the hills and track Gunnar and so Skin Varney, all on his own.

Even this welling of conviction ebbed within him as he trailed down the path and entered the west end of the main street of Promise, the very town he had fled as a wanted man, a murderer.

Whom to see first? The lawyer? Fletcher suspected the other man might well be sympathetic to his cause, yet he could not be certain.

To his left, a man dragged a squat barrel of something heavy, shoving and kneeing it along a loading dock. He saw Fletcher and glanced away, then swung his head back, his brows meeting. His open stare did very little to help convince Fletcher that he'd made the right choice.

Fletcher glanced back over his left shoulder and saw that the man had hastened inside what looked to be a depot office. That might well mean the man was looking for assistance to apprehend the killer returned to their midst. Oh, dear.

Fletcher groaned and beelined for the one place he knew he shouldn't go. But it was closer than the rest — just ahead to his left, in fact.

Millie's Place.

How ironic, he thought as he mounted the steps and knocked, looking up and down the street. *I own this place and yet I wither inside to enter.* He glanced once more behind him. So far, no one else seemed to be out and about. At least nearby. There was sign of people at the east end of the street, but nobody seemed to be running toward him or shooting at him. Yet.

He knocked again.

Why am I knocking? I own this place. Even that cold comfort of a thought slowed his hands, though he did reach for the knob and depressed the thumb latch. He was about to shove the door when it jerked inward, fast.

A wide-eyed woman stared at him, and he at her. It took him as long as it did her for recognition to bloom. "You!" she said. Then he knew it was Hester, the woman who had let him in that day when he'd first arrived. "You have some nerve, boy, showing up here again!" She spat the words through nearly clenched teeth. Never had Fletcher felt so very uncomfortable.

He looked to his right, eastward, and saw that the folks he'd seen from a distance were now drawing closer, moving in a determined way, four, perhaps five of them. Still too far away to know.

He looked to his left, from the direction he'd walked down into town, and there was the man he'd seen moments before, the one who had shoved the keg. But he was not alone. A burly woman strode with him, and twenty feet behind, another man was tugging on a coat, and in his other arm, he lugged a shotgun. The keg dragger wore a gun belt, one weapon on each side of his ample hips.

"Let me in, damn it!" Fletcher shouted at the woman, only mildly bothered by the fact that he had uttered a foul oath in the presence of a woman, and then shoved past her as she stumbled back in shock. She recovered quickly and grabbed for him. He expected it and shook her off, spinning on her.

"Close that door and listen to me. I'll stand right here and keep my hands visible to you, okay?"

She stared, glared at him. But she didn't close the door.

"It's a matter of life and death!"

"Your life? Why should I care?"

Once more, he shoved toward her, reached past her, and slammed the door shut. She didn't move.

"No, not mine. Well, yes, my life." Fletcher heard sounds behind him and looked up the staircase at the several women who had gathered there, no half-dressed men in tow. *Good.* He backed a little toward the big clock and held up his hands at chest height, palms out. "I'm not looking for trouble,"

"Then you came to the wrong place." Hester's words were spoken low, through gritted teeth. Her slitted eyes told Fletcher he'd better make haste with an explanation.

"Gunnar Tibbs is in trouble and I need help."

"What? What did you do to Gunnar?" She clenched and unclenched her fists, glanced quickly to the women on the stairs behind him. He edged farther back, keeping the clock to his back so that he might be able to see them, too.

"Skin Varney."

He heard breath drawn in, as if the very name he'd uttered was that of someone who held them in his grip, yet feared and reviled in equal measure.

"What about him?" The woman who asked in little more than a breathy whisper was Dominique, if Fletcher recalled correctly. This time she was fully dressed. Around her eyes, red puffiness belied the fact that she'd been in the midst of tears when he arrived. A woman next to her rubbed her on the shoulder.

"Well," said Fletcher. "He's a killer and a thief. He's the one who robbed the town twenty-four years ago with . . . Samuel Thorne."

"You mean, your father," said Hester. She didn't take her eyes from him.

Finally he nodded. "Yes. Okay, fine. But look, I didn't come here to tell you things

319

you already know. Gunnar told me the whole story about what happened that night. And then he told me that Skin Varney has been released from prison and is free once more."

No response. Then there was a loud knocking on the door. Hester looked at him, then at the door, then back to him. "You'd best keep talking."

Fletcher nodded. Maybe he would get through to them. "He also told me that Skin killed Millie." The women gasped; some shouted at him, called him a liar.

"No!" he said with a force that startled himself. "I may be many things, but I am no liar. I have not lied to you, nor will I. Hear me out, and then if you decide to throw me to the wolves, I'll go. But I'm telling the truth. If we don't act soon, Gunnar may be killed."

"Why?"

"He went to track down Skin Varney after we found Horton Meader dead."

Another round of gasps flurried up from the women. Hester walked closer to him. Fletcher backed up a step. She was a formidable presence; about his height, with her demure heels on, she was pretty but thick, solid seeming. She reminded him of a stout tree that could weather any storm.

"You're not making any sense, mister. You'd better keep talking or I'll open that door and let those fools have their way with you. They all think you killed Millie and half of them believe you had a hand in marshal's death and his wife's, too."

With that, the woman on the stairs, she of the dewy eyes, sobbed and collapsed to a seated position on one of the steps. The woman beside her now patted her head.

"And now you tell us Horton's dead, too?"

Fletcher nodded. "Look, I realize it could be construed that I am the guilty party here, but from what Gunnar tells me, my arrival here is coincident with the arrival of Skin Varney, as near as I can figure."

"That doesn't explain a thing."

Fletcher sighed.

Again, loud thumping sounded on the door. It bounced slightly with the blow. Now Fletcher could hear voices out there, too. Many. A small crowd.

"How about this: If I am lying, I'll give myself up, okay?"

"What if you're planning on killing us right now the way you did Millie?"

"I didn't kill her! Skin Varney did, and Gunnar might be in trouble!"

The women stared at him. He returned the look to each face in turn. "Whether you all like it or not, Millie was, well, she was my aunt, of sorts. And she left this place to me."

All the women, save for Hester, burbled with shock and indignation.

"It's true," he said, and saw a resigned look on Hester's face that told him she knew he was telling the truth. "Please tell them," he said.

She stared at him a moment longer, then said, "It's true. She left the place to him, the whole business. I never said anything after she died, because I wasn't sure how much this fella knew. But I guess he knows just about all there is to know."

She sighed and looked at him. "What *do* you know? So Gunnar was right."

"You talked with Gunnar about me? Then you knew? Why didn't you tell me?"

She shrugged. "Testing you." She looked at the women on the stairs. "I think he's mostly telling the truth, at least about not killing Millie."

"You do?"

"Yeah, Gunnar told me himself. But don't get ahead of me now," she said, that hard edge returning to her voice.

"But . . . but," said Dominique on the stairs, "where will we go? What will we do?"

"You'll go nowhere," he said. "Look, I

have the papers in my bag, but I'm not about to drag them out and read them to you, not with an angry mob outside."

"Ain't no angry mob in Promise, mister," said Hester. "It's just Dewey and Melvin and a few others. They're worked up, same as us, because you're someone we don't know much about, and we have had some mighty bad deaths lately."

"Okay, fine. We can worry about all that later. Look, I came here for help. I've grown fond of Gunnar Tibbs. He believed in me when no one else would, and I want to help him."

"We'll talk. You go on through to the kitchen. Your kitchen." Hester nodded her head past him.

"I could use some water."

"Yeah, well, there's water in a pitcher on the table."

He regarded them all. "Please hurry." He walked down the darkened corridor toward the rear of the house and emerged into a kitchen. Not seeing a cup, he drank straight from the stoneware pitcher on the table.

He paused, heard a few voices, whispers now and again. Suddenly he felt cold all over, as if he had just discovered a hunk of ice in his pocket. Something was wrong. He was getting hot prickles of warning, as Gunnar might have said.

Fletcher gulped down the rest of the water and made for the back door. On his way, he spied a cloth-covered platter.

He lifted one corner of the blue-checked gingham and saw a pyramid of tall, fluffy biscuits. He felt a quick twinge of guilt, then decided that, by gum, he owned the building, so he technically owned the food, too. He snatched up a half dozen, jamming one in his mouth, the rest in his pockets. Then he opened the door, which led to a small picket-fenced yard, where five or six hens clucked and pecked at the dirt beneath a small coop.

"Ladies," he said, touching his hat brim as he bolted past them. He leapt the rear of the fence, not a huge feat, as it was less than a couple of feet tall, and glanced back toward the house. Nobody had seen or heard him yet. "Gunnar," he whispered, "I'm not much, but here I come. I hope."

He cut left, following the same path he'd taken into town. This led him behind the other buildings, all with backyards, most with fenced-in chickens. One held a fat brown-and-black dog with one perked ear that stared at him and didn't seem to have ambition enough to bark.

Coming to town had been a mistake. He'd

wasted precious time, thinking he could replicate the posse of all those years before. In truth, he'd been afraid to set out on his own. He'd not been confident he could find Gunnar. He still wasn't, but now he knew he had to do it. And do it alone. Those women, the townsfolk, all of them, maybe they didn't believe him. Maybe they were too afraid of Varney. Whatever the reason, he was on his own.

All he'd accomplished in coming to town was wasting time. But Gunnar had been adamant that he do so, and he'd fallen for it. He'd still been so reluctant to accept who he really was that he'd blindly followed the old man's orders and marched to town. All Gunnar had wanted was to get him out of the way so he could go off on his vengeance quest alone.

Instead of leaving him feeling angry and violated and untrusted, it came to Fletcher that the thing Gunnar had done for him, sending him to safety, at least a safer place than where Gunnar was headed, had been an act of kindness because he didn't want Fletcher to be killed. The old man had trusted that Fletcher was smart enough to convince the folks of Promise that he was in the right, that he was innocent.

Yes, it was kind of Gunnar, but it was

misguided. If Skin Varney was half as dangerous as Gunnar had said he was, then Gunnar was in trouble, and he knew it. The full force of the realization smacked Fletcher as if he'd been hit in the temple with a split of stove-wood.

Gunnar knew he was going to his death. Or at least that he stood little chance of defeating Varney. He was forlorn at having lost Millie and Horton. He knew Fletcher meant much to Millie, having heard of him for so long.

What a disappointment I must have been to him, thought the young man as he ran toward the hills. He glanced back once more toward town, but saw no one following him.

Let the townsfolk track him. What did he care? They weren't interested in helping him. Maybe he had to do this on his own. He wondered if, in some odd way, this was how he was meant to seek retribution for all the ills caused to Promise by his father and Skin Varney.

As he strode into the hills once more, Fletcher reached down and felt the two jostling guns that rode low on his hips, the ends of the holsters tied down about his thighs. He reached into his coat and patted the bulge that was the hideout gun. His guns. And about his neck, there sat the locket. The locket with the pictures of his parents. His parents. His family.

"What have you gotten yourself into, Fletcher J. Ralston?" he asked out loud.

Then he laughed, because Fletcher J. Ralston, he realized, no longer existed. Indeed, he had never existed. He had been a fabrication, a lie twenty-four years in the making, in the living, in the telling. Now it was time for the truth.

CHAPTER TWENTY-NINE

Fletcher made it back to Gunnar's cabin after dark. How the old man managed to walk to and from town without benefit of a horse to ride for all those years, hauling his supplies on his own back, he'd never know. Maybe it was the whiskey that had enabled him to do it. Either way, it had been a hellish journey.

Fletcher had scraped his shins, smacked his shoulders, and even knocked his bowler off his head twice on the journey. But he made it. All of a sudden, though, he did not feel safe there. Even earlier in the day, he'd felt plenty safe, but that had been when Gunnar was there.

"Now," he said aloud to the empty cabin. "Now there's nobody here but me." Then he paused. What if that wasn't true? What if Skin had already killed Gunnar and lay in wait for him?

Did Skin know about him? Did he care?

How would he even know about him? Unless he'd spied on them, which was possible. Yet surely he'd not know or care that Fletcher was about. Would he?

That thought stayed the greenhorn's hand as he reached for the matches to light the oil lamp by the woodstove. No, maybe Gunnar had it right. Maybe a cold camp was the way to do this. All he intended to do was gather what gear he thought he might need.

He'd not counted on needing much because he had no idea what to take. He'd only been passing by the cabin anyway on his route to tracking Gunnar. How did one go about tracking a man anyway?

With a calming breath, he lit a lantern and turned the little wheel to keep the flame low. Keeping one hand on a pistol butt, Fletcher prowled the cabin, looking for things he might take. He felt as if he was violating the old buck's privacy by peering into the few closed spaces, a drawer and two wooden boxes he found beneath the bed.

One contained a bundle of twine-tied letters that Fletcher hastily put back. In the end, he settled for a short sheath knife that he strapped on his belt. Then he filled a flour sack with the remaining dozen or so biscuits he'd made.

He bit into one and winced. Gunnar had been correct. They were awful. He also packed the last of the jerked meat hanging from lengths of twine from a ceiling beam. Then he snatched a small wool blanket that smelled horsey from the bed, draped it over his shoulders, lifted down a wooden canteen, slung its strap over his neck, and walked into the night.

He strode down the path Gunnar had taken, walking slowly for ten minutes, doing his best to avoid more knee-height rocks, and thankful for the three-quarter moon, the glow of which lit the trail well enough. Or rather it shifted enough shadows to give him a general sense of the path.

It would be all too easy for him to miss some clue as to Gunnar's direction. Maybe he had taken a side route some minutes back?

Fletcher paused, shivered, and pulled the blanket tighter about his shoulders. As he considered his situation, weariness, deep in his bones, began settling on him as if it were a pair of gentle hands pressing on his shoulders and not letting up, but pushing down and down. He stumbled backward, landing on his backside against a rock, and felt the night's coldness creep through the rock, through the thin fabric of his trousers, and chill him. He shivered once more.

What I need, he thought, *is a cup of coffee. A cup of hot coffee and maybe a biscuit or two. Yes, that would be the ticket. Something warm. Warm . . .*

CHAPTER THIRTY

Gunnar woke slowly, as if he'd been trapped in river ice for months and it was only then beginning to melt. He'd spent the afternoon and evening before cold and wet some miles from his cabin. He hadn't gotten all that far, because the hills there-abouts were a jagged challenge.

He had often ruminated on the fact that if he were able to fly like a red-tailed hawk, he'd finally get himself a good look at the local terrain, from the Rondo Basin to the east clear on over to the Jawbone ridgelines that grew up to form the foothills. Everything between them was Promise country. At least that was how he'd always thought of it. When he'd imagined that from above, the whole of it looked not unlike a churned-up blanket atop an unmade bed.

But he wasn't a red-tailed hawk — just an old man, frigid and tired and damp all over from a rainstorm sometime in the night.

Still, he thought, it was better than staying in the cabin any longer with the kid.

Fletcher Ralston was a decent fellow, just not somebody he wanted to be around right then. He had things to do, things to figure out. Besides, he had to keep the kid out of this. Wasn't his fault he was a greenhorn.

The kid hadn't asked to be born into a mess with no end. No, Gunnar knew he had to be the one to end it. As soon as he was able. Had to draw Skin out into the hills to have it out with him.

But right then all he wanted was a cup of hot coffee and a decent biscuit or three with sugar syrup poured over the top of them. Maybe some berries . . . He adjusted his feet and rearranged his hinder end to find a more comfortable spot amongst the rocks and roots and duff — too much of the first two and not enough of the last.

He sighed and groaned. It was still dark enough he should get going, make up some distance in hopes of drawing Skin farther from the kid, farther from Promise, before he killed again. Gunnar was pretty certain he was the killer's target, so luring him away was as sound a plan as he could think of. The trouble-some part was he couldn't be sure where the killer was, let alone if the man was going to follow him. But his gut told him it was the move to make.

After he'd left the cabin and the kid, Gunnar had spent the few hours of daylight yesterday making distance, kicking stones, snapping branches, scuffing extra footprints, away from Horton's diggings and more northward. He hoped it would be enough of an obvious trail.

Maybe just another few minutes of catnapping, he thought, letting his lids drift closed once more. The day would be a long one as it was. *A few minutes more of snoozing time can't hurt, now, can it?*

"Where you at, old man?"

The shout caught Gunnar by surprise. He'd dozed again. His eyes jerked wide open. It was full daylight.

"I said, 'Where you at, old man?' "

It was Skin Varney, sure as the devil knew he was a bad seed. Gunnar spun his head, growling and biting back a curse. He didn't want to give away his location and risk Skin seeing him before he caught sight of the bastard. Bad enough he'd snoozed too long. *Curse me for a fool,* he thought. And now he was knotted up worse than a stunted shrub of wind-tortured cedar.

"Who you callin' 'old'?" mumbled Gunnar in a whisper, even as he suppressed a groan as he tried to straighten his stiff legs.

He'd figured that since he wasn't able to see in the dark, neither could Varney. That might have been a mistake, he now realized. Not only was Skin a dang night hunter, but now he was close, and the bastard knew it.

If Varney moved and called again from a different spot, Gunnar figured either he was not certain of where Gunnar was hiding or maybe he was playing a round of cat and mouse with him.

Within a minute, the crusty miner had his answer.

"Oh, Gunnnnnar? Where you at, old man? Time to show yourself!"

The voice teased out as if released from a passing bird's mouth. And it came from Gunnar's right this time, somewhat southeast of where he sat. He continued to massage his knees.

He'd been gimped up many mornings in the past, and he'd come to depend on the fineries of his home for far too long now. This was the first time he'd felt helpless, as he couldn't get up and go. He was willing, but his legs throbbed with aches the likes of which he'd never before felt. What was wrong with him?

His quarry's voice shouted once more, farther away, more northeastward. Could be Skin was walking away from him because he didn't know where Gunnar was. That seemed likely, given that Skin used to be a spur-of-the-moment sort of fellow, a dangerous trait when coupled with the fact that he was also a killer.

Gunnar knew Skin had killed Millie and Horton. The other two, the marshal and his wife, they weren't so easy. Gunnar felt mostly sure they'd been killed by Skin, but folks in town thought Reg's shenanigans at Millie's were what had brought about their ruination. No matter now.

Even as he rummaged in his pockets, Gunnar knew it was more than morning stiffness he felt. It was the brave face of something he wasn't used to — his own weakness. He rummaged again and found a mixed wad of dusty medicinal leaves, comfrey and whatnot, that he'd stuffed in haste into his breast pocket while he'd been gathering his goods from the cabin.

He'd been so intent on getting out of there before the kid could talk him into taking him with him that he'd overlooked too many items he should have taken, more tinctures and medicinal plants among them. Age was a scurvy-ridden beast that would not leave him be.

Gunnar chewed the leafy blend, wishing he could avoid tasting its bitterness. Though the mixture was unpleasant, he hoped it would limber him enough that he could get himself upright and moving. Now that he knew he was on the snake's trail and that Skin was close, he didn't want to lose him.

"Come on now, Gunnar Tibbs," he whispered to himself, chewing and swallowing back the bite of the medicinal leaves. "Get cracking."

"Yep," said a voice right behind him. "Get cracking, Mr. Tibbs."

Gunnar froze, eyes wide, hands on his knees. There was only one person who'd called him Mr. Tibbs of late, but this voice wasn't the kid's. It was low and gravelly and cold as a fresh-dug grave at midnight.

"You," he said, without turning.

"Yep," the voice chuckled. "It's me. Ain't nobody but me."

Everything Gunnar had throughout his long years — all the work he'd put into his diggings, all the hours he'd spent with Horton jawing away the hours, all the evenings of happiness he'd found in Millie's arms, all the hours he'd spent alone with his thoughts in his cabin or out front overlooking Chillowaw Rim — all that time of his life had led him to this.

He snorted. Should be something better at the end of it all, should be something softer, gentler, kinder than to end up killed by the very man who'd fouled the lives of so many others, including those Gunnar most loved. And now he'd fallen right into that trap himself.

"I've been a fool," he said out loud.

The snake of a man replied, "Yeah, you have, old man. An old, stupid fool." Again, the vermin laughed, this time long and loud. The laugh tailed off into a ragged, wet, raspy cough. Didn't sound right to Gunnar. Was something wrong with the man? Gunnar shifted, began turning around.

"No, no."

He heard a steel snicking sound, a hammer being pulled back.

"You keep yourself facing away. Do as I say or you'll end sooner than I intend you to."

Tibbs spat. "Figured on smokin' you out, Skin Varney."

"Yeah, well, I got to you first, Gunnar Tibbs. Wasn't hard. You still smell like homemade sin, and them bowed legs of yours never did get any better."

Despite his situation, Gunnar chuckled. Varney was a lot of things, but boring wasn't one of them. "What is it you intend for me, Varney?"

"I intend to gut you slow, peel your hide

from your bones until you're a screaming sack of muck — that's what I intend. But it ain't gonna happen yet. First off, we got to get somewhere, just the two of us. Somewhere that will be familiar, I promise you. That is, if you can rouse your useless old bones and walk there."

That, more than any leafy tincture, riled Gunnar. "You bet I can, you foul stink of a man!" As he perfumed the air with all manner of raw talk, Gunnar slid a hand up from his right knee toward his holstered gun. "Get away from me and watch out. I intend to give as good as I get, and no mistake!"

Again, the laughing erupted behind him. "I'll give you this much, old man. You got a bigger set than most folks I ever did meet. Usually, they're whimpering and pissing themselves about now in the proceedings. But I'll wager you are full of ideas about how you can get the better of me. Well, we'll see about that. Yep, sir, we'll see."

Gunnar sought to distract Varney and alter the tone of the palaver. "I see you are on foot, Skin. Hard times befall you of late?"

"Shot my horse."

"Well, why would a man do such a thing?"

"Beast didn't walk fast enough to suit me. Let that be a lesson, you old fool. Now get going!"

Before Gunnar could pluck his revolver free, rapid footsteps thumped and crunched, coming up close behind him. Something whapped down hard on his left shoulder. He flinched and yelped. He lurched and shoved at the ragged, worn end of a long, straight branch. He spun his head, holding tight to the thing, and saw Skin for the first time, not but three feet behind him, staring down at him.

"You keep trying to unbridle that gun, old man. You do it again and you just see what all's going to happen!"

The man's face was recognizable to Gunnar. Other than a whole lot more lines and a beard now steel gray and flecked with strands of coarse black, he looked about the same.

It was the eyes, always the eyes, that gave him away. They were hard, dark, and hateful. And they gave Gunnar pause, as always they had, never more than now.

They were the eyes of a killer, after all. The man who'd laid low his love, Millie, and his friend, Horton. The renewed resolve of revenge bloomed hard and bright in Gunnar's chest. He sneered, returned the stare, and noticed that while Skin Varney did have him covered with a revolver, the killer's other hand held the hastily whittled

340

end of the very branch he'd slammed on Gunnar's shoulder.

It looked to be a walking stick, recently made, and not with any craftsmanship, Gunnar noted. He took pride in his own ventures with carving, from decorations to practical implements.

What's more, Varney favored his left side, sort of leaned that way, as if he didn't even recognize he was doing so. As if he was wounded, maybe?

Gunnar would keep that in mind. Maybe hit him with something low and on the man's side. Might not take much of a hard, swinging blow to render him a kneeling beggar. At least long enough to finish him off.

"What's the matter, Varney? You ailing?"

The dark look on Skin's face almost made Gunnar forget he himself was ailing.

Skin sucked air in between tight set teeth as if he were holding something back, and jerked the stick from Gunnar's grasp. "You never mind about me. I was you, I'd worry about your old, sorry hide! Now get up and get along, I tell you!"

Skin raised the stick once more as if to strike Gunnar, but the older man rolled to his right and snatched for his gun. Too late. The stick came down once more, harder this time, striking Gunnar across the head.

His old felt hat collapsed against his skull and the blow dizzied him.

While he fought a sudden gush of heat and confusion that blinded him in a wash of pain, Gunnar felt Skin's presence closer than ever, and he lashed out blindly.

All he felt for his effort was a whoosh of air, and then his arm thunked the pine against which he'd been leaning all night.

Skin jerked the revolver from Gunnar's belt, likewise the old man's big-bladed knife.

"No, you don't!" Gunnar lashed out once more and heard laughs for his efforts.

"Now maybe you'll get up when I tell you to. Start behaving like a whupped schoolboy and you might — just might — live to the end of the day. Why, I take a notion, we could share a pot of coffee together. Now wouldn't that be nicer than you settin' here like a brain-addled old donkey in the cold, thinking you was trailing me when all the time I was doing that to you?"

"Huh?" Gunnar rubbed his head and did his best to stand. He groped the rough bark of the ponderosa and used it to gain his feet slowly.

"That's right. That's good. Gonna need you to heft that pack of yours, slow and easy, and haul it on up onto your shoulder and carry it like the good donkey you are.

Then we're going to march. Maybe all day, if I take the notion to."

"Won't share coffee with you. Nothin' . . ." Gunnar knew his mumbles amounted to less of a threat than he intended, but Skin heard them and laughed once more.

"Anything you say, old donkey!" He chuckled and prodded Gunnar in the back. "Walk on, beast. No, no." Skin rapped him hard on the side of his upper right arm. "Thataway. Northeastward. And don't drag at it."

Gunnar took a single step and his guts rushed up to meet his throat. He bent over and vomited the jerky and biscuits he'd taken in the night before.

"Gaw, you are a mess, old man. Walking will cure you of it. Now move!" Skin whacked Gunnar once more, and the old miner, on cramped, unsteady legs, picked his way forward, slowly angling downslope and northeastward, herded by hard raps from Skin's walking stick.

A few hundred yards ahead, Gunnar saw the lower edge of the gentle slope where he'd encamped. Beyond the trees bright sun flooded down. He was sunk, he guessed, but at least he'd have the warming sunshine to ease his bones. The medicinal leaves were beginning to take hold and soothe his joints.

But his knees, worst of all, gave him sharp, hot needles of pain slicing up and down inside his legs with each gimpy step he took.

His senses slowly began to clear. He tasted the bile and smelled the stink of sour food on his breath, and he was grateful for it, because it reminded him he was still alive and he had a job to do. Somehow.

That bastard had forced him to leave behind his sawed-off shredder, the one Millie had given him. He'd sorely like to avenge her with that thing. It had been the fondest part of his plan.

But now, unless by some miracle he somehow lived through all this, that gun was destined to rot, leaned against the ponderosa where Skin had chosen to walk on by it. He could hardly blame Skin — lugging that short, heavy brute, if he had to be honest, had been a sore trial, like hauling a length of stone around the mountainsides. But it had been Millie's.

Skin had robbed him, too, of his old revolver, so Gunnar took stock of the one weapon he had left on him, his Barlow folder. It sat where he always kept it, tucked in his buckskin tunic, in a pocket within easy reach through the garment's flap on his breast.

He'd find a use for it, he vowed, before the day was out.

CHAPTER THIRTY-ONE

Fletcher twitched. Something, a sound, had startled him. His eyes opened. It was daylight. Barely. Very early, and very cold, but it was dimly light out. What had he done? Fallen asleep? Gunnar . . . He had to find the old codger before . . .

Somebody cleared a throat. That was the same noise that had awakened him. He spun his head right, then left. Somebody stood nearby, not ten feet away. He blinked, then rubbed his eyes and looked again.

It was not a big frightening killer. Not Skin Varney. It was a woman, a woman Fletcher recognized. Hester from the bordello. And she was holding a rifle cradled in her arms. Behind her stood two, three, four other women. The women from Millie's Place. From his place.

He opened his mouth, but nothing came out. So this was it: They were going to kill him out here in the wilderness. Or truss him up and drag him back to town for the rest of the townsfolk to do what they would with him. Perhaps hang him! That was their way out here in the wild lands, was it not?

Fletcher sat up.

"About time you woke," said Hester.

"I . . ."

"You what?" she said; her eyebrows rose. "We've been waiting on you."

Fletcher noticed the woman directly behind her, Dominique, held the bail of a now-quenched lantern. And beyond her, the other women stared at him.

They'd walked all night in the dark to get here. He looked past them.

"Where are the others?"

"Others?" she said.

"The others from town."

"Ha!" She shook her head. "Too lazy and scared."

"Then how come you . . . ?"

"Us?" said Hester, half turning to look at her friends, who had spread in a semicircle about her. "Gunnar is our friend, too, you know. They all were. Besides, we have nothing to lose, Mr. Ralston. Nothing at all. Except our dignity." She smiled at that word. "Yes, we do have dignity, Mr. Ralston. We also deeply believe in ourselves — two things that really are one anyway. That's one of the things Millie taught us."

"She sounds like a remarkable woman," he said, sitting up and rubbing his neck. He was still confused, but he let her talk.

"You're damn right she was."

"Then does this mean you no longer think I . . ."

"Oh, no," she said, shaking her head, though he swore he saw a thin grin on her face. "Not so fast on that score. We just think you're maybe not as guilty as you are innocent. We'll find out. Now, if you're about through with your rest, we'd best be moving on."

She walked past him on the trail, followed by the women. "We have Millie's man to rescue and a killer to catch."

Fletcher struggled upright, shaking himself back into wakefulness, and tugging the blanket tight about his throat. "What will you do with him should you catch Skin Varney?"

"Oh," said Hester over her shoulder, "we'll catch him. And then we have a number of possibilities open to us." They all giggled low and kept walking.

It was then that Fletcher noticed not all of them held guns. One carried a double-bit ax, one wore a bandolier of rope, and another wore two massive kitchen knives riding at her hips.

He swallowed and fell into line behind them. Fletcher had some thinking to do.

CHAPTER THIRTY-TWO

As the morning wore on, Skin grew quieter, and his comments were reduced to random grunts and curses. It sounded to Gunnar as if Skin was drinking, what with all the growling and slurring. If he was lapping up whiskey, it would provide Gunnar with an advantage in the situation.

Now that he was limbered up, Gunnar was moving pretty near as good as he did back home. Of course, if Skin was liquored, his fuse, already short and sputtering, might prove even shorter, were Gunnar to kick up a fuss. He had to get that Barlow knife out of his tunic without Skin seeing him. He couldn't afford to risk losing it, but he'd rather have the bastard in view when he went for it.

He decided to leave it where it was until an opportunity came up. It had better show itself soon, though.

The sunlight had gone a long way toward

warming his bones and limbering him enough to keep from stumbling up and down the graveled slopes and falling on his face. As it was, every time he stumbled, Skin howled with laughter. *Soon,* Gunnar thought as he dusted himself off from the last drop to his knees he'd taken. *Soon I'll gut Skin like a fresh-caught trout.*

The terrain had become unfamiliar to him, though they were still within traveling range of his cabin. Little more than a day's worth, at his reduced pace, and well less than a day for someone with young legs, like the kid. *Oh, that kid,* thought Gunnar.

He hoped he had done the right thing in sending him to town. Hell, Fletcher Ralston was no dummy. Green about the ways of the West, sure, but he was no mental sluggard. Maybe he'd think for himself and hightail it away from Promise. That was what Gunnar would have done were he the kid.

But would Fletcher? That would only offer a lifetime with his head on a swivel, like a songbird did every time it lit somewhere for a drink or to pick at a bug. No, that was no way to live.

But then again, what would going to Promise bring Fletcher? Misery and a whole lot of angry townies who all thought the kid had killed Millie and perhaps even suspected him of the deaths of the marshal and his wife.

Though given that they were found dead together, he with a gut wound, she with a shot to the bean that nibbled into Reg's head, too, maybe Edna really had done the double deed herself.

Maybe she had gotten tired of sharing her man, such as he was, with the women at Millie's, notably Dominique, the one woman he'd been seeing regularly for years. Everybody in Promise knew, and though they never mentioned it, everybody assumed Edna knew, too.

But what was between a man and his wife was just that, between them. Nobody else's business. And Gunnar knew deep in his gut that the townies were wrong about what had happened to Reg and his wife. They'd not had their final fight. No, they'd been laid low, somehow, by Skin Varney; of that, Gunnar was certain. At the very least, the filthy animal had had a big hand in their deaths.

"Hold up, old donkey!"

The shout from behind Gunnar was farther back than he'd expected it to be. He stopped, grateful for the break from trudging over and between rocks, and looked over his right shoulder. There was Skin, stumping along himself, putting awkward weight on the stick. The revolver hanging loose in his right hand, swinging by his leg.

He caught Gunnar peeking at him and raised the gun. "I told you before: You keep your eyes front and forward. I have to tell you again, I won't tell you at all. I'll just open up on you!"

Gunnar complied as Skin walked closer. When he was still five or six feet behind, Skin said, "Any of this terrain starting to come to you now?"

Gunnar looked about himself and shrugged, shaking his head. "Nope. Should it?"

That seemed to anger the killer. "You're damn right it should! Get moving through them bushes ahead, past that big reddish rock. Yeah, that one. And keep going. Now, you get past them bushes, you tell me what you see."

Gunnar sighed and ambled forward. He was bone sore and tired, and he could have used a long pull on his canteen. His shoulders and upper back muscles were twitchy, aching, and tense from the rucksack riding there. That put the shotgun in his mind and he felt a twinge of regret at not having it, and an even bigger twinge for losing something Millie had given him.

Before he shoved through those bushes, he hesitated; maybe this was where Varney planned to kill him. *End of the trail, pard,* he thought, then shook his head. No, that was no way to think.

Millie deserved justice. Horton deserved justice. If he failed the people he loved, why, Gunnar reckoned, he'd twist and spin and scream for eternity on a red-hot spoke in hell. He had to try.

A hasty plan took shape. He'd slow up. Then as they both got through the bushes, he'd lunge to his right and get that Barlow knife out, maybe start working it loose before he dove to the side.

It was a lousy plan, but then again his entire situation was lousy. Best he could do. "Guide me, Millie and Horton," he whispered. "Help me through it. . . ."

He slowed as he shoved through the bushes and saw the scene before him. His plan was forgotten. *Of course,* he thought. *How could I forget this place?*

There, ahead and below him, sat the ravine, the very spot he'd tracked Skin to all those years before. The very spot where that dumb bastard had tried to cross the gap on the back of an old log, a log that had sloughed its bark and bucked off his inching weight.

All he'd had to do was scramble down the ravine, then cross the dry wash bottom and climb up the far side, but Skin had been too stupid or too lazy or both. And now, twenty-four years later, here they were once more.

"Can't get enough of tormenting yourself, Varney?" said Gunnar, risking a sideways glance. To his surprise, Varney had joined him at the edge of the ravine, well to his left, the revolver aimed loosely in Gunnar's direction. Skin was staring down at the gravel below.

"Yeah," he said, his voice calm and low. "I believe you're right, Tibbs. Every day, all day, week after month after year after decade, I dreamed of this place, of walking to it with you, getting you down there where I was laid up, where you lorded over me with your gun." He turned with reluctance toward Gunnar.

The old miner had his right arm resting inside the front flap of his tunic, as if he were in need of an arm sling.

"All you had to do was turn away, let me go. That's all you had to do, Tibbs. All I did was help Thorne steal money. I didn't even have it. Ain't nobody got harmed too bad back then. All you had to do was nothing. Simplest thing in the world to do is nothing. But you couldn't even do that right."

His snarled beard quivered in counter-point to his twitching bloodshot eyes. Skin's voice was low, even, and deadlier sounding to Gunnar than it had ever been.

"You bastard. I will never forgive you." Then the killer smiled. "Lucky for me I don't have long to wait. Now get on down there and stand by the last of that old log. I expect it's the same one we both know well."

"Yeah," said Gunnar. "It's the one you tried to get across on. Years ain't been kind to it, though. Looks about as rough as I feel."

Skin snorted. "You're about to feel a whole lot worse than that, you old donkey."

CHAPTER THIRTY-THREE

As fortune would have it, it was Skin's ailing side that faced Gunnar, the one he had seen the outlaw favoring, rubbing gently. He figured the man had received some sort of wound, maybe a glancing blow with a knife or a bullet grazing, or maybe something he'd earned in prison. Gunnar didn't know or much care.

That Varney had a visible ailment, one he took no pains to disguise from Gunnar, told him all he needed to know. It gave him an extra edge of confidence. He wasn't ready, still had his hand on his Barlow nested in his tunic, but he had no time to reconsider. He'd take the chance when he got it or forever live in regret. That notion had served him well in life so far. He was still alive, after all. No time to abandon such a time-tested belief.

Gunnar dove for his captor, ramming the killer hard in his ailing side. The blow caught Skin in the waist, above the belt. Gunnar's moccasin slipped on scree and he lost a pinch of momentum. When he hit the big killer, his own shoulder buckled and Gunnar felt something inside pop, but he kept on.

His right arm was still nested in his tunic, with the Barlow knife gripped tight in his palm. Now he'd have to wait to get away from Skin before he dared pause to jerk open the blade.

His lunge folded Skin Varney like a poor hand of cards, and the big brute collapsed as if gutshot. Skin's grunt of shock and raised eyebrows told Gunnar the killer could hardly believe it was the old man who'd driven himself like a wedge into Skin's midsection. Gunnar had bent low and sprung at him sideways, hadn't offered a shout or growl to warn Skin he was about to take a fast, short journey.

Gunnar hoped to gain a few precious seconds, enough to disorient Skin and give himself time to ready the small knife. They rolled together to the ragged lip of earth atop the ravine, a tangle of limbs as the thrashing killer's surprise turned to seething rage. Varney bellowed as he snatched at his attacker.

Gunnar tried to roll from the clawing

man's big hands. As he shoved away from Skin, he felt wetness against the side of his face. He jerked away and saw on Skin's shirt the singular seeping dark redness that came only from a bleeding wound. He scrambled with renewed effort to get away from Varney, his mind savoring the facts that Skin was indeed wounded and that Gunnar had just reopened whatever wound had been troubling the killer.

Varney regained one knee, but wobbled, fell down on his backside once more, then collapsed to lean on one elbow, his back to the open air of the ravine. His hands clutched at the sopping reddening wound in his left side. His right hand snatched for his revolver, then up again to hold the wound, then down once more. He did this several times while groaning and cursing, "Aah, aah," over and over, sucking shallow breaths through tight-set teeth.

If it had been anyone else, Gunnar might have felt bad for them. But for Skin Varney, he managed a grim smile as he worked with fumbling fingers to open the Barlow's blade. That was as far as he got.

Skin's flailing legs smacked into Gunnar, and when the killer felt he'd connected with his foe, despite his own pain, he jerked his feet hard. Gunnar fell to his left, pitching down the graveled drop, and he felt the Barlow fly from his grasp. He jammed his feet downslope and slowed himself to a dust-clouded skid.

As Skin struggled once more to regain his knees, Gunnar's departure had knocked him off-kilter, and Skin leaned too far to his right. He jammed an arm outward to catch himself, but he was turned around and his outstretched mitt grasped nothing at all.

Varney uttered a short, loud bark of anger and surprise as he tumbled downslope, headfirst, end over end, before skidding toward the bottom of the ravine twenty feet below. As he thundered downward, he caromed off head-size boulders and jags of spiny rock exposed by floods of the past. Grunts and moans marked the last few feet until he collapsed in an unmoving sprawl at the rocky base.

Gunnar also lost the fight, despite clawing efforts to snatch at something, anything that might slow his fall down the near-vertical drop. *I am a fool and a half,* he thought as he slid, slammed, and rolled, unable to stop himself. *I caused this and deserve every damned broken bone I get.*

That was all the time Gunnar had for thinking because he slammed once more into Skin Varney at the base of the slope and bounced off the big brute's unmoving body. Then the old miner's wispy head smacked something bigger and a whole lot harder. The day's crisp gray-blue sky turned grayer and grayer, darker and darker as he gazed upward. Then he knew no more.

CHAPTER THIRTY-FOUR

Gunnar came to with a jerk, as if someone had tossed a bucket of water on his slack bearded face. But he felt no water, only brightness and warmth. He cracked an eye. Yep, had to be he was still alive. There was the sun, hot and bright high up in the big blue sky.

He lay unmoving. *This is getting to be a habit,* he thought, recalling how he had begun what had become this, the most troubling day of his life. Then he remembered where he was — at the bottom of the dry ravine with Skin Varney.

Gunnar scrabbled in the gravel, his head not liking the effort one bit. His vision blurred, cleared, then blurred once more. If he'd had anything in his gut, it would have worked its way up and out by then. Still, he retched and crabbed, the heel of one hand pinning for a moment his buckskin tunic to the earth. He shoved himself up onto all fours and swayed like a strange bony bear, swinging his head slowly to rid himself of the dizziness and buzzing and headache. Nothing he did worked.

He finally did see Varney, though, sprawled not but six feet upslope of him. The bastard was hunched, flopped on his side, maybe dead. He didn't look too good. But no, Gunnar saw the killer's right boot twitching, and his fondest wish was whisked from him. But was the brute's boot actually twitching? Everywhere Gunnar looked showed something jumping and jerking.

Varney had to be alive — Gunnar had not gotten so close to be robbed of this prize. Gunnar needed to kill Varney himself. He needed to see the man's life drain away in front of him. It was the only way. He crawled toward Varney, upslope, sliding as gravel gave way, and finally reached the killer.

Gunnar's vision doubled, trebled, and he reached a callused hand toward one of the three black boots before him. His fingers closed on air. He reached again, and his fingertips brushed the killer's boot toe. He crabbed forward and snatched at rocks, at Varney's leg, and dragged himself up to the man.

Gunnar shook his head slowly, but all that

did was make the cannon fire inside his skull boom louder and threaten to crack his head wide open. He finally noticed one of Varney's revolvers a few inches from his shaking hand. Gunnar lurched forward, felt his fingers close over the butt, and tugged to free it, but wouldn't you know it? The man had it tied down. A long piece of leather looped over the hammer.

The old man gritted his teeth and tried to make his twitchy fingers do his bidding. They felt the rawhide thong as he fumbled with it, but it wouldn't slip free. Then a big grimy hand slammed downward and smacked Gunnar's own flat as if it were squashing a fly.

"You!" thundered Skin Varney, shoving himself up to a sitting position. While still retaining a grip on Gunnar's hand, he swung a wide, looping round-house of a punch with his other big fist.

The old miner saw it coming in hard and fast, and jerked his head down like a gun-shy turtle. The big mitt whistled over and Skin grunted with the effort. The grunt turned into a growl as Gunnar yanked his hand free and jabbed a fist once more at the big man's bloodied side.

As Gunnar's hand smacked into the middle of the bloodied patch on Skin's shirt, the killer's fist swung hard again and connected with Gunnar's cheek. This sent the bearded old buck sprawling backward.

He reached the bottom and, with a buzzing and clanging in his head, caught sight of the gasping Varney rising up. The big murderer appeared to be in better shape than Gunnar thought.

"You son . . . of . . . a . . ." Skin's curse trailed off as he freed a revolver and slicked back the hammer in one smooth motion.

The shot whipped wide and spanged off a boulder on the far side of the ravine. Gunnar jerked low and scrabbled to get behind the largest thing close by — the remnants of the big old log.

It was not enough to prevent himself from receiving a second shot. It caught him high on the right shoulder and he howled and spun, snatching at his shoulder and watching hot red blood pump through his clamping fingers.

"Curse you, Varney!"

Gunnar's lifelong bet with himself that he'd make it to his grave without ever having tasted another man's thrown lead had finally been spoiled. This was the first time he'd been shot, and it hurt, stinging and throbbing and lancing inside like lightning trapped inside him, worse than any bodily pain he'd ever felt.

Varney's laughter snagged out into a ragged cough. He spat and dragged a wrist across his bearded face. "You'll taste more of the same before this hour's up, old man!"

He shoved to his knees once more, in full view of Gunnar, confident that the old miner was now weaponless and incapacitated.

"You're about to taste what Horton Meader got, what that foul marshal and his simpering wife got, and what that old whore Millie Jessup got — death delivered one way or another by Skin Varney, a man who keeps his promises . . . even if they are twenty-four years in coming!"

I have to keep him distracted and talking, thought Gunnar. *It might buy me time to think of a plan.* "Why are you so bent on revenge, Varney?"

"Why? Just look at you and those idiots back in town. Hell, I didn't figure anybody was fool enough to stay around a place like Promise. Boy, was I wrong. I got me a hell of a surprise when I came back. Not much has changed. Not many from the old posse still alive, but the town's still a dusty little hole full of fools and dreamers. Makes my job easier."

Gunnar clamped his hand tighter on his

bleeding shoulder and eyed the man. "Yeah? How's that?"

Varney smiled. "I'll tell you, since we got time and you asked so nicely. Once I'm done doing to you whatever it is I feel you deserve, I am going to do the same to the rest of the idiots in that foul little town. Figure I'll lock them all in the saloon and light them on fire. Perch myself on a rise and cut down anybody who runs from my flames of vengeance!" His dry chuckle echoed in the long, high-sided gulch.

"Sounds like . . ." Gunnar sucked in a breath as pain washed through his body. "Like you've put all manner of thought into this, Varney."

"You bet I have. Had plenty of time to do it, too. And you're to blame."

"Bah! What is it you really want, Varney?"

"Don't play the fool with me, Tibbs. You know what I told you all them years ago right here." With a long finger he poked the dusty earth beside him. "When you broke off from that posse and followed me, you had to know something was going to happen. Ran me aground like a hound on a squirrel. But it all worked out." Varney smiled.

Gunnar saw for the first time that the man's teeth were blackened and greened and pitted, like wormy apples.

"You told me all I needed to know," said Skin.

"How's that?"

"You don't remember, do you? Ha, that's rich. That day in this here gulch, you told me you was glad Millie sent Thorne packing that night of the robbery."

Gunnar's guts tightened at what he was hearing. "That . . . that don't mean a thing."

Skin snorted and shook his head. "Why sure it does!" He laughed. "It told me Millie was maybe the last person in town to see Sam before he left. That got me thinking that she might well know something of use to me. Something to give me a direction to begin my search. So I started with her! All thanks to you, Tibbs."

Varney's laughter was a vile thing to hear. Gunnar felt his grief rise up his gorge and threaten to choke him. He grabbed a handful of gravel and squeezed. "No! I'd never betray her like that! I couldn't. It don't mean a thing!"

"Comfort yourself with that thought as I tell you about the fear I saw in that old whore's eyes. You should have seen them eyes as I dragged my keen blade across her old chicken throat!" His cackling laugh grated like sand against glass. He eyed Tibbs as rage shook the old man like a wind-worried branch.

"Yeah, yeah, that's about right. That angry feeling boiling up inside? That's how I felt all them years ago when you and that useless old grubber Horton Meader rousted me up in the high rocks that day. You came up on me at my raw camp whilst I was squatting over a hole, relieving myself of a mistake of a meal of bad meat. No lie! It about killed me. And then all you posse folks treated me like I was some sort of farmyard vermin."

"Good reason for that. You are vermin, Varney. You've left a trail of death behind you your entire life. You . . . you're filth."

"I can take a lot of things, even foul names, but not from a stupid old man."

"You'll take it and you'll like it, demon!" Tibbs lunged, raging and weaponless.

Before Gunnar managed to reach more than a few inches, a shotgun blast thundered loud, cracking the air of the ravine. Lead shot sizzled a path between the two shouting men, pelting and spattering against boulders, pinging shards of rock, gravel, and earth like grapeshot from a cannonade rooster-tailing into the air.

"Gaah!" Skin Varney cursed, spinning to his right in an effort to avoid the vicious missiles. He squinted down at Gunnar. "But you ain't got your shotgun! I left it back yonder where I found you!"

"Wasn't me!" Gunnar felt a flutter of hope in his breast. The old mountain goat dropped to his knees and cradled his right arm, sucking in breath through tight-clenched teeth. A dark stain had spread over the old supple buckskin sleeve of his tunic. Soon he spied movement high up, behind a cluster of boulders, a twisted-trunk pine leaning across the near face of the biggest one.

Varney hunched low behind a tumble of rock and broke his careful scrutiny of the old man. Somebody else had crashed their party with a shotgun. He looked over his shoulder. "Well, it damn sure wasn't me, you old bastard!"

"Got a surprise for you, Skin!"

"Oh?" said Varney, drawing his revolver once more. "What's that?"

"You'll find out soon enough when you're barking at the gates of hell!" Gunnar shouted, despite how awful he felt.

"I've had enough of you!" He leveled on Gunnar and let loose with a shot. It buzzed and whined off a rock to Gunnar's right. "All them years in prison messed with my aim."

"Not mine," said a third voice.

"Who's there?" Even as he shouted, Skin swiveled his head back to face Gunnar, then beyond, then back behind him.

"Why, it's me, Skin," said a man's voice.

"Who's that?" shouted the big killer, trying to look in all directions at once.

"Me . . . Sam Thorne."

Gunnar smiled as Fletcher stepped out from behind a Ponderosa pine, holding his father's pearl-handled hideout gun before him. He had the wee derringer cocked and aimed at Skin Varney's broad chest.

"Ha! What's that, boy? You going to scare off a bluebottle fly with that thing? And who in the hell are you anyway?"

"Why, Skin, you don't recognize me? I'm
—"

But Tibbs broke in, smiling a tight, grim smirk between huffing breaths. "He's your worst nightmare, Varney!"

"Well, that must mean I don't dream near as bad as I used to 'cause this little fool looks to be a child."

"A child, yes," said Fletcher. "The child of Rose McGuire and Samuel Thorne."

"What?"

It was the first time that Gunnar saw Varney's squint-eyed, smirking gaze alter. His eyes widened and his lips parted, revealing tight-set stained teeth, two of them were black, dead at the root, and others were already well past that stage, stumpy and painful-looking.

"Ah, I see it now, sure. You got the mangy look all right. You and that double-crossing, treasure-thieving bastard could be brothers! And since you are the spawn of that filthy animal who left me to swing all those years ago, where's my money?"

"Why, right here, Skin." Fletcher waved a hand at himself.

"What?" said Varney. "You waste it on ugly clothes?"

Fletcher shook his head. "You people have no sense of fashion. I'm the treasure. I see it now." He glanced quickly at Gunnar. "Me, my education."

"All them years stuck in that hellish hole, all them years, and you tell me this?" Varney waved a dismissive hand toward Fletcher. He gritted his teeth and fiery rage once more filled his bloodred eyes. "By God, you'll taste my lead, you son of a whore!"

"Aww, you two stop talking each other to death and get to it! Man can't hardly bleed out around here without palaver this and palaver that!"

The prompt from the old man spurred Skin Varney into action, and he snatched at the revolver at his waist, hanging down low on his left side. He clawed it free of the holster and in a single smooth motion raised it to bear on Fletcher. He paused but a moment to smile wide, revealing to all who stood by that he was taking great delight in the coming shot. But it was a moment too long.

Fletcher squeezed the little gun's trigger and it snapped off a shot.

A long, thin, piggish squeal streamed out of the puckering hole of Skin Varney's mouth. Above that, his pimpled nose twitched and ran yellow. At the top, centered betwixt the killer's rheumy, mad eyes, a neat round hole welled red and pumped out thick dying blood.

The big man who'd caused so many people so much grief for so long dropped to his knees, still staring straight at the young man before him.

In his fading moments of clarity, Skin Varney saw his old pard, Samuel Thorne, the man who'd fed him to the wolves all those years before. It looked to him as if time had been most kind to ol' Sammy Thorne. Most kind, indeed. He hadn't even aged.

But, came Varney's last thought, *it can't be . . . can it?*

"Son of a whore?" said Fletcher, looking down at the dead killer. "You bet."

CHAPTER THIRTY-FIVE

Varney had not shuddered his last before Millie's women descended like vengeance-seeking angels and surrounded him. *Angels with deadly weapons,* thought Fletcher as they bent low and made damn certain the worm who'd killed their beloved mother figure was good and dead.

They worked in near silence, save for grunts as they kicked and flailed and savaged the killer's corpse.

Fletcher left them to it, certain it was not something he wanted to see, but knowing it was something they felt they had to do.

He turned his attention to Gunnar Tibbs. "Are you okay, Gunnar?" He knelt before the seated man, regarding the old miner's drawn face, as ashen as his flowing beard.

"Been worse. Good to see you, boy. Good to see you. Help me up."

He raised a hand and Fletcher steadied him and helped him over to a sizable boulder near where he leaned. They each re-garded the flailing mass of women, then turned away and said nothing of it.

Gunnar nodded toward the sawed-off shotgun clutched in Hester's hands. "Looks familiar. Nice entrance you made there."

"Yeah," Fletcher said. "We found it back there along the trail, leaning against a pine tree. We figured we were on the right trail then for certain."

"Might make a tracker of you yet, boy. But I ain't holding my breath." Gunnar winced and squeezed his bleeding shoulder tighter and Fletcher helped him bind it.

A few moments later, Hester walked over and set the shotgun next to Gunnar, brush-ing wisps of hair from her face with the back of a wrist, and took over tending to Gun-nar's wound. The other women walked up behind her, smoothing their dresses and dabbing sweat from their faces with their skirts. A few of them wore flecks of gore on their hands and cheeks and dress fronts, but, Fletcher noted, they were surprisingly clean.

He glanced at Skin Varney, then looked away. The corpse was foul and not a sight he needed to dwell on in his life.

"Should . . . ," said Fletcher in a quiet voice. All eyes turned to him. "Should we bury him?"

"No, sir!" growled Gunnar, who, despite his pain, shook his head and pushed away from the boulder to stand upright. "That bastard liked this gulch so well, let him have it all to himself for all eternity. Me, I aim never to visit this dark place again."

He turned and began walking back up the trail. "Gives me the creepin' willies."

Fletcher followed, and the women strode silently behind him, their grisly assortment of weapons hanging at their sides.

Gunnar stumbled once and Fletcher bolted forward and caught him. He bent down to drape Gunnar's good arm over his shoulder.

The old man resisted. "Boy, I managed to walk through life all these years without no help. . . ."

"I know that, Mr. Tibbs," said the young man, suppressing a grin. "But who's to say I'm not the one needs a little support?"

"Ha!" cackled the old miner. "And just what, Mr. Thorne, do you think I been doling out to you for weeks now, you mooching young hound dog?"

"Mr. Thorne," said the young man, smiling. "Not a bad sound to it."

Gunnar Tibbs nodded. "Course, it's tainted some by the one who wore it before you. But ain't nobody saying you can't polish it up as you go . . . Samuel Thorne."

ABOUT THE AUTHORS

Ralph Compton stood six foot eight without his boots. He worked as a musician, a radio announcer, a songwriter, and a newspaper columnist. His first novel, *The Goodnight Trail,* was a finalist for the Western Writers of America Medicine Pipe Bearer Award for best debut novel. He was the *USA Today* bestselling author of the Trail of the Gunfighter series, the Border Empire series, the Sundown Rider series, and the Trail Drive series, among others.

Matthew P. Mayo is a Western Writers of America Spur Award winner and a Western Fictioneers Peacemaker Award finalist. His short stories have appeared in numerous anthologies and his many novels include the Westerns *Winters' War, Wrong Town, Hot Lead, Cold Heart, Dead Man's Ranch, Tucker's Reckoning, The Hunted,* and *Shot-*

gun Charlie. He contributes to several popular series of Western and adventure novels.

380

The employees of Thorndike Press hope you have enjoyed this Large Print book. All our Thorndike, Wheeler, and Kennebec Large Print titles are designed for easy reading, and all our books are made to last. Other Thorndike Press Large Print books are available at your library, through selected bookstores, or directly from us.

For information about titles, please call:
(800) 223-1244

or visit our website at:
gale.com/thorndike

To share your comments, please write:
Publisher
Thorndike Press
10 Water St., Suite 310
Waterville, ME 04901

X X